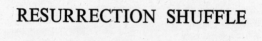

RESURRECTION SHUFFLE

BY THE SAME AUTHOR

The End of Something Nice

ANGUS WOLFE MURRAY

RESURRECTION SHUFFLE

A NOVEL

PETER OWEN · LONDON

ISBN 0 7206 0519 9

The author gratefully acknowledges
the generous support of the
Scottish Arts Council

PETER OWEN LIMITED
73 Kenway Road London SW5 0RE

First British Commonwealth edition 1978
© Angus Wolfe Murray 1978

Printed in Great Britain by
Villiers Publications Ingestre Road London NW5

For J. T.

The Blues are beautiful because it's simpler and because it's real. It's not perverted or thought about : It's not a concept, it is a chair; not a design for a chair but the first chair. The chair is for sitting on, not for looking at or being appreciated. You sit on that music.

John Lennon

1970

LAS VEGAS

I watch the sun melt the curtains. It must be noon. Rain Fortune is smiling. She's asleep. She hates Las Vegas.

There is no quality but the quality of stillness. Words convey feeling, indulge imagination in a style that excludes reality. We are warped by the process of age.

When I was a child I believed in a golden future. Now I believe in everything that has passed.

Second week of the tour, rituals repeating, airport to hotel to gig to hotel to airport, interrupted at intervals by news freaks, columnists, ('Do you believe in astral inevitability?' 'Do you recognize your own reincarnation?'), chicks tucking their tits under scarlet handkerchiefs, ('Do you ball?'), snatching burgers and Cokes before sound checks, avoiding crowds, trying not to denounce the movement of liberation, having as much sympathy for rat-faced farm boys from upstate Kentucky as the murderous Cong in the Delta paddies, remembering always that music composed in silence a long time ago was for them, these kids, trying to believe it, the audience being an object, having its own style, its own weight, and remembering also to retain the instincts of origin, conscious of the need to perform, to be like anyone who ever stepped on a stage, and yet a myth, a legend, more real, higher than actual, being there, bathed in brilliant light.

There was a gale blowing. Figures huddled in doorways. We drove through Detroit.

I wanted to tell them how much it reminded me of places where I had lived.

The theatre was large, a revamped Edwardian cinema. The promoter said he'd been thrown out of two alternative sites already. He was small and skinny with pebble shades and pale piss hair. I asked, 'Why not bring soul bands up from the south?' It was conversation. He was born in San Francisco. His father, a gynaecologist, believed that the infusion of hard drugs into the ghettoes would destroy America and so opened a free clinic in Haight Ashbury. Six months later windows were smashed, files burnt and a part-time nurse called Ella May Peabody raped. Police arrested a group of black militants, one of whom was reported as saying, 'White ants come scratch our bag, man, get a taste of our disease', subsequently denied as 'pig rap' and 'unlawful'. There had been an interview on local radio in which the doctor discussed the problem of convincing kids he was *concerned*. He talked of the corruption of human dignity by the inequalities of the capitalist system and how ironic and fitting it would be if the ideals of the American Constitution degenerated into a fascist philosophy that curbed self-expression. What angered the militants was his assumption that only white liberals had the ability to cure them. They didn't want shit and sympathy. They wanted guns. Love was cruel. Hate was strong. They wanted *real* identity.

Afterwards I doubted his story. He talked of bands like they were precious metal.

12

We build from inadequacy. We make use of pain. Pretensions placed on us by others are barbed with lies created by publicity departments to increase a hold on the imagination of kids too young to recognize the tragedy of the world. Morality cannot breathe in an atmosphere of commercial hype. The trust of children is used to the advantage of whores and pimps, always the bad devouring the qualities of the good. We are taught at school values that don't exist in life. The fact that we reject them is to our credit.

My father believed the guitar to be a profane instrument and my mother suspected the insidious content of all literature, insisting that people who called themselves intellectuals were miserable and unhappy in their private lives. I told her, 'So am I.' She hadn't thought of that. She had no curiosity.

I learnt two things. We are created by the influence of others and we are alone. School was an echo of life's restrictive authority. I owed them nothing, least of all my effort. I felt no point of contact, resenting the loss of freedom.

I questioned my father more and more. There had to be something of him in me. I behaved opposite to my nature believing that denial was stronger than aggression. I thought, we are born empty, it's other people who fill us. I drifted away. I let the waves wash me. To be still was to be true. And yet at no time did I recognize the future as an act of faith. I told myself, 'I am not the same. I am different.' But I was the same. I had my father's blood.

Rain Fortune scrunches up her eyes.

"I don't wanna know what that goddam desert is doin," she says.

"It's doing the same as it did yesterday," I say.

"What's that?"

13

"Nothing."
She burrows deeper.
"Don't let it move, honey."

    – How would you describe your beginnings?
    – Uncertain.
    – What do you remember?
    – My mother living with my father.
    – Did you have a formative youth?
    – I took my sister into the forest that was over the other side of
      the hill from where we lived and told her that one day the
      world would end and we'd find ourselves in a forest like this
      and would have to begin again, eating grubs and sleeping
      under trees, and my sister began to cry and I thought, no
      one is telling us the truth anymore. What matters most are
      the elements, the seasons, the animals and the flowers, not
      in any aesthetic sense, not because they happen to be more
      organized, but because they belong absolutely to the con-
      text of their surroundings and are governed as much by the
      movement of the planet as by geographical faults. I don't
      understand American kids who demand freedom *and* the
      breakdown of monetary systems. They want to be thrown
      back into rural dependence without recognizing that this
      leads to a worse kind of slavery. Ask the country poor.
      Have they prospered in body and spirit? Do they believe?
    – Do you?
    – I believe in myself.
    – And yet are involved, ironically, wouldn't you agree, in the
      noisiest overpublicized ballyhoo of the entire entertain-
      ment industry?
    – I'm not involved.
    – What are you doing?
    – Waiting for the next meal.
    – Would you admit, seriously, that your music, not the
      message behind the music, the songs, I should say, literally
      speaking the *content*, even the *lyrics*, might be interpreted
      as belonging to the movement of protest?
    – I knew a cow once, a beautiful dung-coloured cow that
      wanted to be a bird. She was called Belle Matrix. All the

cows at that place were called something Matrix. She had
Walt Disney eyes. She was a Walt Disney cow. A lady. She
watched swallows with longing.
– That reminds me of your last album. The sentiments of
ecological self-destruction. What happened to the cow?
– She jumped off the barn roof.

Ken telephones. I sit with my toes out of bed.
"Press conference at six," he says.
I shiver and shake.
"Okay."
I dreamed my father was a cavalry officer and we rode to-
gether, he and I, one beside the other, and he kept turning to
look at me as we galloped over dead fusiliers and he was shout-
ing, 'Plug the wound with earth and moss', and I looked and
couldn't find anything and all the time he was screaming and
pointing and I thought, Christ, I'm dying and I don't know why.
Ken says that Terry flung the lead amp off the back of the
van and smashed it.
"What he do that for?" I ask.
"He's a cunt," he says.
I am naked.
Four thousand canaries were released last week as a gesture
to hawks before a selected audience of television cameramen to
celebrate the opening of a new casino. The glamour is cellophane. It's difficult to predict. I stretch my arms. The bones
crack.
It was hard in California but it's worse here.
I walk to the window. The curtains are drawn. American
hotels know nothing of nostalgia. I wrote a song called 'Lakeside
Memorial Motel Blues' in Delaware two years ago and I remember those rooms exactly, even now, how the screws came out
of the walls and a pipe in the shower leaked brown scum over
patterned lino. The place was six months old and warped. To
touch the door handle or the knob of the TV was like taking
risks with your life and I was touching them all the time and

15

having these sharp electric shocks and being told by sympathetic scientists dressed as cleaning staff about brush nylon carpets building up static electricity, and thinking, what's the purpose of progress, what's the meaning of movement? When I was sixteen I carried a pocket dictionary to dazzle snotty chicks with words longer than 'piss', enjoying the music of language ('altruistic', 'loquacious', 'belladonna', 'maid servant', 'flint'), words as weapons, as toys. The phase passed. I went back to believing that speech idioms were recognizable symbols like stations on a bus route and that clichés contained more power to the people than perfectly pruned prose.

Life runs in conflicting circles. I cannot carry the conviction I did three years ago. Once progress meant recovery from illiteracy. Now it's technological infanticide, spiritual and ecological decay. Kids starve in Calcutta while those in New York queue for analysts. There is no answer because every answer has a reason and every reason is relevant. If I tell chicks who give me the organic rap that they're the product of fifteen years' addiction to Coca-Cola they nod their heads and say, 'Yeh, man, that's right.' But it's the product of money too and I ask why they believe there's more truth in dirt and they say, 'When you're poor, like starving, man, you've got *real* hangups', and I tell them, 'That's bullshit because when you're poor you know nothing, you know the day's going to start and it's going to end and that's all you know and in your heart you want to be rich because when you're rich you have something to do during the day and you have something to do the next day too and you begin to look forward and see time coming and understand what it means to have ambition and make time work for you which poor people don't because they lack the ability to control destiny or make use of space.'

Las Vegas is moon town, shielded by orange hills and flat grey sand, example of the madness that makes Americans accept excess as the rational extension of ambition, world capital of steely sham flash, the junk we live with, where private ambulances park at the back of hotels and middle-aged teeny-boppers slash their wrists with hundred dollar bills. Once people approve Caesar's Palace, drive-in divorce shops, poster ads shutting out the sky, they'll welcome test-tube children and World War III.

16

I read in a magazine : 'Las Vegas in daylight is a public urinal.'
Facile word games. What does it mean? Journalists wouldn't
know the truth if it was handed out with groceries, can't com-
prehend the mental constriction of going on tour or what it
means to find no motive in repetition even at the height of what
is called success. They join us for a day or a week and I watch
them finding points of contact, discussing technicalities with
Ken and Terry, admiring a guitar, saying it's like Eric Clapton's
or B.B. King's. Male groupies do this. Anything to stay around.
It's a hype. Eventually they break through because no one
bothers enough to stop them and then they go away, go home,
and dictate a self-congratulatory piece, full of pop star chatter
and DJ jokes, about how they survived 'the rigours of the road'.
Parasitic insects. Living off other people's talent.

Ken drove to Las Vegas from Phoenix with Terry, Jug Meat's
roadie, in a hired Hertz and said it was like Death Valley,
a straight run through dust and desert, littered with snake skins
and giant prickly cactus. Ken's been a road manager for five
years. Matthew says he's 90% reliable and 110% loyal. He tells
the story of a Scandinavian tour when Ken's Transit broke down
in a blizzard eighty miles north of Stockholm, how he called out
the Army and brought the gear to the gig under escort with out-
riders and jeeps. Terry heard from a mate of his who was humping for the band at the time that Ken sat on his arse in the warm
van and bitched while the other guy, this friend of Terry's, stood
in the freezing wind, waiting for a lift. When a car did come he
was driven to the next village and telephoned the promoter's
office where there happened to be a kid with a cousin in the
transport service who arranged for a truck to be sent from a
barracks eight kilometers away.
Ken and Terry have a mutual disrespect for each other that
Matthew doesn't want to hear about. Terry's nervous, randy
and fast. Ken's slower and heavy with flat shovel paws and damp
seaweed hair. When he was ten his mother abandoned him to a
sixty-five-year-old relative called Uncle Toggy who preferred

horse racing and rabbit breeding to a dull gerk who wet his bed. Terry says, 'If I suggest anything for the band, a new spare leads box or a floor mike for the drums, he says, you've fuckin chicks in your head like some poxy hen house. He thinks it funny 'cause he found out I had crabs in Dortmund last year and had to shave meself. Fuckin great! I can't tell him turn right when we're driving without him turning left, getting lost, and then lecturing me for half an hour on how dope corrodes yer nuts. I sit there like a stuffed rubber and let the bastard bang on. He's round the fuckin twist, man. No bother!'

Matthew left after the San Jose gig. Beccy was dying. He knew it when we began the tour but wouldn't cancel or send anyone else. He hated going to the hospital, thinking what was happening inside her. He had that energy, that life force, and Beccy, lying in bed, her face turned to look at him, must have recognized and longed for it. He said, 'I can't watch her giving up.' She wasn't. I knew that. She was asking for help.

He waited in the lobby of the San Jose hotel for a taxi to take him to the airport. I couldn't speak. There was nothing to say. We stood in silence. It was pathetic. Beccy told me once that no one's more down on you than a disillusioned romantic. She said, 'The world should be a constant wonder. Why isn't it?' Matthew didn't know. He wouldn't attempt to answer. She said, 'Don't lose contact with home.' We argued for hours. I said, 'I don't want that.' She sighed. I said, 'What is it?' She said, 'I'm tired of hearing how you'll change the world and seeing it the same like there's no justice and no common sense.' I said, 'It can't happen tomorrow.' She said, 'I'm tired of *feeling*.' Matthew laughed. He said, 'Feeling *me*?' He bought leather clothes in Hollywood because he knew how much she liked them. She said, 'It's crazy! I can have it all. I'm the girl who dreams of marrying a star.' I said, 'What's wrong with that?' She said, 'I never dreamed of marrying anyone. I don't enjoy rich things.' I said, 'Do you love him?' She said, 'He believes money binds a marriage. I know it doesn't.'

18

My hand rests on the bed sheet.

Love is a word of many meanings. The recognition and the act. Separate phases of the moon. I must retain in this vacuum a sensitivity that distinguishes difference. There comes a time, and often it has always been, when accident is accepted as the whole. We see ourselves blithely as children of darkness, unable to contain the passion or control the journey.

Rain Fortune breathes gently now, her face in the pillows. She was born in Chicago. Her uncle was a street musician who taught her bottleneck guitar. When still young she wrote 'Rain Makes Me Weary', the story of a man who comes north from Mississippi, sleeps in a bus depot and steals food to live. One day he's caught taking oranges from a stall in the market. He's attacked by his own people and left bleeding in the gutter. An old blues singer finds him and tells him to get up off his ass before the rain comes. The man lies still. He says he doesn't care about the weather. He's from the south. The rain's going to wash away his trouble. The old singer tells him he's a fool. Nothing changes the nature of a city except music and it's music that's going to make people recognize the truth of their repression and let them stand together and see each other as brothers. She told me, 'It wasn't *real* blues, honey. A girl don't understand how a man truly lives. My Pa said, every woman's gotta work for a man. I told him, I *do*. I work for my uncle. I sang in church too with my sisters and my brother. We'd scream an shout crazy stuff like *I wanna see the light, Lord, I wanna feel salvation like a great black mule ridin down the sky on me with God's own hooves!* We were kids. It was city imitation of country gospel. Bugs beatin at the frame like in old southern movies.'

I stroke her shoulders.

"What you doin in the streets this time o' the mornin, Captain?" she murmurs.

"I lost my road," I say.

She licks my eyes.

"You should be ashamed. A fine-talkin gentleman like yourself."

19

"I was looking for Miss Rainberry Fortune. She lives here-abouts, I understand."

"I believe that's right, soldier."

"Thought I recognized a gentle intonation, Ma'am. Are you resident in this neighbourhood?"

"I *own* this town."

She bites me under the arm.

"You do a great service, if I may say so."

I tease her nipple with my tongue.

"My father's a rich sea raider, Ma'am, and my mother's too fine to be a Hollywood star."

I kiss her fur.

"I'm honey summer," she whispers.

She's warm. She licks my back and buttocks.

"That's the whole truth."

I feel her sorrow, her life, as if her heart lay open beside me. I want to tell her *yes yes,* the distance electric between existence and dreams. I'm a snake in the fire, twisting through ashes over rocks to her fountain.

"Shit! *Baby!*"

Heat enfolds me.

"Jesus!"

Shaken at the violence of the shimmer in the run, ripples pass and pulse, shining like the sea.

"I wanna eat you when you fuck me."

Lips are flowers. Nothing moves. I float like paper.

My arm falls across the bed. I ring Room Service and ask for food.

She turns her neck to look at me. I touch her face.

"What you thinkin?"

I would live in a monastery if I understood the forces that control instinct. Communion is damaged by our belief that speech is man's most precious possession. Children of the mountain walk on water, fly in air, buoyed by the bliss of their secret revelation. The real world lies beyond, separated by rules and emotion, pressures and language. The mountain is magic. The real world is not.

She rolls like a puma.

"I'll eat horses."

She lands on the floor and crawls.

"When he comes through that door I'll claw an I'll scratch."
She's circling. "The rawest red ram you ever known, man!"

"*Aieee!!*"

She's groaning on the ground, rubbing her stomach.

"Heap nasty hotel manager. Not good," I say. "Coffee shop
daughter. *Ah!* Much tender monkey."

I slip away from the sheets.

"Hunger for plenty fat man. Never satisfaction."

We chase each other on all fours.

"*YAAaaa!!*"

She plays. She's intuitive. Baring her natural skin.

I scuttle out of sight into the bathroom.

Lips lie me like laurel down softly in silence, Rain Fortune
on her haunches. My roots in her teeth. Flows on the ebb that
moans and glides. I am coming to a meeting, I am late on the
journey, I am calling through sea spray, I am walking on high
waves, I am running, I am lava. . . . Sweet Fortune, how she
lives! How she swims! Life changes. Darkens. Cruelty heals.
Time is bleak. Our moments are our visions. Hold! Hold! I
listen. She is laughing.

The service waiter enters the other room. I hear his voice.
I snatch a towel from the rail, wrap it round my waist. He is
laying the tray on the table beside the TV. He stops when he
sees me. He is Italian or Mexican, very dark and puffy. I
imagine him as a child rubbing oil into his cheeks to preserve
the texture of his skin.

He waves a piece of paper. I make a pretence at checking the
food. Rain Fortune enters wearing hand towels.

"I like The Beatles," he says. "I have most of their records."

Rain Fortune takes a plate over to the bed.

"We get a lot of English groups here," he says. "My brother's
in the bar downstairs."

He wants to unfold. I look away. His hand reaches for mine.

"Kiss him, honey!" Rain Fortune says.

21

We don't make our lives. We move naturally into areas of isolation. What is left may be the shadow of originality. Once the image becomes the man then the man is forgotten. Matthew worries where I'll be in five years. I have lost my sense of belonging. I say, 'I'm not in it for the bread.' He worries where *he'll* be in five years. Money debases people. We learn to live enclosed. Catherine asked, 'Why must we change?' I said, 'We grow used to each other.' She said, 'Nothing makes time pass more slowly than lying under plum trees watching wasps.'

How we invent beauty! How we build dreams out of slender hope! I recognize phases in my life like layers of coloured chalk. I am not me. I am multiplied and divided, added and subtracted. I am algebra. We lose our innocence by condoning corruption, accepting the darker deceits of man's injustice and cruelty. I was born ignorant. I cherished it. Shyness was armour. God made animals and birds and trees and fields (all that) and mountains and seas and fish and insects and earth and sky (all that too) and then, being vain, a creature in His own likeness. But that creature was not God. It was man. Man knew greed. God said, 'Be good and you'll make it to the next world.' The Devil said, 'Do your own thing, man. There is no next world.' We have faith in ourselves now, in our ability to build landscape gardens and potted fish factories and china geese factories and cottages in the country and stables with horses and fifteen miles of barbed wire fencing and little children dressed in satin and holidays abroad and Continental cars. We believe in practical myths. I don't fall on the floor now. I don't say, 'You're doing a wonderful job, Lord. I appreciate these emotions you're handing out.' God has no power. He can do nothing. He's tired of trying. He's asleep. Perhaps He's dead. Perhaps He never lived. I know He didn't make the land or the animals. He didn't make us. We evolved like everything else. Science destroys belief in heaven and yet fables excite the imagination. Without mystery we have no excuse. I am a dreamer in the lit morning. If truth hurts I soften it. I say, 'God made the land and I have lived on the land and the land is good which makes me good', forgetting that the land is hard and strange, demanding of man's body and blood.

Driving through Santa Barbara, the second gig of the tour, with the Pacific stretching away to the left so perfectly blue, past low ranch-style houses in quiet suburban areas, I talked to one of the promoters in his butterfly-painted VW. He said, 'The kids are scared now. They're not together. The pigs shoot anything that moves. Revolutionaries say you're either with us or against us.' He wore frayed faded Levis, leather sandals, a beard. Three years ago he would have been a surfer. He said, 'They're arresting hitch-hikers, frisking them for guns.' He looked across at me to gauge reaction. I said, 'That's bad.' He was a beach dude, salt flecked and honey skinned. He said, 'This used to be a sleepy town. No one knew there was a University here.' I imagined him reading aloud to his lady by the light of an Hawaiian moon (Kenneth Rexroth, Chinese Love Poems, Dylan Thomas), oh the softness of the wind, the complimentary softness of his voice as he lay with her, thigh by knee, hair tangled at the water's edge, rolling half asleep, in like a thief, as she moaned, he kissing *mmmmmmm*, she snatching his hands, bringing them to her breasts where they fluttered like gulls, and he would whisper, 'I feel your soul shake', because it sounded so fine in the darkness, and she would bite his neck suddenly and he'd take fright, losing control of the poetry in motion as she bucked like a zebra, afterwards brushing sand from his beard, bathing it off in the sea. He said, 'Everyone wants to go to this concert but a lot of kids' parents won't let them because of Nazi hassles and students getting back in time for curfew.' I felt his joy, talking from personal experience of brutality and repression when before he would have argued the price of buggy tyres. I said, 'Do you like Richard Brautigan?' He looked surprised. He said, 'Sure.' I said, 'Better than Hemingway?' He said, 'Yeh.' I said, 'Why?' He said, 'We can't go on living in these bullshit cities, man.' I said, 'What's that got to do with it?' He said, 'Trout Fishing in American Shorty, man.' I laughed and said, 'Treat This Wino Like An Angel.' He said, 'Yeh!' The streets of Santa Barbara were clean and empty. We drove through. He said, 'Brautigan is Woodstock Nation, right? Woodstock Nation is Earth People's Park. Earth People's Park is The Grateful Dead. The Grateful Dead is Bobby Seale. Bobby Seale's in the pigpen learning what you've got to do to eat shit in white capitalist society. Everyone's

23

together, man.' He talked like he had microphones in his breast-bone. His name was Jackson. He was a student. I asked, 'What kind of student?' He told me. Some category of sociology. I didn't recogniz it. I said, 'That's cool.' The gig was at an out-door amphitheatre in the hills on the edge of town, sheltered by trees and thick green bushes and a thirty-foot cliff with a ten-foot wire fence running along the top. Jackson said, 'They cut it last night.' I said, 'Why?' He said, 'They want to put us out of business.' I thought he meant the police, but he didn't. He meant rival promoters from L.A. He said, 'When Joe Cocker was here kids came storming in like buffalo.' The concrete stage was the size of a parking lot. A San Franciscan sounds company was setting up the PA. I remembered their name from a year ago. Chicks in bare feet and denim were moving around in the sun. It was four o'clock in the afternoon. Jackson said, 'They banned concerts after that first bank bombing.' He recounted incidents of kids peppered with birdshot, cops tossing tear gas canisters into campus pot parties. I said, 'Easy, man. Okay? I've been driving six hours. I'm fucked.' He said, 'It's happening all over, right? In Germany, Japan, France, Italy. . . .' I sat on a folding chair against the wall of an outbuilding. Matthew was hassling Jackson's partners about which PA to use. Ken and Terry had arrived with our gear and were un-loading. I began to worry about the size of the stage and how they had fixed the lighting and how many other bands were booked and who they were. I sat in the sun wearing my Spanish straw hat. Rick Burns from the record company came over carrying a chair. He placed it beside me and sat down. He was dressed in a white cotton suit with rope-soled shoes. He pulled a folder of cuttings out of his briefcase. I glanced at them. They were press reviews of the first gig. I read two of them while Rick told me why this was going to be a sensational tour and how they'd arranged a poster for the new album on Sunset Strip and what he'd said to Bill Graham in San Francisco on the telephone that morning and how excited he had been to have me back and what a great show he'd put together. I disliked the reviews. They talked of *losing ethnic roots* and *imitating North American concepts*. Patrick, Steve and Charlie of Jug Meat had arrived in another car. Steve waved at Matthew. Terry was setting up

24

Charlie's drums. Ken shouted over to Patrick, 'There's no power. The gig's off.' Patrick grinned. Ken was plugging wires into the cabinets. Steve shouted, 'Git yourself togevver, lad!' He tickled Ken's tits. Ken squirmed, kneeing him. Jackson's partners stood on the grass in front of the stage talking to Jackson. Terry was setting up the mikes for rehearsal, his curly black hair tied in an Arlo Guthrie ponytail. Rick Burns asked whether I had met Rose Crumbie. I said, 'No.' He said, 'Remember Don Musquat? Handled PR on the West Coast.' I said, 'Yeh.' He said, 'Blew his fuse.' I said, 'How?' He said, 'Acid.' Matthew joined us. He wore the leather bronco hat he'd bought in Colorado last year. He was tall and muscular like those butch male models in American cigarette ads who lounge about on horses and have their balls muslin-wrapped. Rick started telling him all the things he had told me. Matthew pretended not to listen and then asked, 'How's the album selling?' Rick said, 'We're trying Dick Cavett in New York.' Matthew nodded. Rick said, 'Seen the cuttings?' I walked off. A warm breeze was blowing. Terry tapped the mikes. No sound. I said, 'Where's the organ?' Patrick said, 'They're borrowing one from a French History professor.' Terry jumped the wires. He said, 'Why haven't we got juice?' Ken said, 'The dam burst, cunt.' Terry said, 'What fuckin dam?' Charlie couldn't nail his drums to the concrete. He shouted, 'Hey! Ken!' Jackson dropped a wet hamburger into my hand. I passed it to Patrick who opened it, examined the greasy shrivelled meat, the yellow red sauce, the burnt onion peelings, and then closed it again, wrapped it in its tissue and handed it back to Jackson. He said, 'I might even like it here if the grub wasn't dog shit.' Jackson laughed. I knew he was going to say something about capitalist meat manufacturers or bastard bun bakers and so I stopped him. I said, 'What are you charging for the concert?' He told me. I said, 'That's a rip off, man.' He said, 'We're not aiming to make a profit.' I said, 'Open the gates. Let the people in free.' He thought I was serious. He said, 'You can't build a nation on hope and prayer.' I said, 'You're right.' Steve was chatting up chicks beside a dry stone stream that cut through the trees at the side of the stage. Terry shouted, 'Gerr em off!' Steve turned his back on us. One of Jackson's partners, Moby, appeared with a fat man in blue dungarees. Terry and Charlie

25

were fitting blocks under the drums. Moby introduced the fat man as an electrician. Ken told him the fuses had blown. The electrician said, 'Must be overloading.' Ken said, 'Your box is buggered, mate.' Jackson offered me a tin of rolled joints. I refused. Patrick smiled, shook his head. Jackson said, 'That's cool, man.' He closed the tin.

Patrick's taller than me, thin and bony. He wears crushed velvet trousers, faun zip boots, crimson T-shirt. Jug Meat's only album, *Locked Inside Your Head,* sold better than expected, but what interested Matthew was Patrick's arrangements on two of my songs. He enthused about their seriousness, something I would have taken for granted, I suppose. That was a year ago when I was refusing interviews, becoming increasingly nervous of performance. We were playing Chicago, I remember, and Matthew came into the dressing room and said the security cops were beating kids off the aisles. I went to look. There was a spade band performing loud soul rock with a white singer out front. The cops were backed against the stage, a line of twenty or thirty of them, shiny crash hats gleaming under the spots, guns in holsters, night sticks dangling from leather belts. The kids were on their seats screaming and the band incited them more and more. I returned to the dressing room. I said, 'They want a fucking *riot*!' Matthew knew what in my mind and yet I believe, even now, that if he had stayed, waited a little longer, reassured me, I would have come through. But he didn't. He said, 'Don't worry about a thing.' And left. I packed my guitars, walked out of the dressing room and stood at the stage door. Two security guards barred my way. They had orders to stop anyone leaving. I said, 'I want to go.' They said, 'Do us a favour, buddy.' I sat on a trunk in a corner in the dark. A blonde chick came and sat beside me. I closed my eyes. I didn't move. I didn't look at her. I felt the heat of her body, heard the kids screeching as the spade band returned for a pulverizing encore. I began to slide. Matthew held me under the arms. I said, 'It's okay. I'm okay.' I was taken into the dressing room. I lay on the floor. The room was crowded. One moment it was empty and the next it was full. I was carried into a chair. The blonde chick offered me a sesame seed biscuit. I laughed. In her face. She had pearl-shaped eyes. Her lips opened. She was speaking. I couldn't hear. There

26

was nothing. Next day they flew me home, wrapped in blankets, and the newspapers published predictable pieces about THE PRICE OF FAME. I wanted to go away, begin again. Matthew saw it differently, as he would, valuing the publicity and talking of 'This important chapter in your life.' He said, 'Pain and suffering is the garnish.' I said, 'To what?' He said, 'You know . . . life.' I said, 'I don't.' He said, 'The kids dig it.' I said, 'If they think I'm dying for them, I'm not. I'm dying *in spite* of them.' He said, 'Keep writing, rest and come back soon.' I went to see Beccy, feeling the spirit of Rimbaud thrash across her balcony. I was outside, able to perceive clearly other people's motivations. Matthew had been a student at one of those northern universities. He drank beer and wore a long scarf down his front and had short hair and talked without an accent. His father was a Civil Servant who commuted daily into London from a rustic cottage in Surrey. Matthew called him 'self-consciously cultured' and said that both his parents would sit in the front room listening to Philharmonic concerts on the radio like characters in a 1940 movie, the radio on the table between them, one of those big bulgy pre-war things, real *objet d'art,* and he talked always of the silence in that house and the green fence surrounding it and the books in the bookshelves that couldn't be taken out without permission. Everything they did embarrassed him. Beccy understood. She liked them. She said, 'They don't make a big pretence. They're gentle people.' Beccy was Jewish. She had a hunger for family. She told me, 'Matthew depends on you as a friend.' It wasn't true. I left three days later for Spain. Catherine came with me. She whispered, 'I want to carry you in my pocket.' The aeroplane floated like a bottle. Catherine said, 'Are you sad?' We held hands. I felt her blood in my veins. The villa, her uncle's, stood on the Andalusian border. We were alone except for Pietro, the gardener, and Angelina, the cook. Days existed like extensions of our own bodies. Catherine walked in the wood. She became the wood. She swam in the sea. She became the sea. She lay in my reeds like a swan. I told her, 'You *are* me.' She said, 'I am myself loving you.' I said, 'I am you also.' She said, 'I have ugly insides.' I said, 'I am all of you.' She said, 'That's too much.' My life had reached a wall. She said, 'I've never known anyone like you.' I raised my tongue, remem-

27

bering my mother's tears, how my father's faith had frightened us. I said, 'Do you believe in Jesus?' She said, 'I don't need confession. I have you.' Our differences were our strength. We wandered through the cork forest over dry cracked earth. She ran ahead. I belonged to a fantasy of childhood, hidden beneath rhododendrons with dead squirrels and voles, the leaves of games long passed and played. I watched her. She turned laughing. She called my name. We reached the sea and swam. We walked back through the stunted forest to lunch in the shade of the vine-hung patio. I wondered, is love a tree that hides the world? I was aware of the weather, each day a little different, the wind a little stronger, a little lighter, the sun hotter, softer, the rain, the dew, the temperature of the air. People are not what they seem but a culmination of life's span. The roots remain, our reality a reaction, itself indicating involvement, mine a continuation, simultaneous rejection and acceptance of that sulky scruff lifting neeps from a damp field sixteen years ago. Catherine said, 'As a family we're together.' She was talking of herself. I said, 'All I ever wanted was to run.' She said, 'Why are you so proud of that?' Her moods changed so fast. I said, 'I never belonged.' She said, 'Sometimes when I'm unhappy I feel the same but it makes demands on people, especially those close to you.' When I met her father he spent an evening discussing music with me. I was flattered. Catherine said, 'He's a lonely man.' I said, 'Isn't the house always full of people?' She said, 'Yes.' I said, 'How can he be lonely?' She said, 'He was trained as a diplomat and diplomats know how to talk to people.' I said, 'How do they talk to people?' She said, 'It's a technical thing. They make them feel interesting and amusing.' I stayed three days. When I think of it now I wonder how I survived. Catherine's mother asked, 'Are you comfortable? Do you have everything?' I thought she was joking. I said, 'It's a nice house.' It was a castle. There were coal fires in every bedroom, hot water bottles in every bed, breakfast on silver trays. I hated it and yet Catherine had a quality of strength I had never discovered in other girls, a confidence that became protective. I enjoyed the danger of the journey because, for me, it was dangerous. I never wondered, never asked myself what it was that she wanted, thinking, she loves me like she says, and yet there were

28

times, later, when everything seemed mistaken and incredible. At home she changed. She was happy and nostalgic which only intensified my feeling of isolation, the contrast so striking, lawns as wide as corn fields, a private chapel, a billiard room, a squash court in the stables with doves nesting in the eaves, a butler older than my father who called me Sir. She said, 'We had no need for alternatives. We went to school, boarding school, like going to prison, and then came home and had each other.' Standing at the french windows in the summer drawing room I could see forever across a wooded valley where deer and cattle grazed and pheasants hatched under chickens to be shot by civilized, educated men wearing houndstooth tweed and water-proof shoes. Catherine said, 'My mother has her own things. Village things. She leads a disciplined life.' I said, 'Does your Dad work?' She said, 'He's away much of the time and when he's at home he stays in his study. He's not the strongest in-fluence.' She liked to listen to me talk of my childhood, imagin-ing how she would have reacted if she had lived with us. Her admiration for my mother was entirely sentimental. When I accused her of this she said, 'You don't appreciate such sacrifice.' I said, 'Without choice there is no sacrifice.' In Spain I began to work again. Catherine leaned over my shoulder, kissed my neck. It was not enough to know my life. She had to feel it and understand it and I had to feel hers and understand hers also so that together we shared the language of our souls. I told her, 'I am not used to love.' At the start I had been afraid to give myself completely, believing that once you did so you were left with nothing and your emptiness became as a dry well in the desert. Catherine said, 'Lead me.' The garden was heavy with the scent of roses. She said, 'It'll be fantastic.' She believed that life was simple. Only people complicated it. She said, 'We pretend how important and intelligent we are and how cruel and savage animals are. And yet we're like them. We are them.' I said, 'We're not. We're nothing like them.' She had a child's capacity for pleasure and a child's impatience. Looking up, seeing me coming, her cheeks burned. She said, 'I'm not as innocent as I look.' But she was. So was I. She said, 'Imagine we are birds. How free! How wild!' She stretched her arms in anticipation of the miracle. I said, 'We'd be shot by your father's gamekeeper.' She said, 'Perhaps.' There were places that didn't exist where she wished to live and yet when I questioned her she stopped me. She said, 'I believe in you.' I said, 'Why?' She said, 'Because you love me.' And yet there were areas of her life that I could not reach.

"Why did it take so long to suss Vietnam as a bad scene?" I ask.

I'm standing at the window, looking out. Everything feels larger, even the sky.

'They had blacks coming into the streets sayin they was goin to kill people. An they did. They killed white folk," Rain Fortune says. "Now that was a strange thing. A black man thinkin he could turn aroun an talk right back. Senators said, we got somethin like revolution movin aroun here, we got trouble coming, man; we're goin to have to do something to change all that. So they make this other revolution in Vietnam which they say's a danger to y'all, bein a million miles away an concerning *Chinese*. They tell the white kids, don't fret y'ass, brothers, we're not takin you out of school; we're takin the dumb kooks an the niggers. That's what they wanted, that's what they planned all along, to clean us off the streets an save the country. But when the war's over, honey, all those kids is coming home. They goin to know about killing an bombing. The war ain't *never* goin to end."

"Do you believe that?"

"Why you risin me?"

"I'm serious."

"Yeah?"

"What else?"

"I hate this world sometimes. Those cats who go get theyselves sick on pills and junk, they have my love, honey, they have all my love. They don't have it, not mine, not nobody's right now. They can't see *nothin*. No way. An they *feel*. They got feelings in them you never *dreamed*. Maybe you, honey, but not many. . . . They suffer their colour like you suffer dead baby chil'ren. When we was kids we went to church. We dressed us in white, real fancy clothes like to a wedding, an washed clean, made us feel we lived the same as everyone, and we looked aroun there in that church at cheeks running with tears, not from sadness no more but from freedom; that *was* freedom. We had feelings all inside that the music brought back. We had these feelings so strong we wanna scream 'n' shout. They ain't hurt. They jes *there.* They *always* bin there. White folk say, you got real soul, man. They make it sound like some rich thing. Like only a few found it. Muddy Waters an Bessie Smith maybe an Otis, yeah! They talk of soul and say, sure, *Otis,* he got soul. Then they think awhile an remember, *hey! James Brown,* yeah! Although they never properly *known* him. Only *heard* of him. Then they think some more. *Hey!* Little Richard, Chuck Berry! But they're *names.* Figures from the past. Not like kids in the street though kids in the street are the same. They got soul. They all got soul. It ain't no special thing, God's hand touchin you an sayin, you feel me handlin you something special, chil, you feel this piece o' soul I'm handlin you, honey? I say, I'm feelin every little bit of it, Lord, an I'm grateful 'cause I can go out an make me a big roll of money from the white folk who like t'hear this whole thing happen. But I *dig* it, honey. Soul's havin feelings up inside an findin ways of bringing them out real slow. If you don't they turn you bad an you need that junk to stop yourself killing everybody an startin a war 'cause of the conditions you're living in an the prospects you learn to accept, bein black. The Mafia's s'posed to control junk an the Mafia's white folk. It's to their advantage to keep niggers strung out. They make that junk the only release for soul that's turning kids crazy."

Heat hangs over the city. People lose faith in their ability to remember where they're going. When the world dies Las Vegas will remain a lasting replica of American enterprise, the secret desire for live magazine art, the romance, the electricity, the hunger for magic.

Rain Fortune combs her hair.

"When you're rich and famous you'll forget all this and buy a big house in the suburbs and have Mexican servants and a pebbled driveway and an agent called Miss Annabelle Crabapple," I say.

Rain Fortune laughs.

"I'll build me a pool an have all the black kids in the neighbourhood come splash aroun in it," she says. "You *like* that?"

"They'll give you candle-lit boudoir banquets and unlikely honours like Master of Contemporary Rock at some far out mid-western university."

"Rows of diamonds, honey! Will you be there?"

"I'll wear my gold lamé suiting with green umbrella epaulettes. I'll be your *man*! I'll drive your car."

"Hey! *Shang-a-dang!*"

Life is fruitless expression, one-armed bitch bandits and rat dice rollers moving to the wonder of surprise and hope, somnolent Eskimos dealing cards like in dreams, and yet it isn't as I imagined, a white road star trekked with hotels and casinos and high class eating houses leading for miles and years into a dark desert peopled by gangsters and cabaret singers and rich freaks from every country club and cocktail bar in the nation, fat men in pungent clothes making us wonder what's this beauty called money and what's this money made to do but lather us shimmery and lay us down dead too soon leaving little old ladies with body bags of booty, wrapped in furs and wigs, rolling and groaning for lost baby youth before the rushing cold freezes their lips and sex tastes tetchy and swollen. Las Vegas is a big town, wide and substantial, the buttress of fantasy a proportion of the whole, reminding me, yet again, of the delicate balance between image and reality. Freedom for Rain Fortune is escape from the ghetto, opportunity to live like a real person which wasn't possible before because of the knowledge that in the ordinary scale of things black people can't pull themselves out by hard work and effort because the economic structure is bent too far the other way. It was different for me. My father raged with pride, opposed every motion towards change. I was afraid of him, remembering what he was, what he had been. My sister clung to my mother's skirts. We were timid. We had a feeling of dread about the world. Home was my father's word, his *sound*. We knelt at the table in the draughty kitchen as he prayed. The schoolteacher read books about Africa, Canada, Australia. She said, 'You have *eyes* in your head. Now *use* them.' She made us stand at the window and look out, come back to our desks and write everything we had seen, not everything we *thought* we had seen. I wrote: 'I saw a bird fly into the tree and dirty a branch and fly away again. It does not have a nest. The tree is next to the road. The road bends uphill towards our house. I saw the clouds. They were moving fast.' She corrected: 'How do you know the bird has no nest? You think so because it flies away. Also you cannot see your house from here.' She spoke to Janet Munro one morning. She said, 'Do you believe what you are told because you *want* to or because you *think* there's nothing else?' Janet said, 'Pardon?' The teacher said, 'If I told you the sky was yellow, would you agree?' Janet said, 'Yes, Miss.' The teacher said, 'It's not, is it?' Janet didn't answer. The teacher said, 'What colour is the sky?' Janet said, 'Dark black, Miss.' The teacher said, 'It's not yellow, is it?' Janet said, 'No, Miss.' The teacher said, 'It's not black either. It's grey.' Janet said, 'Yes, Miss.' That was all. I remember everything, Janet's eyes shining with tears, the teacher's face turning away. I thought, we're like wasps in jam. She took us on bus trips, hikes, rides, and slowly we began to understand, to look at ourselves in a different way. Nature was examined, explained. The dissection of life started on the first morning. Spring was a rebirth, a resurrection. Autumn had nobility. Summer had breadth of feeling. Winter was death. We watched a weasel and a rabbit in a field. She said, 'Cruelty is *passionate*.' We said, 'What's that, Miss?' She said, '*Listen!*' I caught a pigeon that blew against our house in a storm. I kept it in my room. It would not eat nor drink. It stood puffed up in a box and then fell on its side, blinking. I stared at it for hours. I waited and watched. I wondered how birds understood death, how men lost in the jungle felt God, how sailors in the sea experienced water flooding their lungs, how dogs knew when to crawl away and hide. It was hard, so hard. I thought, surely a tree is a tree. Surely leaves die because the wind blows them off. The teacher said, 'Death is like the coming of the evening. You grow tired and then you want to sleep.' Gordon Walker whose father died of cancer said, 'Your blood dries up and then you shrink and when there's nothing left you're dead.' We held our breath with fright. People tried to have the teacher removed. They said she didn't understand country ways, was putting ideas into our heads. I thought of her in the pigeon box, toppling over without a sound, her eyes going

up into her skull and not coming back. I prayed that she might
live, anyway for as long as I was at school. On Sundays she went
for bike rides with a knapsack tied to the pillion bar, collected
wild flowers and fern grasses to press into thick volumes of
Encyclopaedia Britannica. My father called her heathen because
she talked of Jesus as 'remarkably clever for someone with only
limited education'. When I think of her now I remember the
bones of her hands. She was a heron, a water bird, small-voiced
and shrill with a lanky body and claw-shaped shoes, nibbling
home-baked biscuits from a tin under her desk. Jim said she laid
eggs and ate them, ate cabbage and lettuce too. One evening in
summer Flora saw her fly through a hole in the school-house
chimney. She said, 'She's a witch! She's an angel! She *can't* die.'
Kathy said, 'Everyone dies. My Gran died.' When we left, when
we sold the farm and packed everything into crates, I felt a
bitterness blowing through me for those years of obedience and
prayer, discovering school where her influence exposed new
territories, only to be brought back so soon, finding myself in the
compartment of a train, my father saying, 'Be a bit brave, lad',
when I was already, refusing to cry until we were out of sight,
refusing to stare, my sister curled in my mother's arms, the train
moving slowly, the country passing, trees, rivers, hills. Sadness
was inconsolable. We bruised forever. My father said, 'There
was nothing for it.' My mother said, 'Look on the bright side.'
City school was bigger than our village. I lived in cinemas, shops,
in cold broken regions, alone. I was fearful of education now,
unable to explain to anyone, especially my father, what it was
that had gone, remembering her always, the heron, her silver
hair nesting, her bones like sticks. I reread her books and went
on to read others. The man at the library smelt of mints and pipe
tobacco. He was pleased to have me on his list because it proved
something important about 'literary culture's battle against
anarchic youth trends'. When offering to indulge the wealth of
his experience, including tea in the café opposite and Sibelius
somewhere else, I told him to piss off. The street we lived in
ended at a brick wall. Over the wall was a cemetery. Beyond
the cemetery were houses stretching for miles into grey twilit
smoke. The grass in the cemetery grew to my thighs. I watched

coffins lowered into the earth, mourners filing downhill, hired limos parked at the roadside. The city was heavy with practical architecture and machines. I was born in another place, my senses tuned to different sounds. The cemetery became the mark of independence. I exaggerated its romance.

- When did you discover your talent as a writer?
- I'm not a writer.
- Are you ambitious?
- Everyone is ambitious when they're young. The difficulty is to know what to do with it.
- Do you believe there's too much affluence?
- We're talking about energy and ego.
- Why ambition? What drives you?
- Singers are creative. Don't make them question more than they've worked out in their heads.
- You talk like an actor.
- Songs exist at their conception as genuine articles of faith. The feelings are real. I work on them until they're right and then tape them. Later I might lose those feelings. The songs remain. Sometimes I can recreate emotion on stage but it's not exactly the same. Feelings are instantaneous, otherwise they're artificial. It's a problem of technique. I'm less aware of the audience now, which is good, less dependent on them. We do a fully rehearsed set as you've seen and it's the *sound* that produces the response. On the last tour I was getting paranoiac. I needed to *feel* what was out there, what was *really* out there, and I wasn't doing that, I was feeling myself anticipating negative vibes. I needed *support*. Still do. Not the roar of the living dead.

I step out of the hotel into blistering sunlight. Patrick's there, lit with the glow of Californian fireflies. He loves it.

At Long Beach police massed in the balcony and at exit gates armed with night sticks, revolvers and gas canisters, doing nothing, outnumbered, the air thick with marijuana smoke as kids clambered onto the stage and were hurled off, Ken and Terry fixing our gear, joints flying from every direction, cries of 'Far out!', 'Get it on!', a child freaking on acid under the stage, being dragged away, bleeding. We could have played Beethoven or Bach. They wouldn't have noticed. We weren't the object of their adoration as Patrick believed but reflections of a peculiar self-love. By entering the experience of our performance they entered themselves.

YOU CAN'T BEAT THE SYSTEM BY EXISTING WITHIN IT. Messages scratched on walls. H GATHERS SPEED. I see it as a fact, the way we are. Human nature's a bitch. Jesus had a stronger hold on life than these guys. Listen how they talk of the country now, hyped into believing that peasants and Red Indians are the true men. Lie down in the corn like they do on Madison Avenue storyboards. It'll all come true. Whatever it is. California is polluted with rotting dreams. If you can't make it in the Golden State you won't make it to hell. This is Eden Garden Motelerama. Bread enough to ease your pain, Mother. Sun enough to soak your sin. But it's no good. Beauty can't be bought any more than happiness and the responsibility of fulfilling perfection proves too much for fifteen-year-old runaways. We can't live with truth. Why pretend? Death is the only freedom.

The mythology of shimsham summer music fades visibly on impact as longhairs panhandle Fillmore and chicks shuffle in the dust outside The Whisky on Sunset, so tired of hungering love their tears blister like boils. It's another scene, a religion, freakout on Pacific Drive that's going to crush convention and destroy straight society forever, such imagery of wilderness prancers, doom ships, Big Sur romantics, Macrobiotic Man retching in supermarkets, crawling through mountain allotments chanting fertility rites over peyote and marijuana, chewing weed like a goat.

36

What is relevant about kids who can't relate to their past? At least I am aware that once I was young and whatever I have become was influenced and moulded by that time and that place and the scars remaining are as much a part of me as the experience that followed.

Patrick admires the ability to change and adapt.
"You're a hippy," I say.
"What are you?"

I cannot gauge what the kids are into like I did at the beginning when my thoughts and feelings mirrored theirs. Once confidence fades there is nothing left but repetition. Success isolates the spirit. Beccy said, 'Rock'n'roll's a reflection of our unconscious desire to shit on bourgeois values.' I said, 'It's nothing to do with the unconscious. It's out and out expressionism.' I hate the practice of analysis. It kills instinct. Information, news, gossip is worshipped like the Holy Grail until there's no difference between fact and fiction. Flattery destroys integrity faster than fame. Parody mocks praise.

After Chicago when truth in music felt wasted and worthless Matthew began to suspect I might be serious in wanting to stay away with Catherine. He worked fast on a new plan. Jug Meat were approached to consider the possibility of a combined album. They agreed. Later we met. Patrick and I decided to record in Nashville. It seemed like an interesting idea. Matthew said, 'You'll be doubling the Dylan thing two years late.' I said, 'It's good PR. Especially in the States.' He said, 'It's been overexposed.' I said, 'Tell Leonard Cohen.' We rehearsed for a month while Matthew thought of alternatives. Finally, after arranging with the American record company to share costs, he said, 'Okay. Do it.' I was back. Folded like a pancake. My sister worked in Matthew's office. We shared a flat. She wrote home every week to say how I was and what I was doing. I didn't write. Once my mother came to London and stayed with us. She told me I must be patient with our Dad as he was getting old. I said, 'He won't let me *talk* to him.' She said, 'All we do is lead our lives. That's all any of us do.' I felt then as I had felt before that I was still a child in her eyes, still angry and foolish. She wanted me to know how hard she had tried and that she was right even though it ended like it did. She wanted me to recognize her life and carry it with me. I said, 'Go home, Mam.' I was tired. I stared at her. Why fight when all we have to do is pull off our knickers and wave them in the wind for a bit of peace? Don't preach stinking fish to a fishmonger's daughter! Don't line the path with grit! Don't wash your socks in public or talk sly of your soul's damage! Who's mistress of your bandaged tangle, for God's sake? Who's running the scum through your front room now? Not me, Mam. I'm so far gone you can hear the bells on my balls ring in Cincinnati, feel the waves lap your rump as I fuck little children on the other side of the world. I'm another man, sick of the memory of Our Father Who Farts In Heaven, thick stools of porridge in the milked windy mornings, seeing my sister's eyes sodden with sadness for Elspeth Grant who had an accident in the cowshed and never came back, or my father's body steaming in the tin, his great black cock like a hunk of dung in the scummy water, so terrible that I imagined myself fouled forever, and in the nights would dream of gull-white steamers riding their moorings, plunging through shoals, all hands asleep, hooting their toots, giving birth to dinghies in small yards by the port, brave silken boats, sexy as carp. I am concerned with my relevance to a life of conflicting influences, my experience going back as far as I can remember and the interpretation of that experience, my feeling of isolation and desire for involvement that will eliminate suffering. Friendship, achieved now as a result of success, has a tendency to corrupt. I am suspicious of brother love on the scale advocated by American kids. It's a wake for the death of family. Mindless multitudes rise as one to the chorus 'Love Is All You Need', offering flowers to the fuzz with such withering naivety. Group therapy insults the individual as friendship proves too delicate for definition. My mother tied labels to her natural love, believing that only women understood the child in men. I was her element, she mine. No one died of pleasure in the wood. We showed our bums to the girls. They showed their cracks. I walked to school kicking rocks, my sister's hand on my coat. I prayed, 'Please dear Jesus God don't kill us.' Wind blew the corn flat. We harvested with scythes. I cut my foot. I wore no socks. Blood was in my shoe.

Always I am growing, deflating and deflecting commitment, a boy in the dust of an alien civilization, unaware that death lies along broken stones like the dew, calling for protection to the birds and the clouds, believing them part of my life as the air and the earth and the bright sun, becoming, in time, a living creature in the empty spaces, filling them with movement, changing their colour with the rub of my body, forgetting the voices of the past and the joys of human companionship, making things happen as I believe God did once although God has changed into the great mountain behind which the sun rises in the morning because I know in my heart that God is a protector, not an innovator, and the great mountain protects me like a mother, God being a woman, and I have no fear of Her grandeur, only of snakes and spiders in the rocks, green lizards, ants, chameleons in the forest, and as time passes, summers and winters fall, I lose faith in speech and begin quietly, through an understanding of silence and the movement of heat in air, to uncover the mysteries of the world and find it is enough to know that loneliness makes me strong.

On my return from Spain I visited Beccy in hospital. She said, 'You've been away so long.' I told her Catherine had flown to Marrakesh and was staying with friends. She wasn't interested in Marrakesh. She said, 'I thought you'd never come home.' She sat in bed with a schoolgirl's white sweater over her nightdress. Her face was thinner, hair shorter. She said, 'They prick pins into me every hour and rush off to make tests. I keep telling them I feel lousy because of the prison camp food. They don't listen.'

In Nashville I thought of her often. I telephoned Matthew. He said, 'Don't worry about a thing. We're celebrating. It's Beccy's mother's birthday.' I heard people laughing. He said, 'Beccy sends love.' I asked, 'Is she there?' He said, 'She's coming home next week.'

Musicians moved through air-conditioned studios and rehearsal rooms. Tennessee was clean and fresh, full of energy at last. The columunists from music papers seemed younger than me. There was no jive.

Rain Fortune, lying on a mattress in a downtown motel room, fanned herself with a copy of *Ebony*. She said, 'You make it hard on yourself, honey!' I asked, 'What's harder than it is already?' She told me to stop snapping around the toes of things and *do it*. I said, 'You're just a showbiz blues singer.' She said, 'Blues is blues. That's one kind.' I said, 'What's the other?' She said, 'White dudes protect the sanctity of their sweet ass, dig *nothin* they don't acknowledge. That's not *blues*, man. That's Hollywood movies. We're all niggers in the dark.'

Gigs are alike. The details change but the approach is the same. Arrive early, check equipment, take sound test for acoustics, see the man on lights, wait in the dressing room for hours, drink coffee from plastic cups, chew hamburgers, roll joints, rap with strangers who've nothing better to do than look dangerous in dime store Indian beads and JOHN WAYNE IS A FAGGOT on their stovepipes, waste time as other roadies from other bands set up their gear or push it back so that we can get ours on.

The Tucson gig was in a disused wrestling hall at the centre of an empty lot on the edge of town. Two boxing rings had been pushed together to make a stage. Terry laughed when he saw it. Ken bounced the canvas. The ropes had been taken off but the corner posts remained. There were three kids standing in the shadows. One was short with a black pioneer beard, no shirt, workingman's dungarees and cowboy boots. He said, 'I'm Ralph. I'm getting it on.' The others stood beside him, thumbs in the tail of their jeans. Ken said, 'You can get it right off for all I care.' The kids looked embarrassed. Ralph said, 'This is Hicksville, U.S.A., man. They don't dig rock concerts like they do out there in the real world. They figure their little girls are going to get laid or spiked or some goddam thing. They wouldn't let us do it at all unless we came half-way into the fuckin desert. I tried to tell them who you were. They need to be told things. Like what day it is, right? I said you're a country boy. You play quiet music. They said if he's Merle Haggard's mother that's okay. No one's going to shit on Grandma Moses unless they're zapped out of their fuckin minds, man.' Ken said, 'That's your hangup.' He was enjoying himself. I asked Ralph, 'Can anyone use a hammer and nails?' We wheeled the boxing rings back and spent the afternoon building a stage. By the time it was finished half the longhairs in Arizona were stripped to their cut-off Levis and *working*. Ken refused. He said, 'If they can't get their own thing together, screw 'em.' He waited in the hotel. Terry set up the gear. No one told Ken when it was ready and so he wandered over an hour after the gig had started and told the kids at the door, 'Ralph knows me.' Ralph said, 'What's the hassle, man?' Ken said, 'I want in.' Ralph said, 'Were you here this afternoon?' Ken said, 'I've been here all day.' Ralph said, 'What kinda bullshit's that, man?' He wouldn't let him through.

In the years before star hype I performed alone, carried everything with me, used a small box amp that fed through one of the cabinets. Now we have Jug Meat, two roadies and a vanload of gear. Patrick worries about sound quality but won't aggravate promoters if the PA's poor. He's nervous with strangers, won't push to the limit. Ken is different. He began with Love Stone Convention, a bluesy soul band from Birmingham, in the mid '60s. After they broke up he stayed with Mick Hammell, the lead guitarist, and Moonshine Pirate, a black drummer who had worked as a session man in Hollywood. They formed Gomorrah, a prototype heavy metal band, with Dave Wells, a bass guitarist from another English group, Soldiers of

41

Fortune, and a wild Scot called Fraser Dalgliesh on organ. I met Ken for the first time at the Montreal Summer Festival a couple of years ago when Gomorrah caused confusion by exploding their organ on stage after the set. On tour, during days off, he stayed in his hotel, watched TV, drank milk and slept. He was making good bread and saving it. Terry said, 'The guy's a freak. He hates everyone.' Matthew said, 'He's a hard man with promoters and that's what we need.' Mick Hammell ODed three months after the Canadian gig. Moonshine Pirate continued with what was left of the band and Ken split. He said he wouldn't hump gear for any nigger.

Patrick's impressionable. He comes from a southern English town, Bournemouth or Weymouth, one of those, and met Steve and Charlie at Bromley Art College when he was eighteen. Steve's a clown, a raver. Charlie's quiet and dedicated but lacks the flair that gives Patrick's guitar work such unique quality. I know I'm taking risks with Jug Meat because they're good enough to blow me off any time they want but the fact we're involved together in a group that includes three black chicks doing an Ikettes harmony with Rain Fortune climbing up for a couple of solos like Rita Coolidge in Joe Cocker's Mad Dogs spreads talent enough so that the individuality of Patrick's playing melds rather than breaks continuity.

If I had lived all my life in the States I would be like these kids now, rapping about revolution and freedom, into acid and food stamps and commune sex, crashing pop festivals, dodging the draft, believing sincerely and absolutely that to die for a tattle rag state in southern Asia was sheer fantastic madness. But I wasn't, I was born elsewhere, and so find it hard to forgive them their greed, their arrogance, their lack of sensitivity. When I was sixteen I was aware that the sky was empty. I didn't feel part of anything, didn't realize that over the mountains on the other side whole forests were shaking, separated, it seemed, by arid distance and heinous ignorance. Even then, subliminal, something was growing, a faith, like a seed, a faith in

42

luck, in God, although it wasn't God.

- Was your family musical?
- My father tampered with the fluegelhorn when he wasn't killing cows.
- What were your influences as a child?
- I went to school. I played in the street. I watched other kids play in the street.
- You had an interesting childhood?
- It went on for a long time.
- When did you become aware of a musical consciousness?
- I might sit down in a room in a motel in Minneapolis and work something out but I'm doing that because there's nothing else to do in a room in a motel in Minneapolis. Glamour's an exaggeration of the banal. You know that. I find myself looking at one of your magazines, amazed by the sheer weight of invention. I ask myself, what's wrong? Why don't I notice this fabulous glamour? Why don't I feel these vibes? I'm not saying you're irrelevant. You're not. As a person. You go home at night. You do all the things that everyone else does. You go to bed. You get up in the morning. You go to work. That's your *life*. It's the same with me. I go to bed. I get up in the morning. I think, it's another day. Or I don't think anything. I look at my face in the mirror. It's the same face as it was yesterday. I wash it. Life would be more glamorous if we changed. On Monday, Elvis. On Tuesday, Garbo. On Wednesday, Walt Whitman. What you're going to write isn't about me, it's about your impression of me. That's not me. I haven't told you anything. Your impression is as much to do with you as it is with me. What about you? Did you have an interesting childhood? When were you aware of literary consciousness? What's your family think of you? What do they think of me? It's *you*, isn't it? It's you looking at me, remembering everything you've ever read about me, fitting that into what I do now, what I say which isn't much because all I'm saying is there's nothing. Chick journalists should be groupies. Then they'd understand.
- There's something fundamentally wrong with your analysis

43

of what a reader expects.
- I don't know who reads your stuff.
- You implied that writers falsify their evidence to suit editorial policy.
- I didn't. But I will if you like.
- Kids are *interested*. That may come as a surprise. No one gets paid for *enjoying* their jobs. If they do it's a bonus.
- You're offended because I'm not answering your questions.
- I learn a great deal from the avoidance of questions.
- Why not invent the whole thing?
- Exactly.
- I sleep in the nude. I have a cat called Litz. I own a farmhouse in Oxfordshire. I write jingles for Cleenaire Deodorant. I'm an environmental poet.
- That's predictable.
- It's also untrue.
- I'm surprised. I expected another kind of person.
- Who?
- I'm intrigued.
- Are you married?
- Does it show?
- Do you like being married?
- I have a nice husband.
- What does that mean?
- Are you thinking of marriage?
- I'll make a deal with you. I'll answer your questions if you answer mine.
- What are your questions?
- I'm not bothered by what you write. I won't read it.
- You realize how dangerous this is?
- Everything's dangerous. Otherwise it's dead.
- Perhaps some things should be dead.
- Interviews sell records, right? I want to sell records because it's crazy doing what I do without getting something out of it. I believe we have two lives, the inner life and the outer life. I'm more into the inner life but can't escape altogether because I've got to move around and be seen. When I do interviews I loon about because I know the guy who's asking the questions doesn't want real answers. He wants to flash a bit, join us on tour, have groupies and dope and free booze because it makes him feel like he's part of the action which he isn't and never will be. When

44

I play bad music and kids think it's great because I'm famous and people know me and write about me I lose all sense of proportion and that shit about image being the master of art begins to make sense and I stand there screaming and they think it's part of the act. What can I do? It's not enough to be a person, to understand that I exist. I've got to know *why,* like I want to know about you, why you think things, why you enjoy being married, why you do your job, what you feel for me, for other people. You're *outside.* You have a lot to offer. If I write a song that says, woke up this morning, saw the rain running down the hillside where it's never run before, and say nothing else, leave it there, not meaning much, making you imagine flooded fields, ruined crops, how this beautiful water rushing over the rocks isn't beautiful inside my head because I know the destruction down in the valley, and don't wrap it up sweet with fancy riffs and double tracks, just play it soft, that's *true,* a true song true to me, but when it's taken to mean a whole load of other things because of the rubbish that's written about songs, it becomes something it never was, and that's the shadow again, the plastic shadow, what I'm trying to avoid.

We turn off The Strip. There's a crowd at the front of the Convention Center. I can see them in the distance squatting on the concrete patio. To the left there's a new hotel, The Landmark, and we slip through its parking lot to the back of the Center where Ken's van's parked beside five or six cars. The sliding doors of the building are locked.

Patrick laughs.

"We're stuck."

"Try the other side."

"You try. You know the way."

We stand in the sun arguing until the idea of forcing a way through the kids at the main door becomes absolutely unacceptable. We decide to go to The Landmark and telephone Ken but the thought of his reaction is too strong a deterrent and so persuade ourselves that the commissionaire at The Landmark wouldn't let us in, wouldn't let *me* in anyway with my jeans and army surplus running shoes. I tell Patrick he looks enough like a male hustler to make it. He offers to change his clothes.

"Admit that all you want to be is Donovan," he says. "In fact, that's not a bad plan. Donovan would walk through that crowd, no bother."

"I don't want to be Donovan," I say. "I don't even look like him. Donovan sings nursery rhymes and has this Celtic mythology going for him which is more than can be said for me."

"You don't have to sing, for Christ's sake! You say, 'Hi kids, I'm Donovan', and they'll be so surprised they'll say, 'Wow, crazy man! Far out!', and you'll be through grappling with the glass doors before they know what's happened."

Images of Donomania are too much. Patrick suggests Lee Marvin and Pancho Gonzales.

"Who's Pancho Gonzales?" I ask.

He looks hurt.

"I'd rather be Jackie Onassis," I say.

"You can't," Patrick says. "If Lee Marvin and Jackie Onassis are walking through a crowd of dangerous Las Vegan deviants Lee Marvin would suss it out first to make sure everything's okay because if the lady was damaged Ari wouldn't dig it, would he? He'd pay a lot of bread to have the gig cancelled, unearth some phoney fire restriction and give every kid in the audience a free copy of 'Frank Zappa Sings Mary Poppins' plus a signed photograph of Princess Grace dressed as the young Queen Victoria, and if that happened, which it would, we'd be stuck here for the rest of the night."

"Since I'm Jackie Onassis I feel confident that a man of Lee Marvin's reputation would come up with something."

"I don't even have *white hair*."

"A little thing like the colour of your sidies doesn't worry Lee Marvin. He's too good an actor."

"John Wayne could do it."

"Lee Marvin's faster."

"The kids would fold up at the sight of John Wayne, especially on his horse."

"He hasn't got a horse."

"He was *born* on a horse."

"That's Roy Rogers."

"A horse to John Wayne is like a white suit to Elvis."

"Elvis didn't wear a white suit in *Jailhouse Rock*."

"It's a known fact that Elvis never sets foot in Nevada without his white suit. Las Vegas and the white suit are one. Las Vegas and Elvis and the white suit."

"I don't have a suit. It wouldn't work. John Wayne's better."

"Okay."

"Git on that hoss an do y'thing, Dook."

"Hold it, Frankie. I'm Lee Marvin. *You* git up."

"Who's Frankie?"

"Frankie the Rat."

"You're too skinny to be Dean or Peter or Sammy or Joey."

"I could be Mia."

"She married the other guy."

"I could be the other guy."

"What other guy?"

"The guy she married."

"The Maharishi?"

"She didn't marry the Maharishi."

"Who did she marry?"

"One of the Beach Boys."

"She didn't. She married that musician."

"Who?"

"Tchaikovsky."

"Yeah, that's right. You be Tchaikovsky and I'll be Hamlet's ghost."

"Tchaikovsky's Russian and can't speak English and wouldn't have a chance of getting through the door because the cops wouldn't understand what he was saying and if they did they'd arrest him as a spy, but Hamlet's ghost could make it because no one would see him."

"Hamlet's ghost wore armour. They'd see that and stop it at the door and read the rules which discriminate against any form of armour on account of a series of thefts at the Museum of Arts & Indian Crafts so that anyone seen walking about in armour is arrested on the spot and held without trial until satisfactory psychiatric reports."

"I can't see the armour."

"Of course you can't. You're Tchaikovsky and Tchaikovsky was terrified of armour due to the fact that his mother used to dress him in suits of the stuff because she believed it increased his musical appreciation like being locked in a soundproof booth and playing twenty-four hours of Nelson Riddle at 78 revs. Of course Tchaikovsky lost his cool and half his mind and whenever he came across a suit of armour in later life he thought it was Nelson Riddle and his friends were worried that the KGB might arrest him for fraternizing with subversive Western band leaders and so persuaded him to make an appointment with Rasputin's ghost who hypnotized him into thinking that suits of armour were dead chickens because when he was a kid he wandered into the kitchen when the cook was plucking a hen and . . . for $10,000, *what* did baby Tchaikovsky think the plucked hen on the kitchen table *was*?"

"Nelson Riddle's mother."

"No."

"Frank Sinatra."

"No."

"Buñuel."

"Who's Buñuel?"

"Nelson Riddle's father."

"Nelson Riddle's not called Nelson Buñuel."

"His father's called Buñuel Riddle."

"Very interesting but it's not the answer."

"I give up."

"You lose the chance of $10,000. Or would you prefer to open the box?"

"I'll open the box."

"He's refused a $10,000 gold watch, ladies and gentlemen, in favour of Box Number 13. *How about that!!?* You be the audience – boos, hisses!"

"I want to open the box."

"He wants to open the box, ladies and gentlemen! He wants to risk a lavatory brush, a soiled Tampax toilet requisite and a bent copy of 'Frank Zappa Plays My Blue Heaven' instead of accepting, here and now, on the show, *live*, from your sponsors, Rat Pack Inc., sellers of crappy movies and worn out handlebar moustache jokes, a $10,000 trip to Miami Beach, Florida, and

48

the opportunity of an invitation to cocktails with Tricia Nixon and assorted members of the FBI."

"I wasn't offered Tricia Nixon and the FBI. I was offered a lousy Mickey Mouse tick-tock."

"He won't be swayed, ladies and gentlemen! He believes that Box Number 13 holds more for him than 10,000 free tickets to Disneyland, Cal."

"I don't! I'll take Disneyland!"

"Too late! Tricia Nixon just called to say she's protesting against Sylvester's aggression against Tweetie Pie and will be picketing all cartoon movie emporiums up and down the country and won't be *in situ* for the annual bombout at the FBI Lounge, Miami Hilton, blah blah apologies peep peep. Anyway she's just married a guy. One of the Beach Boys."

"Open the bloody box! I don't care whether she's married Frank Zappa."

"*She has!* You've won the Brilliant Bumper Bundle! Or, if you prefer it, the Customary Christmas Crumble. What's it to be? Bundle or Crumble?"

"I'll Crumble."

"Good lad. We open the box . . . click click fumble pull. . . . You've won. . . . *Hold it,* ladies and gentlemen! Our contestant, Mr Frank Sinatra Junior from North London Polytechnic for Further Studies Into Phantasmal Phenomena, otherwise referred to as Look And Learn About Mia Farrow And Her Fantastic Rise To Fame, has turned down an evening in front of the telly with Mamie Eisenhower for . . . fold unfold squint shuffle . . . *Big John Wayne*! Congratulations, Mr Tchaikovsky. The answer to Nelson's riddle about the baby and the dead chicken is 'Popeye Meets Mighty Mouse' starring His Grace The Bedford of Monaco and Mr Terry-Fred-Thomas with Happy Rockefeller as Sophie, the maid, and Twiggy falling over the furniture in the famous Catsup underwater dance sequence which cost $4 million and took three years to film."

"Why?"

"What do you mean?"

"Why did it take four years to film and $3 million to make?"

"I don't know. You're John Wayne. Ask yourself."

"I'm not John Wayne. I'm Tchaikovsky."

"You're not. You've just won yourself."

"You can't go back on it."

"You've seen the armour. I'm Hamlet's ghost. I'm covered in armour from head to foot."

"I refuse. I was never Tchaikovsky in the first place. You tried to make me Tchaikovsky. I didn't agree. I was someone else. Ethel Merman, I think."

"You *were* Tchaikovsky. You just said so. You said, I'm not Big John, I'm Tchaikovsky. Now you're 'Popeye Meets Mighty Mouse'. Get stuffed!"

Ken walks past towards the Hertz van. He ignores us.

"Don't look now," Patrick says.

"I won't. I'm not. Who is it?"

"What shall we do?"

Ken unlocks the back of the van.

"Wait."

"Do you think he's seen us?"

"Who?"

"Old meatjaw, the mad monk."

"Old junkyard, the sheep thief."

"He has eyes – "

"In his flies."

"No one tells me anything."

Ken walks from the van with a mike stand, his brown hair, even in this heat, looking dirty and damp.

"You locked us out, you sod," I say.

"What happened to the press conference?" he says.

"The door was bolted. We couldn't get in."

We go through the sliding doors which are open now into a wide high passage. Terry's testing the mikes, calling, "One, two! One, two!" Steps lead up onto the rear of the stage. Martha's sitting on a drum case behind the cabinets. Patrick asks about his guitar. Ken says it's in the dressing room, pointing to a door at the end of the passage on the right, closest to the stage. We enter. It's bright and freshly painted with hooks on the walls and an individual lavatory at the end and a shower. There are two chicks sitting on a bench against the wall. Guitar cases and clothes are lying about the floor. Patrick acts as if the chicks aren't there. I'm uncertain how to approach them. They look

50

very young.

"I'm Bobby," the blonde says. "This is my friend, Bernice. She's called Bernie."

Bobby smiles. She's pretty.

"What are you doing here?" I ask.

"Stephen said it was okay."

"You know Steve?"

She makes a little laugh.

Bernie is dark. She wears jeans and baseball boots and a strange white embroidered shirt with beads at the collar. She has a round puppy face, fat lips and spots.

"How old are you?"

"She's seventeen," Bobby says. "We had this groovy party out in the desert. With a *snake* hunt! On *horse*back!"

"Can she talk?"

"Sure she can talk."

Patrick attempts to slip out behind me. I catch him and push him into the shower.

"She's got *all* your *albums*," he mimics.

"She's fucking Rock Hudson!"

"The blonde one?"

"I'll kill Steve. She's a *kid*! She's *twelve*!"

"She's Bobby Vee's younger brother."

"That maniac Terry picked her out of nursery school."

"She's hot for a gobble."

"*Christ!*"

"What do we do?"

"Tell 'em to piss off. *You* tell 'em."

He leaves the shower, walks through the room without saying a word. I'm trapped. They're sitting in the same place. They haven't moved. Bobby's wearing Bermuda shorts and ankle socks and little white shoes. Her cheeks are built to be crushed against the shoulders of Parental Guidance Officers on front-room settees and bucket seats, her hair never fingered by drunken rednecks, never burnt in the fire that killed her cousins, never cut by the gang that rode her wild. She says to Bernie as they walk to school, 'I *love* Robert Mitchum. He's so *soldier*.' But if Robert Mitchum forced her against a drugstore stool and rammed her like a ewe she'd die. Her innocence disgusts me.

51

Without dreams chicks like Bobby choke in vomit, their bodies found in baths, swimming pools, drains, lakes, miles from home, and when the story's told it's full of hate and lies, how they tortured tame squirrels with sharpened Coke cans, murdered dogs and cut off their genitals, became whores at thirteen and bought themselves a habit, fucked vicars in vestries to alleviate the pain of discovering that buttercrunch sundaes aren't made of kisses and Daddy's business trips hive him horny for pussy in low-slung dives where middle-aged Mormons masturbate to striptease dykes out of Sunset skin clubs and Mummy's arse shimmers and shivers on a wicker saddle in a downtown dosshouse every Tuesday at three, where prime-cut niggers slap their pricks between hamburger rolls bringing them on plates to the lathered ladies who plunge like dolphins in simulated steeplechase. However they interpret God's truth it can't last. Kids who filter into rock bands feed off glory's turds. No chick, no *person,* can be treated as fodder, feeling, if they feel at all, that part of the energy, those rave blades revolving and wild phallus signals from the stage, are for them. Inevitably they are used and broken. No one stays, nothing changes. Acts of revelry continue. Big band multiple lays are myth-making fantasy fucks that destroy every last inhibition, revealing chasms of insensitivity as harpies squeal out of clouds like crazed bats to be tumbled onto tables and humped stupid by guitarists too pissed to hold hard ons, the annihilation of the birth of the world, their senses disconnected in a climax that imitates dying, the long exhaustive mind blown break into spent labouring night that offers nothing but a body bruised by its insult and a heart numbed by loss. Whores and superstars roar against defeat. I don't notice. I don't see them now, more hurt by the chicks who *believe,* quiet inconspicuous small town cherries with soft freckled faces and brown kids' sandals who bring flowers wrapped in tissue and stand outside my door, touch me, touch my arm, their eyes filled like pools. And yet these also have faded, knocked back by a new phenomenon, the fierce corps of emancipated groupies, front-line guerrillas in a sex war that aims to destroy penis power forever, too sophisticated for English bands who gladly sacrifice imaginary status for a hot tongue sandwich or a handful of pink tit. Parity agreements, half-digested Women's Lib dictates, fly clean across the board as Steve and Terry pinch pubes, yank knicks with the subtlety of moose in rut. Poster ads plead for mercy. SAVE THIS CONDITION. Love is hidden. A case for charity. Gay Liberators do their thing in full view of the pigs. I'm confused. Devonshire Downs, southern California. Second week of the tour. Hottest day in forty years. No ice. I remember warm Pepsi in a broiling caravan at the back of a ten-foot stage, imitative Romanesque orgy, the music secondary to the real show in the dust bowl. Chicks danced, their breasts like pigeons in pillow slips, buttocks undulating beneath frayed sailcloth pants, racing in their minds along spume-speckled shores, barefoot through lapwaves as cameras turned and horses leapt, the light of the sun on the water, hot thighs and hair, gambolling limbs in the summersheen haze towards Hobo Prince, their starfuck movieman, boots buggered by the long burn from Galveston, skin chafed and split by those highway winds. I walked out on stage to do the set and the sound was so bad I wanted to leave, forget it, and would have except for the knowledge that the kids had fried for six hours like spaced zombie Martians, their arms in the sky, beautiful child faces washed clean as pearls, and I turned to where Rain Fortune stood with Martha and Bella Prentice and she saw me shake, knew I was falling, the sun like a truncheon beating down upon us, word chains broken, guitars out of tune, and she shouted above the speakers, 'Climb on that hate, honey! Bring it on up!', and I finished alive, mucked sweat, slipping and sliding, Patrick behind me soaring like a bird. Afterwards I was ill in L.A. and had to cancel the San Bernardo gig and change the date for Tucson. There was no news from Matthew. He was still in England. Feelings of paranoia exaggerated the temptation to make comparisons with the first years when things felt easier, working small clubs and bars, making £12 a week, not seriously striving, simply glad to be paid. The man who put me on the road was a Roman Catholic priest called Brother Mark who ran a community centre for delinquent teenagers. I admired him. He wasn't God-stoned or sexually subversive. He *cared*. It was a strange understanding. I battled against my father's religion and sympathized openly with the Israelites who followed Moses out of Egypt suffering daily doses of fire and brimstone to keep them out of each other's pants and wasn't surprised after twenty years that the kids who didn't remember what they were running from questioned the need for temperance. Why swallow that hype about celibacy being closest to holiness when the place was heaving with nubile chicks stirring stewpots and collecting manna and sitting at the back of camp-fire hymnalongs bored out of their fucking minds? The answer was golden calves, sex, gigs, the old established order exposed as powerless against successive waves of go-go raveups, Jehovah baits, balling and vandalism. Finally the Mums and Dads who for years had been imitating desert mules with sore arseholes and boils, gave up the struggle and jumped in with the kids, wife swapping and boozing, until Mo the Po, furious at the failure of yet another five-year plan, rushed up the hill with a hammer and chisel and tapped out the Top Ten, knowing only too well the advantages of an illiterate and superstitious multitude. I was high on heresy. Brother Mark called it *'extraneous motivation.'* He enjoyed the imagery. Unlike dowhah social workers he didn't emphasize the need for sincerity. It existed or it didn't. He said, 'If you've got into trouble that's your misfortune and your business. I'm here to help you make the next move.' He avoided consultation with parents, wasn't a member of any Youth Organization or Civic Authority, suspected publicity and talked often of the dubious moral standards of national newspapers, refusing to let us become public showcases to satisfy the masochistic guilt-ins of a sucked-out generation. He expounded elitism *from the bottom,* and said, 'You can't fit disturbed kids into a society that's crazy enough to reject them. You've got to build confidence and self-respect so that they understand they're *real* people with *real* talents, not discarded rags in someone else's dustbin.' He wanted to create a sanctuary for these qualities to develop away from the emotional strictures of home and school. He said, 'Life stunts the spirit with its petty snobberies, bad laws, social class structures and bureaucracy.' He believed in meditation, what he called *'soul ointment'.* I questioned the sanity of a man calling himself the Son of God. He told me to remember the temptation in the wilderness. He said, 'Jesus found himself there.' I said, 'What else would he find in a fucking desert?' He said, 'Don't worry about the story. Think of the fabric. The fable. What it means in your life.' I said, 'I can't swim. I can't walk on water.' He said, 'You can if you believe. You can walk in the sky. Why not?' I said, 'I'd kill myself.' He said, 'Given a few years and a bit of concentrated effort faith might move you.' He took the palms of my hands and pressed them together and knelt on the plank floor. He made me do the same. We were alone. I pulled myself up. I stood away. He said, 'Doesn't matter a damn what you make of yourself as long as *you* make it.' I was trying to remember his words. He said, 'You wouldn't pray in public if your life depended on it, would you?' I said, 'Yes.' He was walking now, his hands hidden. He said, 'You don't want people to categorize you. You are *yourself.* You exist in your own right.' I said nothing. He said, 'Jesus didn't care that others called him a revolutionary or a heretic. He *knew.* That's what gave him his strength. He could stand alone. He had learnt that.' I said, 'We're not *all* mad.' He ignored me. He said, 'If you knew who you were you would have got down on your knees. You would have done it for me. I want to show you the *meaning.* I want to activate a part of that wilderness within you.' I felt my eyes prickle and my throat ache. I was crying. I *never* cry! He said, 'You can't mock Christ without understanding his importance.' I said, 'What's that?' He said, 'Self-discovery.' I thought, I'm not safe here, I won't listen. I had daydreams, nightmares, moods of turning screws on practical experience, getting my father on the ground and making him eat the Bible, page by page, recite Te Deum backwards in Arabic under sentence of crucifixion, the fires of hell blazing through our front room and fiends with ruby breath clambering over the furniture, blaspheming and belching, ripping off my mother as she brushed at them wildly with prayer book and duster. I was dying of religion. I was fifteen. It is difficult to understand what happened. It was an illness. I told no one. I awoke one morning with a sense of overpowering loss. I forgot elementary things. I forgot the way to school, where our house was, the name of our street. I followed my sister to the bus stop, onto the bus. I recognized the houses. I recognized the school when we came to it. My sister began to run. I shouted. Other boys were passing us, staring at me. I was shaking all over. My sister said, 'You're daft.' I begged her, 'Don't leave.' The clock chimed. Everyone was running. I couldn't move. I crouched

55

against the railings. I knew the building. It was my school. I couldn't stop shivering. I clutched my satchel tight to hold myself together. I was afraid someone might see and ask what I was doing. I could smell the shit in my pants. I crept along the railings, doubled up. The street led downhill into the heart of the city. A woman came out of her house with a pram. She pushed it along the path to a gate and through the gate into the street and down the street away from me. I waited until she had disappeared and then opened the gate and went down the path. There was a patch of grass and garden at the back with a washing line hung with clothes and a shed at the end against the wire. I looked over into the other gardens. They were empty. I ran to the shed. It was full of old rakes and garden tools and broken toys and beehives. I took off my trousers. The shit had smeared my legs and arse. I stuffed the pants into a beehive, opened the shed door and peered out. The clothes line was between me and the house but through the flapping shirts and dish cloths I saw another woman in curlers and headwrap and thick woollen dressing gown step out of the back door with a cat in her arms. My stomach was running. I couldn't control it. I was ill. I couldn't hold anything in. I sat on the rim of a beehive. I waited. I must have slept. The next thing I heard was a baby crying. I crawled in behind the rakes and squatted on the floor. I thought I was dying, waited for the sound of wings beating at the bitumen. When Rain Fortune's kid brother was hit by a garbage truck in Chicago and lay on the sidewalk with his guts crushed he had cried out, *'Hold me down,'* because he felt he was flying and as they took him in the car to the hospital he screamed because one of the windows was open a crack and no one closed it and he died in that car and Rain Fortune said, 'Maybe it wasn't *his* voice talking. His body was so hurt.' Darkness had fallen. The clothes on the line had gone and there was no one in the garden. I was cold and hungry. I crossed the grass under the glow of the kitchen window. I saw the form of a woman moving inside. I went round the house and out of the gate into the street. The city sparkled below me like a fairground. I began walking downhill. My legs were weak and stiff. I remembered I had left my pants and satchel in the shed. Without a satchel I couldn't go to school. Everything flowed from

56

there. I was the water oozing from Christ's wounds, away from him. The intensity of the vision exaggerated my fever. I thought, we are not responsible and yet we are, it is impossible to know.

I am sitting on the tiled floor of the shower. Bobby comes round the door.

"Aren't you taking a bath?" she says.

I don't move.

"Why not get it on together?" she says.

Bernie appears.

Bobby pulls her T-shirt over her head. Bernie does the same. They're wearing nothing underneath.

I scramble to my feet.

"Split shit!" Bobby says, holding me.

Bernie's nipples are giant pimply grapes. She puts her arms inside my jacket from the back, up along my shoulder blades. I feel the whole length of her bones. Bobby's on her knees, unbuckling my belt. Bernie kisses me. Bobby unzips my fly, grips my cock with both hands. Bobby's whispering. Bernie strokes her. Bobby licks my thighs, my balls. I move quickly, dragging at my jeans. Bobby's face is flushed.

"It's okay," Bernie says. "She gets like that."

She takes her shirt from the floor and puts it on, very cool and practised now.

"Her mother had this negative relationship with her father," she says. "She went with this guy who made her dress like a fairy and called her Angel Power and made her wear his old Junior High football jerseys and say things like 'Hot diggedy' and 'Crazy horse Daddy'. She was a woman of forty-five."

Bobby sobs at the back of the shower.

Pictures on screens, rerun of death clips, trailers at The Fillmore and Whisky, purple bags bursting on neon plains, further and further, Manson and the Californian cannibals, castration, murder, salvation's ruin exist here like everywhere else, the scream of sick children pillowed in blood. Man's more evil than he imagines, breaking rules of common decency, exposing truth and violence in the body as terror freewheels towards a bitter end that once held hope and meaning. Days of light have passed. Butterflies flatten against the windscreen on desert roads. America is losing. There are no prophets. And yet I remember when every stimulant we experienced, every movie, song, poem came from the States. It wasn't Actor's Studio or black and white realism that saved Ike and Joe McCarthy and the long sleep of Apple Pie Wonderland. It was the sheer visual splendour of Colorado, Wyoming and Montana. No one wears MOTHER MADE ME now. They wear Vietcong flags and STICKY DICKY buttons and labels that read AMERIKA IS ALREADY DEAD. In the '50s there was nowhere else to look. From post-war pavements and black-lace guest houses and dusty meth halls and smog-greased chip shops and five-bob wank shelters, slippery with puke, the image of Big John crossing Red River with the sun falling behind the mountains on an autumnal evening was like talking to Hemingway about things that mattered, man's loyalty to man, man's understanding of God, man's strength of purpose, man's relationship to nature. And yet, simultaneously, we spoke with bitterness of 'sodding Yanks' and 'fucking gumchews'. I listened to early blues records wondering to whom they applied. I liked Al Capone's pinstripes. I liked Robert E. Lee. I liked Memphis and downtown Manhattan. I liked Motown, Massachusetts, Martha's Vineyard. I liked anything Red Indian. I liked California's lush and neurotic promise. I liked the honey-hot ripeness of Tennessee's fading beauty where ladies in tassled silk whispered, 'Ah waited aowl mah laife fore this oane taiste of ahbidin playsure.' America is a collage of imaginary pictures. Information demands more information and more information demands more until a mammoth industry is established inventing and gathering information, speculating as to what that information will be, speculating as to what the speculation of that information will be, until a pattern emerges of a nation hooked on faddism, twenty-four-hour newspeak trapped into producing predictions, facts, gossip, action every day, hour, minute, becoming monstrous and insatiable, feeding a culture that worships the individual and yet individually conforms. Brother Mark's attitude towards the Press was right. Ignore and repel. I've seen too many musicians ruined by publicity, not because it was bad but because it was too good. There isn't such a thing as objective criticism. Praise and fame are a reflection of those doing the praising and every artist must endure it and become proficient at creating the stuff of his own legend and bring body to the myth which is larger than life and therefore not life. We grow slowly. We change. We shed skins and construct others until arriving at the shape we like best and hold it, hang on, use it forever, and it is a different skin from the one we started with although psychiatrists say that the ego is formed in the womb and changes we appear to make are experimental diversifications, testing limitation and stress. I hate thinking that everything we do is preordained in a celestial workshop where personality planners argue over the interpretation of structure. I don't believe it. Religion's all the better for its flash of magic.

It is summer again. My mother lies in the bracken. She is a peasant woman. She understands these things. The dog licks me at my birth. Later they take me by the hand and walk up the mountain and show me the place where I was born. I mark it with a cross of stones. I am five years old, laying my grave. My father is a strong man. We live in a house of stone. My mother's name is Bethlehem. She says there was a time when she saw a vision. The Lord spoke to her of my coming. I feel the dog's tongue in my sleep, the heat of the night over me at my opening. I believe that we are not always the children of our parents but have the potential of becoming other children. We do not recognize this potential and so disown the wilder forms of mysticism in favour of birthright, deathright, motherlove and fatherlove. I asked Catherine whether she realized her imagination and she told me of the games she played with her brothers when they were young. I said, 'No. I mean alone. Making yourself change.' When kids speak of redefining their roots, living off the land, I tell them, 'You don't know what you're saying.' But they do. It's different for them, coming naked at another time, finding it's true that things grow in the soil so easily. Ours was the poorest farm on the hill. Isolation belonged there.

I sneaked up the line through the woods. It was a private life. My father said, 'Where have you been?' My legs were scratched with brambles. I said, 'I went out.' The kitchen was hot and steamy. My mother and father sat on chairs in front of the fire. I stood silent. My mother said, 'It's not good for a boy of your age to be so much on his own.' I said, 'I'm not on my own.' I had discovered whole areas of the hill. I had more knowledge than any of them. My sister asked, 'When you run off, will you take me?' I said, 'No.'

– How does your music relate?
– To what?
– You don't write of the war, for instance.
– No.
– Is there an underlying motivation?
– I dig interviews. They're weird.
– Do you search for truth in action?
– I don't have to.
– Is that your philosophy?
– I don't envy anyone. I don't feel I'm competing, except with myself.
– Songs like 'Jesus Was A Junkie' made people mad. 'Roar Like The Skybark', was another. Do you endorse the sentiments of those lyrics?
– They are anti-religious, not anti-Christ.
– What's the difference?
– I attack the institution, not the man. 'Skybark' is about Communism anyway. It's nothing to do with God.
– What frightens you?
– Prison frightens me.

To play Las Vegas, even for one night, is to corrupt honourable intentions. What Catherine never understood was how close we are to the pit.

The romance of the working class is sentimental moonshine. No sane person can pretend that a factory floor is anything but an asylum for fit men, and yet my father chose it. After thirty-six years on the land he decided to move. Sometimes I wonder what would have happened if we had stayed. And yet I know. I know *exactly*. I would have died young.

Critics enjoy debating whether an artist fulfils his purpose revealing the essence of wasted landscape. Beauty is what life hopes to be. Ugliness is what it is. If beauty is truth then ugliness is beauty because ugliness is truth also and ugly art is as relevant as beautiful art, in fact more so.

"Maxwell!" Patrick shouts.

A kid with a Californian headband stands up from the other end of the auditorium.

At the top of the steps behind the stage Steve has his arms around Bobby and Bernie. Charlie's adjusting tension on his snare drum as Ken nails the stand to the wooden boards. Maxwell walks over. He's like a TV teenager with plastic skin and painted dimples. Patrick says something and he runs back across the floor.

The auditorium resembles a basketball arena with a semicircle of seats looking down onto the centre. The stage is high and wide. We're using a Californian sound system, Histyle Music, which was tried first at Dallas and again at Austin. Ken likes them because they're cheap and less of a hassle than the big pro companies. They have two roadies, Duke and Firefly, with Histyle himself, a fat jovial electrician called Lee Young. Duke and Firefly spend half the year on a commune in Sacramento cultivating marijuana in the forest, having no need to be involved in 'the capitalistic mindfuck'. Firefly is skinny and bearded and moves slow. He is married to a chick called Louise from Macon, Georgia, and has a child called Neon Electra. Louise lives with Neon Electra and a friend of Firefly's called Stoney End. Firefly accepts this arrangement because Stoney End is 'a together person' and as long as Louise is okay and feels happy

61

that makes him happy. I asked, 'What happens when you go home?' Firefly said, 'Nothing *happens,* man. We constitute good vibes.' He used to hang out at Lee Young's electrical repair shop in Stockton helping with blown stereos and busted tapes and when Lee wanted someone to drive the van and carry equipment to local gigs he asked Firefly. Duke was brought in as a third party and together they formed Histyle Music as a community project.

Lee Young is older. He has a wife, Jeannie, and kids, Dave and Lorraine. He's a native Californian who enjoys the irony of Ronald Reagan's reactionary recitations in a state that has a million hippies soaked into welfare. He told me, 'The wealth is incredible. You wouldn't believe it. Everyone living off credit. No one saving a cent. Spending fortunes on ranch-style boxes that fall apart in ten years while the old houses in the hills go for nothing because they're not fashionable. Hippies move there, get rent, food and gas paid by the state, drive Cadillacs. At the same time Mexican fruit pickers in the south suffer nineteenth-century slave-camp conditions and die from crop-spray insecticide poisoning on subsistence wages. It's crazy.'

He sympathizes with longhairs because they're trying to find something better but doubts whether it's possible because the law harasses them mercilessly and the judges legislate against them. He said, 'There's some inherent insecurity in the American makeup that needs to show where it is and what it's doing at all times. California's only eighty years old, filled with migrants from the midwest, Easterners, millionaires, kids run away from home. There's no *identity,* no formulated sense of belonging except money. And if you don't want money, like some of the kids don't, you've got to have a reason. You've got to say what that reason is. Once you've said it you feel you represent something. You *belong.* But it leaves no options. When I think of it now . . . I was twenty years old . . . same as some of these kids. I went to college because it seemed a better thing to do than working in a store selling light bulbs to dust farmers. I didn't know *goddam!* I couldn't formulate the sense of a two-bit candy bar let alone have knowledge of my philosophical future.'

Duke and Firefly are of the old Haight Ashbury. Duke said, 'The best guys went into the country when things began to break

62

up.' Firefly said, 'We're so fucking liberated, man, we're killing ourselves.' Duke said, 'Charlie Manson was testin.' I said, 'Testing what?' Firefly said, 'Gettin the feel of his space, man.'

The sound check and rehearsal is over. Martha and Bella Prentice have already left. Charlie's telling Ken to make sure no one touches the drums. Terry's cleaning out the spare leads trunk. Bobby and Bernie are sitting on an empty case at the back. Steve is with them. Lee Young is down on the floor below the stage arranging the PA control box. Firefly and Duke are sitting in the high seats up to the left, smoking.

"Want to eat?" Charlie says.

"Not now," I say.

He wanders over to Terry who tells him he can't. He hasn't finished. Maxwell returns with a cardboard box full of hot coffee in paper cups. He puts them on the edge of the stage. No one moves. He brings the cups over to us.

"Thanks," I say. "I don't drink coffee."

"Coke?"

"There's Coke in the dressing room."

"Ice cold from the machine."

"I'll get it myself."

Rain Fortune isn't there. I can't see her. Perhaps she's gone. The sliding door at the back of the building opens and a Hertz van reverses down the corridor past the dressing rooms. Two roadies, standing on the tailboard, jump off onto the stage. Maxwell rushes over. The roadies ignore him. Terry introduces himself. Ken watches, suspicious. The driver of the van and a long-haired cowboy in crushed velvet pants, high-heeled boots, embroidered shirt and black leather hat join the roadies on stage. Duke and Firefly climb down from their seats.

"How you doin, Tom?' Duke says.

"Hell! *Shit!*"

They hug each other.

"Where you b'n, man?"

"San Diego."

"That's a wicked place."

"Right on!"

The roadies begin to unload the van. The black-hatted cowboy comes across to me.

63

"Earl Monk in the building?"

"Who?"

The cowboy smiles.

"He's hirin us for this gig."

"There's some hassle about security," I say.

"That right?"

I can smell his perfume.

"Who are you with?" I ask.

"Best fuckin rock'n'roll band in the West."

"I've heard that somewhere."

"You may have heard it *spoken,* boy," he says. "Bet yo'r ass you never heard it *played.*"

I see Patrick slipping down the side at the back as the roadies unload. I follow. We go into the dressing room. Rain Fortune's sitting on the bench. Patrick puts his guitar into its case. Terry comes in.

"Where's the promoter?"

"Why?"

"These guys want to move our stuff."

Beccy marked me early. She said, 'Sometimes I can't believe you're here, half-way dressed behind a wall of trees.' Matthew said, 'She takes a balanced view.' I wasn't prepared to defend myself. Beccy said, 'You don't have solid ground under your feet.' That was two weeks after arriving in London. I was unsure of things, wondering where this change would lead.

My first impression was of style, the way Matthew walked into rooms as if everyone should know him. I was doing a twenty-minute warm up before the main attraction at a better Birmingham disco when he appeared after the set and asked me to join him for a drink. I said, 'I'll have a meal. Ta.' We went to an Indian restaurant. He said, 'You have a good face for TV.' He gave me his card. He said, 'I'm prepared to offer you a contract.' He looked younger then and had a mid-Atlantic accent. I liked nothing about him. He said, 'Why waste yourself here when you could be making real bread in London?'

I said, 'I'm writing songs.' He said, 'Good songs are hard to come by.' I said, 'They're harder to write.' He said, 'I might be of use to you.'

He had been running the agency for less than a year, working from a room off Tottenham Court Road with the help of a part-time secretary. He was in debt to the banks and living off a loan from Beccy's father. Things couldn't have been worse and yet, typically, he wore a Savile Row suit, silk shirt, handmade shoes and drove a resprayed Aston Martin. If he had come dressed in Levis and a corduroy jacket I might have taken him serious-ly. As it was I said, 'Thanks for the curry,' and split.

Brother Mark taught us to respect individuals and demean psychiatrists for the bleakness of their objectivity. He said, 'Once a person becomes a case history he's filed, numbered and posted through the letter box.' He warned us against group protec-tion. He said, 'Gangs are like single people. They think and act as one. They *are* one. The individuals who make them up be-come this corporate thing. And yet when they go to bed at night they understand who they really are. They return to themselves. That's the person I want to find, the person I want *you* to find.' I said, 'We should say our prayers?' He said, 'You can't *see* me, can you?' He was sitting in the corner of the warehouse. I said, 'I'm *looking* at you.' He said, 'Maybe you are. Or *think* you are. But you're seeing someone else. You're seeing the Church.' I said, 'I'm seeing you.' He said, 'Sometimes we appear to hide behind our differences like you hide behind film stars and musicians and footballers without understanding that every-one's hiding somewhere. We're afraid to assert ourselves and yet our dignity as human beings demands privacy and isolation.' He marched up and down, beating his hands as he talked. He said, 'The corporate soul is an instrument of the devil, very powerful and seductive. We're tempted by its luxury, not having to make our own decisions. Protective involvement lulls us into inactive acceptance, gags us as individuals. We *fight* this. We *must.*'

My mother said, 'When I was your age I was pleased to find work.' She filled the kitchen with her big sucked breath. She said, 'You expect so much.' She wanted to touch me, reach out and comfort me. I turned. I ran upstairs. My sister had friends in her room listening to Marty Wilde and Cliff Richard records on a borrowed gramophone. They wore lipstick and bras. I ignored them. Everything was abstract escapism and bitterness. I believed I would die never knowing love.

Childhood was separate. A long way back. We understood the work our parents did. Each had his place, even us kids. Jimmy's Dad and Flora's Dad thinned and cut spruce, brought the tractor along the path to fasten the chain to the felled trunks. Willie's Dad was a shepherd. We helped bring the sheep in from the hill when he was dipping or shearing and went with him also at lambing time. If a fox worried the ewes Willie's Dad knew of it and he'd call Morag's Dad and together they would go to the dens with their terriers. They wouldn't take us. They said, 'It's too dangerous.' We waited behind the broom hedge at the foot of the path for Morag's Dad's van to arrive and then crept up behind – Jimmy, Willie and me – and hung on. Willie's Dad came out of the cottage with his gun. They drove up the hill. We jumped off and lay in the heather. The terriers were sent down. Willie's Dad and Morag's Dad stood above and waited. Once we saw a fox. The dogs had been in for a long time and then Willie pointed : *'There it's!'* The fox was crouched in the entrance, moving its head from side to side like a big red collie, a beautiful thing. Morag's Dad shot it before it started to run. Willie was so excited, he dashed up the hill. His Dad shouted at him, *'Git down!'* There were cubs and a vixen still underground. Jimmy and I stayed hid. After a while one of the terriers came out with blood on her muzzle. Morag's Dad dragged the body of the fox to the van. He took a spade from under the seat. Willie sat on a rock as the two men dug at the den. I touched Jimmy and said, 'Let's be off.' He said, 'They'll see us.' I said, 'They won't.' He said, 'It's *miles.*' I crawled through the heather until I was behind the stones and then ran, ran like the wind.

Every year we cut the corn, every year we seeded, every year we scythed a corner for hay, every year we cut peat, every year we planted neeps, tatties and sprouts, every year we picked rasps, every year the wind blew from the west and rain flooded the steading, every year the burn burst, every winter it snowed and we took sledges up Willie's hill, every year my mother said we couldn't go on, every year I watched the boats leaving, every year I grew older, spread wider, felt the edges of the world expand.

Alone on the hill I was close to the sky. I lay on my face, called, 'Come on, God!' We looked over and saw our house in the distance, perched on the steep side. I said, 'That's it. That's where I live.' God warmed me with sun. He recognized the difficulty of living in His shadow.

Such things evolved with time. When we left the farm and went to the city I lost them, lost them forever, which made me think they were part of that age and that place, a protection country children have against the proximity of nature, fish sensing the changes in weather, ears close to the roots, feeling life in the land rushing through rocks, the cycle and territory of each animal and tree. I knew God was alive as I knew the heather, the bracken, the sea, the clouds, the birds, the corn, the maggots in the barn beams, the nettles, the moss on the stones were alive although I could never tell anyone. I did not believe in my father's God because He was cruel. Mine was a child's God, as much part of the ground as the air, bringing flowers up and rain to feed them. Church wasn't God. Church was a man's thing. Jesus was a man. Later, in the city, I knew God was dead because the city was only people and even the dogs in the city were trying to be people.

- I want to ask you when the disillusionment with early romanticism began.
- The first album was out of my head. I didn't realize what it meant. I was beginning, only *beginning*, to question the myths, *daring* to do so. 'Candy Wore The Tails of Heaven' became the best known from the album, that and 'Lucy Wilder'. The tails of heaven were peacock feathers. I was attacking the Hollywood hype of romantic fulfilment, love burning the bridges to perfect peace, everything dressed in that soft-focus cloud light, blurring sharp outlines. 'Lucy Wilder' was different. She was a real person although that's not her real name. The story's true. She needed to dominate

men. She was the original innocent cannibal, entirely self-orientated. There's a line in it about the seasons of life changing her flavour for love which is a pretentious way of saying that her tastes altered depending on the time of year, which was true. She had big heavy-bearded guys in the winter and skinny pop-star types in the summer. She needed constant reassurance. She could have been an actress or a model. She had perfect looks. The song is a lament, very sad. I'm saying, come down from all that fame and power, baby, it's nothing compared with what I can give you, and she comes down because she can't afford to miss the chance, but she's burnt up, fucked out, doped, brittle and dying, and she tells me, love isn't anything but a plastic key that breaks in the lock, and I say, love is style, and she says, I died in the dance, honey, you weren't there, you could have saved me.

— This stain of disillusionment runs through all your work. Obviously you were attracted to the blues despite an understanding of their limitations. How does a British folk singer relate to ethnic North American black music?

— I can *relate*, whatever that means. It's the music of the heart. It's blood music. Ritualistic, inarticulate. What hit me first when I began listening was the repetition, the simple lyric, the beat. This was music of dog people and it was defiant. I felt immediate sympathy. I was a dog person myself and believed in the fundamental truth of my own lack of experience. Do you understand? It had honesty, something that didn't exist in pop music at that time. I got the same feelings from Woody Guthrie and Dylan, certainly the early stuff, not Pete Seeger, he's too objective, he doesn't roll in the cat shit although can describe others doing so brilliantly. He's an interpreter, very sincere.

— What about English influences? Folk ballads. There is a strong tradition.

— I wanted something that hurt as much as I was hurting. That stuff's too ethereal although I'll admit my first successes with Top Ten were straight steals from soul hits.

— Why was that?

— After years in clubs I believed – because I was told – that I had to compromise to make it. The first album – the one we were talking about – was recorded *after* those singles and was a kind of half-way attempt at escape. I didn't have

68

complete confidence. Not then. Once underground bands became accepted in a commercial sense and The Beatles had wiped out America for what seemed like a whole generation, it was an exciting time and what everyone talked about then, the Swinging Sixties and London being the centre of the new *avant garde,* may seem incredible now as it's moved right back again but it *was* real in the sense that the mood changed completely. We felt we could do anything. It was a great period.

– How are the new songs shaping up?

– I don't know. I'm not sure yet. I'm writing more personal stuff. I want to get away from ecology. I was never a preacher although some critics tried to turn me into one. For instance a lot of the material we're using on this tour is rhythm-and-blues. We have three fantastic chick singers who have helped change our style, even to the extent where people start saying we're covering Joe Cocker. I'm not affected by that as such because I find most critics are after repeats one way or the other and won't respect material for what it is. I'm conscious of change, more and more now. I had a bad period sixteen months ago. Up until then I wasn't committed. That sounds unlikely, I know. 'Colours Green' was supposed to be the one true committed album. It wasn't. I was clearing the decks, attacking *myself.* Few people realized this. The Jesus songs caused offence to the extent that they were banned by the BBC in England although the basis of the album was a personal statement about respect for nature, not nature as religion. It was anti-hippie.

– You say that this was not a commitment and yet make it sound very much like one.

– I mean commitment in a different sense. Commitment to music. Always I've felt outside. What motivates me is not what seems to motivate other people. I don't have friends in the business. I'm not socially integrated. I would never have allowed this interview nine months ago. I was too unsure of myself, expecting talent to be taken away like it was a piece of clothing, and yet when it *was* taken away – or rather when I *thought* it was taken away – I realized it was still there and I could go on. In fact what happened saved me. It proved my worst fears didn't exist. Problems remain. Christ! But they're not the same problems. I can

69

step on stage now and feel that's where I belong. I couldn't
before. I had to create another personality who wasn't
the same as me and wasn't the same as the guy who wrote
the songs. This new commitment is a commitment to *me*.

I had been in London five weeks when I cut 'Moon Rock
Deliver' and 'Furnace Build My Fire Higher'. Both did well.
'Moon Rock' was a slow bluesy ballad and 'Furnace' a screeching
soul number. I wrote them principally for other people as a
pastiche of Top Ten schmaltz. Matthew said, 'You've got to do
them yourself.' I said, 'They're not my kind of music.' Matthew
said, 'You need the experience.' I said. 'What experience?' He
said, 'Working in a studio.' We hired session men and recorded
in a day adding B-sides later. Matthew had a public relations firm
invent lies about my past, plugging the records through pro-
fessional middlemen who had contacts with disc jockeys and
radio producers. He bought clothes for me which I refused to
wear and insinuated I should sleep with a certain influential
lady journalist. I wasn't aware of what was happening, possibly because I didn't allow myself to be. I mimed before cameras
in barnlike warehouses filled with Martian schoolkids. I asked
Matthew, 'What can I learn from this stuff? It's terrible.' He
said, 'It's necessary at the beginning to get maximum exposure
in all forms of media.' I said, 'This kind of crap is what the
Beatles and Stones reacted *against*.' He said, 'The Beatles *made
it* on TV.'

'Moon Rock Deliver' became a minor hit and once it was seen
to be falling Matthew released 'Furnace' and I went through the
whole process again, only worse because 'Furnace' was considered to have far greater potential, being an imitative soul
sound at the time that Otis Redding was the most popular male
singer in the States. Matthew believed I could become Britain's
answer to Sam Cooke. I said, 'I'm Britain's answer to no one.
I don't sing that shit.'

70

I had made the journey south, sickened by the senseless butchery of hassling ex-Bingo callers in Montague Burton suits about bread and time and whether I could use their PA, if they *had* a PA, and if they didn't, what? I was sick of rich pricks who cared nothing for the quality of music as long as it encouraged, not interfered with, the spending of money. Even in the saner atmosphere of folk clubs where serious freaks sat crosslegged on the floor discussing Woody Guthrie's underwear the sinking madness reached me.

The others I met talked of making it to London, buying jeeps, flash gear, smoking dope, pulling skirt. I thought, I'm like them, I'm a singer, I want to get there too, and if I don't what am I doing stealing milk from doorsteps and fruit from the market when I've a card in my pocket that says Matthew Shaw wants to see me? I began to reconsider the advantages and possibilities. It might be interesting. The blues-folk thing could evolve into genuine personal attainment. Failure was nothing. All of us had that. We began there. Now we were learning, everyone helping everyone else, a strong feeling of fraternity, no ego-crazed lead guitarist pulling moodies after a gig because some sod had interfered with the amps, no pretension, little seriousness. Later things became more sensitive once small bands improved enough to have real ambition, backed by a regular following of local supporters, writing their own material, buying bigger, more expensive equipment, having a roadie *and* a van, even a manager, getting into the pose thing, working on stage acts, travelling to Scotland, Cornwall, Wales. There was status in sound. If an engineer invented a cabinet no larger than a shoebox that produced the equivalent amplification of four PA columns at a quarter of the price no pop group would buy it. Filling the stage with gear was half the hype and soon the art of retaining popularity became as vital as winning it.

I had sent a number of songs to Matthew, hoping to sell them. He answered with a letter. He wanted me to come to London. He didn't mention the songs but enclosed a train ticket. Two days later we met in his office. He began sorting out a schedule of gigs. I said, 'I'm through with singing.' He said, 'You haven't come all this way just to tell me that.' I said, 'If you send free tickets I'm going to use them.'

71

For years I lived under the illusion that I was different. I had recurring nightmares about dissolving into yellow liquid and being evenly distributed in the bodies of cats. Literature and music remained constant. Both could be enjoyed in relative safety, without commitment, although the librarian tried hard to involve me in his Boys' Book Club. He was a man of order and conceit. He tried to advise. I ignored him. He was small and old with silver hair and a short white beard. He loved books, he said, because they enhanced an appreciation of life. I felt the same about Leadbelly. Every time I went to the library he brought me something, an old Henty or a new thriller, and I would look at it, turn it over, refuse it, and then he'd ask whether I had liked whatever it was I was bringing back and I would frown and shrug my shoulders. I was at war. Didn't they notice? Couldn't they *see*? The magistrate at the Juvenile Court and Brother Mark were the only two who came close. Doctors and sociologists assume that kids in rage are sick. I believe that you can teach a dog to beg and you can teach it to walk up your arse but that's a man dog not a dog dog and the personality of the dog becomes the personality of the man which is the origin of the saying 'It's a dog's life'.

The magistrate was a Councillor. He was also a butcher. I had been caught taking torch batteries from a newsagent and then two weeks later a bronze lizard paperweight from an antique shop in the old market. The police suspected there was more and took me into a room at the back of the station where they brought tea and biscuits and we sat on chairs. They said, 'What were you doing in the market?' I said, 'I don't know.' They said, 'Shouldn't you have been in school?' I said, 'I don't know.' They said, 'Do you like school?' I said, 'No.' They said, 'Why not?' I said, 'I don't know.' They said, 'You don't know *why* you don't like school?' I felt afraid then because they were forcing me to answer questions I didn't want to answer and there were two of them which made it harder and the room was so empty and cold and I knew in the end they would beat me and I was scared of that. The questions only delayed the moment and somehow I knew that I would prefer it because it wouldn't last long and then I would have a real reason for hating them. The older policeman continued. He said, 'We know you've been doing this quite often. It would be a great help if you told us something more. It would help you too because when you go to the Juvenile Court the magistrate is always impressed by boys who tell the truth. I don't think you really meant to take those things, did you? It was something that happened, wasn't it? Something you couldn't help. Like you might take a newspaper from the counter of a shop and forget to pay.' The younger policeman went out and I was left with the older one. I said nothing. I sat on my chair very still. The older policeman said, 'Unfortunately a charge has been brought otherwise we might have found a way of overlooking this one. What is important now is to make certain it doesn't happen again. We get a lot of kids through here, probably from your school as well. The tough kids are sent away to places where discipline is very hard. They are locked up.' The younger policeman returned with a list of REPORTED JUVENILE CRIMES. We went through them together. I recognized four but denied them all. The older policemen laid the list on the table. He said, 'We can arrange for an identification. It wouldn't be difficult.' I said, 'What's that?' He said, 'A man who saw an assailant run out of his shop two months ago isn't going to remember very clearly because all kids look alike to him. We give him a call and say we think we have the culprit and want him to come over for an identification. He doesn't want to do that because it means leaving the shop, losing trade perhaps. When he arrives he wants to get it over quickly. He's not fussy whether you're the right kid. He's had enough trouble as it is. He says, yes, that's him. But he doesn't know. He's not sure. He wants to get back.' The younger policeman said, 'The mother's here. Shall we bring her in?' I took the list and pointed to the ones I knew. The older policeman asked, 'Is that all?' I said, 'Yes.' He said, 'Where did you take the stuff?' I said, 'I buried it.' He said, 'Where?' I said, 'Behind our house.' We left the room and walked along the corridor, out of a side entrance and into the street. The older policeman stayed. I said, 'My Mam's there.' The younger policeman told me to get into the car. I said, 'My *Mam's* there.' He said, 'She's not. That was a story.' The older policeman came out with a spade. We drove up the hill, past the gasworks, round the top of the estates to the new ring road complex and down into the cemetery from the front gate. I had buried the stuff in a box under the wall. They hauled it out. It was beginning to rain. They opened the box. Inside were beads and nylon stockings wrapped in cellophane, a bottled ship, cigarette lighters, a wrist watch, a silver jewel case, a fur hat, garden tools, a hammer, two screwdrivers, part of an electric drill. They carried the box to the car. I asked, 'Can I go now?' They said, 'Come with us.' They drove to our house. Other women in the street watched as the policemen brought me to the door. I was sent upstairs. The policemen pushed through into the kitchen to talk to my mother. I waited until it was dark. I waited in my room. I heard my father come home. I lay on the bed, remembering the weight hanging over me in the police station, knowing that all they had to do was drop it and I would be dead. I wasn't a thief. I had stolen for reasons of my own, to remain a *living person*. My mother came upstairs. She brought a tray of chips, fish fingers, sliced bread. I ate quickly. She tidied my clothes, my table. I thought of my father downstairs, mutilating his wrists with a toothpick. My mother said, 'You've disgraced us.' I gave her the plate and empty cup. She said, 'You waste time at school. You waste time in the house. What are you telling us? That we're wrong?' I was telling her nothing. The choice was simple. To live by myself or die in their arms.

When the case came up in Juvenile Court I was dressed in Sunday clothes, hair cut, brushed, hands washed. My mother and father came with me. We sat in a hot room overlooking the street. I heard cars, buses, the world outside. My father wore his suit and black laced shoes. He sat close to my mother. I had never seen them kiss. I had never seen him move with any gentleness towards her or take her hand as he did then. I pitied him and hated him. I pitied myself. We were the last on the list and had to sit a long time. My father never looked at me, never spoke to me, until the man who was representing us, the lawyer, entered the room and told us what would happen and asked us not to worry as Mr Rutherford was on the bench. My father was confused. The lawyer said that Juvenile Court wasn't like Magistrate's Court and that Mr Rutherford's style was to talk to the parents and to the child without imposing his authority. I hadn't expected a lawyer. I didn't know what I expected. I didn't know why I had stolen those things, although I did, and it was nothing *they* would understand, to do with *me, my* life, not my mother and father's although they suffered for me because they believed I was an extension of their hopes and dreams, a mirror of their youth.

A policeman appeared and said, 'It's time now.' We followed him along the corridor to the courtroom which was large and light and filled with people. We were taken to a bench near the front below a raised platform where Mr Rutherford sat behind a long table beside a smart middle-aged lady in a brown felt hat. Another policeman read the charge from a notebook and listed the items found in the box. The man from the antique shop gave evidence. Mr Rutherford asked, 'Can you be sure the boy was intentionally stealing the paperweight?' The man from the antique shop said, 'I saw him, sir.' Mr Rutherford said, 'Could he have been looking for someone to ask about the price?' The man from the antique shop said, 'Half-way down the street?' He smiled. Mr Rutherford said, 'You mean the boy ran away once he had taken the paperweight?' The man from the antique shop said, 'That's correct.' Mr Rutherford said, 'You ran after him?' The man from the antique shop said, 'Yes.' Mr Rutherford said, 'How did you manage to catch him?' The man from the antique shop said, 'The boy admits why he was there.' Mr Rutherford leaned forward across the table and said, 'That may or may not be so but you have failed to answer my question.' The man from the antique shop glanced across the room at the policeman standing at the window. He said, 'It's true to say that I remanded him sooner, sir.' Mr Rutherford said, 'Inside the shop?'

He wasn't like a judge. He didn't wear a wig. He was like a farmer we knew called Mr Ross who had pigs and Shetland ponies and a wife called Celline. He liked children and when we watched him feeding the pigs he let us get down and suck the teats. One day he slipped into the shed at the back of the farm

75

where he kept his tools and pulled down a half bottle of whisky from the shelf, but it wasn't the right bottle, it was an old one filled with rat poison, and it killed him. Celline went away. The farm was sold. Jimmy said the walls of their room were thick with dried grasses and flowers. Celline had picked them, pressed them and stuck them to the paper. Jimmy said, 'You couldn't see solid. Like there was something beyond. Another place.' I said, 'What?' He said, 'The edge of a jungle.' I thought about Mr Ross in that room surrounded by the crackling bushes of Celline's mad imagination. He was the only farmer on our hill who had sympathy for living creatures and Mr Rutherford had that same rusty complexion and tilt of the head as he looked down over the table. Mr Ross was always doing that, looking down, being tall, or seeming so to us, and yet never imposing like my father whose height was violent. I thought of my father as a force, like the wind is a force, a *threat*. I thought of Mr Ross as a man who talked to animals and I thought of Celline as a woman who kept parcels tied with wire. I wondered if Mrs Rutherford was the lady sitting on the seat next to Mr Rutherford. She didn't speak. She sat very still, listening. She had a way of looking as if everything Mr Rutherford said was important. The lawyer representing me was talking about my past record which didn't exist and about how long I had been in the city and my problems at school. He read a letter from one of the teachers saying that I was 'a solitary boy who appeared to resist personal encouragement'. Suddenly the librarian jumped up from the back of the room and began talking to Mr Rutherford about my interest in 'good books'. The lady with the brown hat smiled. She said it was 'jolly kind' of him to come and speak up for me. She had a walnut voice like the Laird's wife. I was surprised. She made me think of homemade salad cream and heavy polished dressers and big beds with lace up the edge. The librarian said I had 'a mature taste', meaning I didn't draw faces or write dirty jokes on the back of his books. Mr Rutherford said, 'This isn't exactly relevant.' The librarian said, 'I wanted the court to understand that my colleagues and I are deeply affected by what is happening here. We find it hard to believe that such a sensitive lad could have been the perpetrator of multiple offences.' Mr Rutherford said, 'We appreciate your in-

76

terest.' The librarian sat down. Mr Rutherford asked my father and mother about 'general behaviour' at home. My father said that I had been upset by the move from the country and had never really settled. The walnut lady asked whether it might have been a problem of making new friends at school. My father said, 'I can't tell about that.' The lady nodded. She said, 'Does he have hobbies?' My father thought for a moment and then my mother said that I had always been independently inclined and explained my interest in music. The lady said, 'That's common with the young today', as if it was contagious. Mr Rutherford brought me to the edge of the table. He asked, 'Did you want the things you stole?' I said, 'No.' He said, 'Why take them if you didn't want them?' I looked away. I couldn't explain. I wasn't sure. He said, 'Unfortunately we have laws that protect property and when those laws are broken we have to try and stop it happening again.' I said, 'Yes sir.' He said, 'I am sure your motives were not criminal. But we cannot take what we like from other people. The law exists for that purpose, to protect others, to protect you as well, to protect all of us. If you insist on disregarding the law we have the power to punish you. Now you must try and help me. You must try very hard. Because if I see you in here again I shall have no choice next time.' He spoke slowly and quietly. He was speaking to *me*. He said, 'I am putting you on probation which means that a probation officer will come and see you from time to time and talk to you.' He leant further over the table. He was smiling.

The probation officer called at our house soon afterwards. My mother resented his presence because it reminded her of the experience in the courtroom. He asked, 'Any problems?' I said, 'No.' He said, 'Put the kettle on.' He was practical in his advice and wasted no time sympathizing with sentimental theory about environment and moral responsibility. He shared many of Brother Mark's views about the way society destroys the spirit of its nonconformist element. He said, 'If we can't persuade bright kids that thieving's no good this country's lost its bloody reason and if prisons continue to be filled with intelligent working villains, wasting half the years of their lives, what's the bloody point?' He was the first person I had met who talked openly about politics as a force for change. My father felt that government was too isolated, a vast corporation concerned with the stabilization of other vaster corporations. Jack Field, the probation officer, believed capitalism to be essentially evil as it pandered to the worst elements in our nature and created a vicious class structure that infected the core of the working man's will to resist. He said, 'If I can't be bloody Prime Minister I might as well keep kids out of jail.'

Patrick, Rain Fortune and I walk back from the Convention Center to the hotel.

"I don't see no livin people," Rain Fortune says. "Makes me *zap zap*!" She's laughing. "If we don't get stomped this time, honey, we gotta *fly*."

She hugs me, dances away.

"What do you know about Las Vegas?"

"Every kid who can *read* knows about Las Vegas. There ain't a main street any place, there ain't a city in the United States of America that don't have big hoardings tellin us *this is where it's at*. I mean here. Right *here*! Like you goin t'walk into the sharpest neat shop you ever dreamed of an every time you open your door Dean Martin's standin there with his pants on fire. But introduce black brothers to those tables, honey, and the place gets a bit of *excitement*. White dudes don't dig excitement. They make it look as if they're hot, jivin to that dice like it's a lady, *c'mon baby you do good by me yeah!*"

"You're a racist," I say.

"Because I straighten my hair?" she says.

"Patrick straightens his hair," I say.

"I was born straight," Patrick says.

"You can't help how you're born," Rain Fortune says.

"My mother didn't like curly hair and made me wear a wig," Patrick says.

"Is that right?" Rain Fortune says.

"He can't remember," I say. "He was knocked on the head with a clothes horse when his old man found him tearing the wings off their pet greenfinch. They stuffed him in a bath and made him eat watermelon for five years."

"I ate potatoes a lot," Patrick says.

"He's Irish," I say. "Patrick's an Irish name. Ireland's an island built by the Scots because they couldn't carry those stones all the way to America. The Scots built England too but the English won't admit that. They think they built themselves."

"England's founded on the bodies of dead Brontosaurus," Patrick says. "The old cavemen weren't real cavemen. They lived in whales and killed Brontosaurus by throwing poisoned darts at them."

"The English lived in *holes*," I say. "They lived on a great flat marsh. The Scots lived in a beautiful country to the north full of green hills and heather and wild men dressed as chicks and being a kind and gentle race they felt sad that the English had to live in that boring wet marsh so they decided to give them a present and they all came down one day and built mountains and lakes and put trees here and there and the English came out of their holes and sat under the trees and said, 'Right! Let's get it on, man.' And the first thing they got on were the Scots. Patrick knows. They beat the shit out of them."

"I thought I was Irish," he says.

"You were," I say. "But when you started eating meat you changed. The English eat meat. The Irish eat fish and chips."

"They don't eat fish. They can't catch them. Too much trouble."

"They eat potato salad on Saints' Days. I had a girl friend who was Irish. She told me."

"What?"

"They eat potato salad on Saints' Days."

"What's potato salad?"

"Potato salad is the liquor you make from squeezing the juice from fresh potatoes and mixing it with pure alcohol."

"What do you do with the potato peel?"

"You give it to the cat."

"And the cat dies?"

"Occasionally."

"I had a cat that killed snakes."

"You had a cat that killed snakes?"

"Yes. I had a cat that killed snakes."

79

"What kind of snakes did your cat kill?"

"It killed big snakes and little snakes but it wouldn't kill spiders."

"Why did your cat that killed big snakes and little snakes not kill spiders?"

"There were enough snakes."

"You don't *have* snakes in England," Rain Fortune says.

"We have grass snakes and adders," I say. "Adders kill people and grass snakes kill grass. We need the cats to keep the grass snakes down otherwise England wouldn't be green and that's what people like about it. The cats are paid by the British Tourist Board for their services to ecology. I've met some very rich cats in England."

"We have dogs that kill niggers," Rain Fortune says. "They get medals too."

"The best story's the one about the dogs that killed John Birch," I say.

"Who's John Birch?" Patrick asks.

"John and Joanie Birch," I say.

"An their kids," Rain Fortune says.

"They had so many kids they had to build a jungle in California to put them in," I say. "But the jungle was full of other kids."

"Black-skinned frizzy-haired freaky kids," Rain Fortune says. "An there was this guy called Tarzan who thought he was a bird."

"And there was this other guy called Super Jock who *was* a bird," I say.

"He's someone else," Patrick says. "He's Mr America."

"This guy Tarzan sang in a band," Rain Fortune says. "An the black-skinned freaky kids dug it 'cause he made these weird sounds like *aieeeeee*!!! an John Birch's kids hated to hear that sound 'cause they liked to listen to Ricky Nelson an The Everlys an Pat Boone an they told Tarzan to find another gig an Tarzan told *them* to find another gig an they busted him an all the black cats rose up an had this revolution."

"Tarzan was English," Patrick says.

"That's the TV Tarzan," Rain Fortune says. "We're talkin

about the *black* Tarzan."

We reach the hotel. Someone has thrown rose petals into the pool. Rain Fortune looks at them floating on the clear water.

"They're plastic," Patrick says.

"They're sure as hell not," Rain Fortune says and scoops at them with her hand, showing him the limp pink petals.

A man in bellhop's uniform comes running across the concrete paving stones. Patrick moves instinctively to one side.

"*Keep away!*" he shouts.

He's small, thick set, with greased greying hair.

"*Hey!* Easy, man," Rain Fortune says.

"The pool area is reserved," he says.

"Watering real deep, huh?" Rain Fortune says.

"The pool area is *reserved.*"

Rain Fortune looks around. She opens her eyes wide.

"I don't see no *notice,*" she says.

"Will you please move out of here," he says.

"What kind of bum gig is this?" she says.

The man looks at me. He shakes his head. Rain Fortune has taken off her shirt, boots and pants. She dives into the pool, comes up covered in rose petals. The man turns. He stares at her as she swims a length and then back, drowning the flowers. Patrick's standing at the edge smiling.

"Let's have you," I shout.

Four security police are moving in behind us. A small crowd has gathered outside the glass windows of the hotel. They stand with their backs against the building. They don't come close. Two men in suits try to usher them inside. They won't go. They want to watch. The police arrive at the pool. One of them grabs Patrick by the shoulders.

"Hey! What are you doing?" I ask.

Patrick doesn't resist. They take him away.

"You heard the man," one of the policemen says.

"Nothing that makes sense," I say.

"Maybe *you* make no sense, buddy," he says.

Rain Fortune continues to splash rose petals down into the water. The man in the bellhop's uniform has vanished. The policemen converge on me. I make a run at the pool and dive in.

Rain Fortune's laughing and spitting water.

"You going to shoot us *dead?*" she shouts.

I look up at the windows of the hotel and see faces staring down at us. My clothes are heavy. It is difficult to stay afloat. I wave a hand and duck under. The security police have their night sticks out and are kneeling at the edge of the pool, trying to reach us. Rain Fortune swims underwater close to them. They beat down at her with their sticks. I take off my jacket. Rain Fortune shakes the water out of her eyes. The cops move round the pool. I wade into the centre again.

"I got the feelin she's makin a jackass outta us," one of them says.

"You're feelin right, man," Rain Fortune says.

She swims to the side and splashes them. They jump back. I stop at the steps and begin to pull off my boots. I can see a dark figure moving near me. When he's close I turn fast and throw the boots at him. The others rush me. I dive sideways into the pool. We begin splashing them again and the rose petals are coming up and sticking to their trousers. Rain Fortune is fast in the water. She knows she's safe. She taunts them, flashing her wet tits.

"I'm moving out," I say. "I'm cold."

"Hell, honey," she says. "All they *know* is stomping *kids*!"

I swim to the side and pull myself up. I'm dripping water over the grey hot concrete. I pick up my boots and jacket.

"You got wet feet?" One of the policemen says. He kicks the boots out of my hand.

"What the fuck you doing?"

He's younger than me.

"Waitin for you to pick up your boots," he says.

I don't move.

"There are five hundred people watching us," I say. "If you lay one finger on me – "

He raps my kneecap with his night stick. I'm off balance. I slip. He pulls me up, twists my arm. I drop, pushing my weight into him. He falls across me. His night stick rolls away. I take it and hurl it as far as I can. The other police are running at me now. I dodge them, dive back into the pool. The young one struggles with the gun in his holster. Rain Fortune's hanging on the side. The two older policemen take her and pull her out. I swim to the steps. The young policeman shouts something from the far end of the pool. The others are slapping Rain Fortune across the face, trying to get a grip of her legs. I scramble out and rush at them. I hear screams behind me. Rain Fortune is lying on the ground. I go down, punching. Hands reach for me. Voices. I crawl away.

"Hold it! Hold on, fella!"

"Cover the girl."

"Is she hit?"

"Easy, fella."

"I'm a doctor. It's okay. I'm a doctor."

"Patrick?"

"Jesus!"

Patrick is beside me.

"She's okay."

He ties a handkerchief around my forehead.

"Where is she?"

"They're looking after her."

I can't see any of the policemen.

"What happened?"

"They shot you."

I begin to laugh. A girl comes up and touches my soaking shirt.

I walk through the crowd. I'm hurt. I don't know how bad but can tell from the faces that it shows. We walk into the hotel lobby. Photographers appear in front of us and start flashing film. Officials intercede. People sitting in the lobby stand up and move away. I'm hustled into the elevator. The doors close. We go up. The elevator stops, doors open again. We walk along the corridor to my room, eight or nine of us. The officials are fussing around me now. My head is throbbing. I feel faint. We stop at the door. It opens. We go in. The room is crowded, Martha, Bella Prentice, Charlie, a guy with a beard, another with a camera, a thin woman in chic city clothes, Rain Fortune on the bed propped up with pillows, more, others, so many. I reach across the eiderdown. Rain Fortune touches my face. The room is turning, spinning. Someone's holding my right arm.

"This'll make you more comfortable," a man says.

I pull my arm back.

"You're in shock," the man says.

I crawl over the bed onto the floor, away from him.

"You're in bad shape," he says.

He places the hypodermic in a small black briefcase.

The photographer is taking pictures and the man with the beard holds a portable tape recorder like a box of chocolates in front of him. I'm leaning against the wall now close to the windows. I sit down. I sit on the floor. The bearded reporter kneels beside me.

"I've some stuff in my purse if you need it, man," he says.

He puts his paw on my shoulder. I rest my head against the wall. My hands and feet have lost their feeling. He moves the tape recorder closer.

"Do you remember the bullet?" he asks.

"I'm bleeding to death," I say.

"You'll be okay," he says.

"Thanks."

"What's that?"

"You got chocolates in there?"

"Yeh!" He laughs. "It's a neat machine, right?"

Patrick comes over. The lady in the chic clothes is with him.

"This is Jane Alexander," he says.

"Hello."

"Do you want food?" Patrick asks.

"This guy selling chocolates is breathing over my suit," I say.

The doctor has gone. The photographer is sitting on a chair smoking a joint. Rain Fortune's in bed.

"Will you be staying tomorrow?" Jane Alexander asks.

Her clothes are expensive. She's tall and thin.

"No."

"When are you leaving?"

"Who are you?"

"You may well ask."

"I am."

"I work for a New York literary magazine. They want an

article about you."

"Why?"

"They're very civilized and out of touch."

I imagine her at a Manhattan publisher's party exchanging witticisms with Tom Wolfe about Norman Mailer, quoting French poetry and passages from Proust, living with an ageing doyen of American letters because the younger kids are too hung up with their own image.

I go into the bathroom and shut the door. I look at my face in the mirror. There is a three-inch gash on my forehead at the hairline. Patrick's handkerchief is soaked. I take it off and use it to wipe the wound. I wash my face. I open the bathroom door and call Jane Alexander. She's talking to Rain Fortune.

"Do you want a ride to the hospital?" I ask.

"Why not?" She says.

I look into the mirror again. There's coagulated blood in my hair.

"Have you been to Las Vegas before?" I ask.

"I was married here," she says.

I'm sitting on the side of the bath.

"I feel I've been kicked by a horse," I say.

"A mule," she says.

"What's the difference?"

"Mules hurt more."

"Why?"

"They are vicious."

"Horses can be vicious."

"Horses are gentle."

"How do you know?"

"It's an affectation."

"What's that?"

"Assuming a false identity."

She returns to the bedroom. I lie on the floor. My head is burning. I suppose I've been shot. The bearded reporter implied as much. I remember how scared they were at Santa Barbara and how we didn't believe them because we hadn't stayed long enough to recognize the purple mirrors of paranoia flashing in their skulls. Things are changing, Panthers gunned down in the streets, riots and repression, atrocity stories and statistics from Vietnam too terrible to conceive. I began to think, even then, even before I came back and saw it for myself, that if this country is tearing itself apart the war has done it. Kids talk of capitalism like their fathers talked of Communism and yet alienation goes deeper than that. Jackson and Moby were high on a masochistic trip, bitching against brutality and harassment and yet openly inviting it, *needing* it. At Long Beach kids insulted the police to their faces, lit joints, waved them in the air, threw them on stage as if they *wanted* to be arrested. At Devonshire Downs in the swirling heat they broke through fences, raced across waste ground to where the concert platform had been erected, chased by security guards and cops while jeeps filled with promoter's thugs roared round the perimeter. The spirit of Woodstock is dead. I love America. I love the optimism, energy, inspiration, Abe Lincoln, Marilyn Monroe, Bobby Kennedy, style, hope and passion, all destined for cataclysmic extinction, too radical, too vulnerable and too young. I love America and yet cannot alter the lies, cannot hold the heat at the heart with naked hands. We are born into a society swamped by propaganda and it is this, more than anything, that dulls the will to resist.

I say, who was your father?

Patrick says, he snuffed it.

I count the people I know who have died and write their names on the wall, thinking they will come to me in the night, and my sister rubs their names off with a wet cloth and I tell her, you've killed them now, and she says, they were dead already.

I say, were you happy?

Patrick says, I had a red Raleigh, the fastest bike in the world.

I say, did you have pets?

Patrick says, we had a bird that lived in a cupboard because my mother believed cages were cruel. It was completely wild, this bird. My mother went into the cupboard and closed the door and talked to it in the pitch dark while it flew around her head going mad.

Animals roar in the hills although I never see them. I think, heaven must be lonely.

86

I say, do you despise the poor?

Catherine says, no more than you despise the rich.

I say, I am rich.

Icy rain blows through the streets of Manchester. I carry a guitar under my coat. A big car draws up at the kerb and a man in an Astrakhan coat leans out and says, can I give you a lift to the station? I reply, I'm not going to the station. He says, neither am I.

I say, when you explore inside yourself is there much to find?

Catherine says, more than you think.

I say, I should be prosecuted for trespass.

Curly blonde chick, out of school, brittle-heeled shoes, nervous and hungry, opens her shirt and lets me tumble in the tulips.

I say, do you wonder at the value?

Matthew says, it's not your business to question motive. All the kids need is to believe in something outside themselves.

I say, we have a duty not to cheat people.

Matthew says, your head's full of shit.

Water, water, flowing, draining, water in the sky, in the clouds, sleet and snow covering hills, cities, water like blood, essential to the workings of the world, polluted with poison, garbage, fish heads, birds, the sea slowly dying, the air losing oxygen, people scrambling over the earth and no earth left, the capitalist monster devouring flesh from the body of the land to make wealth, to save us, to kill us, sick blind mothers boiling babies in vats, paying to believe in a future that's lost, sweet rain like acid scorching their throats as the people turn back to the fields too late because the fields are dry and dust covers the façades of palaces built for kings and princes in the years when peasants worked as slaves and believed in God's eternal mercy although nothing stopped famine, flood, war or plague, and now the seasons are changing, darkening, and leaves on the trees are dropping in summer and buds shrivel in frost because the weather has worsened and we talk more and more and make no move, the ecological miracle being the fact of our helplessness, even mine, and the disregard for humanity which is worse, the inability to rage against the fire loud enough to be heard, the smog of freedom like a haze over the country as kids gambol into sundeath oblivious of eclipse.

I'm on the floor. My head throbs. I can hear people talking loudly in the bedroom. My face is stretched, elongated, the bones like boulders under the flesh. I wait.

    — You concentrate a great deal on the environment and so on, subjects not immediately related to pop music. Do you feel committed to that movement? Or is it simply a reflection?
    — That depends where you stand.
    — Don't you think there is a danger of exaggeration?
    — There's always a danger of exaggeration.
    — Protest songs have had a tendency in the past of becoming pedantic and sloganizing. Also they are accused of romanticism and puerility.
    — Politicians spend fortunes on advertising. Slogans sell Presidents the same as they sell beer. Songs sell ideas.
    — I think it would be true to say that politicians do not *desire* the destruction of the world.
    — As long as they get re-elected.
    — The CND movement was defused, you would agree, by the simple logic that Government *was* responsible. It has been said that the emotive hysteria of the Easter marches made a difference to the nuclear test ban negotiations at the time. They might even have had a negative effect. Violent protest creates its own backlash which can seriously affect natural processes. In other words youth movements can hinder rather than help, depending on the degree of their success, working on the principle that protest creates protest as violence creates violence.
    — What are you saying? That if we shut up everything's going to work better?
    — It's a point of view.
    — Hitler had a point of view.
    — I want to take up your own position now as a songwriter

then go back to what we were discussing about the value of the verbalizing media.

– Businessmen see the world through balance sheets and expense accounts. They have no understanding of what's going on underneath because they treat everyone who hasn't compromised as an idiot. I've known kids of seventeen who *killed themselves*. And those kids are considered *sick*. Sociologists produce statistics about teenage suicide and make statements to newspapers in language out of a Kafka *novel*. No one cares about those kids, so scared they can't go home, so empty they're hollow, lying out in some disused warehouse in a city they don't know. Whatever they do or try, wherever they go, they're adrift, without hope. They lose faith, not in God but in the world. They're hurt so hard and so much they reach a level right down where no one wants to touch them, no one wants to know them anymore, and it's not always because they're too stupid to understand, that it's their fault for trusting life, for trusting anyone, because kids who make a run for it have *vision* and it's imagination that kills them, a belief in hope. Rainbows don't last. That's the sad fact. Rainbow makers paint the sky. They go on doing it. Do you see? Do you understand this need for protest?

– I appreciate the reasons. My disappointment stems from their extraordinary lack of knowledge about the workings of Government. Ignorance is no excuse for bad manners.

– The physical landscape is being destroyed and if we can't complain about it because we're not qualified we might as well be dead.

– Utopia is essentially false because it presupposes an unnatural co-operation. The young won't accept democratic muddle.

– Why should they? When politicians learn to tell the truth they might risk it but as long as they don't kids won't respect them.

– How would you define truth?

– A spade's a fucking spade! A bomb's a bomb! Bombs kill children and mothers. They kill people. Let's not talk of Vietnam as a war of liberation, for Christ's sake. It's lust and rage. It's *obscene*.

Jane Alexander returns. She says she's taking me to the hospital.

"Are you on dope?" she asks.

"No," I say.

"You don't use it?"

"Not any more."

The bathroom is sprayed plastic, shiny tiles, bright submerged neon. I walk into the bedroom. I tell Patrick I'm going to the hospital. Rain Fortune says she'll come with me.

"No," I say. "The gig's more important."

The telephone rings and the bearded reporter answers. He says it's a through call from London. I tell Patrick to answer because I know it's Matthew and I don't want to talk to him. I leave with Jane Alexander. We take the elevator down. I'm expecting newsmen in the lobby but there's no one. The hotel desk clerk says Mr Fischer, the manager, wants a word with me. I tell him I'm going to the hospital, I haven't time. The desk clerk looks worried.

"Mr Fischer *insisted*," he says.

"If Mr Fischer would like to send flowers," Jane Alexander says, "that's fine."

We collect her car from the basement and drive out. The heat of the day has passed. The streets are full again. The sadness I felt in the morning doesn't reach me now. We don't speak. I stare through the window. Nothing happens that isn't meant to happen, predictability being the essence of fulfilment. Las Vegas is a controlled environment. Given half a chance America would be too. I felt this in Phoenix and Tucson, a sense of belonging to the nineteenth century where frontier values remain intact and kids are kids, not independent of their parents, watched and fostered in traditions of family, time hanging like moss in the trees, flesh of stone, faces of stone, confirmed reactionary warts resisting the implications of technology. Firefly said of Texas that he had never seen such poverty. He meant poverty of expression. I remember Negroes in the main street of Dallas with slicked-down hair and ill-fitting suits walking three or four blocks into slums, no break in the buildings, rich and poor together, the pawnshops, old clothes shops, windows full of guns, saddles, boots. At the hotel

90

white Texans talked as if humanity had no place in competitive society. It was strange in its darkness after California, almost tribal. I reject permanency, status, fame, and yet involve myself with them. Marriage is a dead issue. I want nothing. No name. I want freedom to dissolve and reappear. If music is a river I let it take me, not noticing that the river itself is a solid thing. We strive for recognition only to discover that recognition is not enough. I can't walk down a street without thinking of myself walking down a street. Writing about the past in the present is a reflection of the past through the present. There are days when I melt with pity for my father and there are days when I hate him. There are days when I wish I could talk to my mother and tell her everything and there are days when I wish she was dead. There are days when I yearn for my child-self again, when the smells and objects of the farm are so rich in my mind and there are days when I dig a pit inside my head and lie there. The lessons I learnt from the white heron remain with me, the ideas our parents resented so much, that we are ourselves free, that a world exists beyond the confines of byre, field, hill, that the trawlers in the harbour have been half across the globe and that we, also, can be like them, that each and every one of us has the potential to grow and move and change. In the city none of these feelings exists because the city is fully comprehensive. I remember sitting in a Kensington bistro with Catherine and she said that when she was with her brothers' friends she felt locked in a glass cage where behaviour patterns related to life outside only superficially because nothing touched them. I didn't understand. I hadn't met her brothers' friends, hadn't been to her house then or realized to what extent the basis of aristocracy depends on land, the use of land, the working of large estates with historical tradition stretching back to the Dark Ages, feudalism, Saxon freakouts and Magna Carta. To me land was farming and farmers. It wasn't riches and power. It was *work*. The Laird spoke with an English voice and was small, neat and very polite, sent his children away to school in Berkshire, lived apart, spiritually and socially, did nothing except employ the fathers of my friends. I told Catherine, 'He was like those trees you find on the shore that can't grow because the wind stunts them, not like real trees

91

that blossom in summer.' Catherine was seventeen, vulnerable and innocent. She said, 'Rats!', lusting after wild and dangerous things, for life to scar the peach pinkness, make her ragged and wonderful. She was romantic in the sense of free fall, not like my sister's friends who bathed in cherry syrup, mooning for sweet star surrender, saying, 'There's nothing to fellas but their standing ovation', the two sides of nature, soft Muzak, hard rock, shielded by girlish chatter, the clan gossip giggles that erased genuine emotion, or so it seemed to me, chicks together, guys together, painted grease dollies and cool midtown cowboys, miles from the boredom of their natural lives, snapped into music, high on Hollywood and role playing, posey as ponies, flashing tongues, tits and Boots' Eau de Cologne, the imagined orgy of love like *beebopaloola* going round and round in their heads. Catherine was convent-educated, a closed and forbidden secret. She said, 'Nuns are frustrated, bitchy, repressed and snobbish.' She hated school, ran away twice, not with boys, but alone, ran home, slept in the stables, creeping into the kitchen when it was dark to steal food, leaving notes for her father, telling him she was safe, waiting until the excitement faded and then coming into the house where she would sit with him in his study and talk about school, why she hated it so, and he would tell her how he'd hated *his* school, the constrictive rules, the compulsory games, the absurd dictates concerning courage and team spirit, the lack of freedom, the intellectual pomposity of the ruling elite, and yet, despite this, how much he had gained from *not* running away, because life, when it came, was never as bad as that, although, at times, similar, and the lessons of survival after ten years of incarceration had prepared him for the world outside. He said, 'You learn nothing from happiness and very little from success.' She said, 'I *need* happiness.' She was a girl. That made a difference. She searched for space and warmth. The claustrophobia of the convent affected her sanity. She talked of embracing experience to make up for lost time. She was naive. She was also a virgin, which surprised me, with fierce loyalties towards her code of behaviour, not promiscuous, not flirtatious, lit with an inner light, unselfconscious and unafraid. She was a child truly magic like the children I never met in the hills although believed were there, children who took the

92

place of parents and never changed, surrounded by an aura of genuine originality. She thought she was ugly. She talked of her body with disgust and hated long party dresses because they made her look like Alice In Wonderland. She broke her nose when she was twelve riding a bike into someone's swimming pool and thought it terrible to admit caring so much as to have it remoulded. She said her mouth was prehensile. I said, 'What's that?' She said, 'Capable of lifting heavy weights.' Her skin was soft. She liked her skin. She said, 'The first blind man I meet I'm going to marry.' I wore dark glasses and fumbled about the room. She pointed at my trousers. I looked. I couldn't see anything. She brought a cloth and began rubbing my knee. She told me to sit down. She said, 'It's quite fresh.' I said, 'What?' She said, 'The blood.' I said, 'There isn't any blood.' She said, 'Bats bleed to death all the time. They're haemophiliacs. They don't know it's happening.' There were moments, not now but earlier, before Chicago, when I felt sympathy for Civil Rights marchers and kids demonstrating against the war, understanding their desire to break with tradition and discover a new life. Catherine approached from another direction to reach a point that was almost identical, talked of *real life* when she meant poverty. I said, 'Where there's no choice there's no hardship. Hope engenders breakdown.' My parents watched the world slide into an abyss of sin and decadence. Kids broke their hearts, winging out of football games and dance halls and picture houses and blues clubs, Spitfired on beer and pills and fantasies of escape before the harpies of the henroost clawed them squawking from race tracks to tether them safe in new council estates on the smart side of town. When I arrived in London I had rooms in a basement at the back end of Fulham Road. There was a bed, a table, three chairs, a chest of drawers, a hanging cupboard and a small stove. The window looked out onto a brick wall and steps leading to the street. If I put my face low at the bottom of the window I could see people walking above me. I could see their feet. The room was littered with paperbacks, record sleeves, clothes, shoes, a pot of honey, bread, reams of foolscap scribbled with half-written lyrics. I didn't use the hanging cupboard or the chest of drawers. I left my shirts and jeans on the chairs. The walls were pinned with

93

typewritten sheets of completed songs, in order, from left to right, moving above the bed towards the window. I worked and slept there, ate down the road in a transport caff or at the Indian restaurant or the Chinese takeaway. Beccy wanted to come and clean for me. I said, 'No. I don't want that. I don't want anyone to come.' I wouldn't have a telephone. I didn't need people. I was in love with Catherine. I saw her every day. I had never been in love although had slept with girls and used to worry that I would die believing it was like the movies, all the colours brighter, the sky bluer, the body like a feather floating in air. Sometimes in the past when I had nowhere to sleep, travelling the northern clubs, I would find a chick at a gig and ask her if she knew of anywhere I could go for the night and she'd take me home and I would think to myself, what does it matter if I don't feel love, I feel everything else, but the chicks were aching with hunger like I was their knight in shining armour and they wanted me forever and promised to love me and never forget me and I wondered about their age because they sounded so young and their bodies were hard and firm, almost like boys, supple and puppyish, smelling of bath talc and lemonade, and I became afraid of what I was doing to them, realizing hopes inside that wouldn't last until morning, this fantasy of a real guitar player although I told them, 'I'm not. I'm nothing. I'm a bum. A faker.' They held me and kissed me and shook their bodies and cried. I disliked doing it more and more and yet couldn't throw them out or hurt them, hating the moment when I would say, 'I've got to go.' They'd blame themelves and say, 'I wasn't any good, was I?', expecting me to tell them, 'You were lovely', which I did at the start, as if it mattered, and so they'd follow me to the bus station, hug me some more, and I thought then, it's not worth it, I don't need it that much, becoming scared of what it was doing to me, understanding the brittleness after so many years, this need for love, this pain, thinking I would salve it on the road, and yet no one cared, no one knew, no one realized my seriousness or the essence of my difference as they laid their longing before me like bouquets of roses. I invented stories as camouflage, lazing in the arms of a pearl diver's daughter across a tartan rug in the back of a van beside a wood one wet January night. I asked whether her

94

father could manage the hundred footers like he did when he was a kid. She lifted herself on an elbow and looked at me. 'What you talkin about, luv?' I said, 'Can your Dad take the high rock dives anymore?' She said, 'Dad's in the foundry.' I said, 'Once I thought my father was a farmer until one night I came home late and found him mining coal in the potato field beyond our house and asked, what you doing, Dad, and he said, digging to Australia, son.' She said, 'Feelin alright?' She wore a bronze sweater with purple tulips over each tit. I told her another story. I said, 'Even when the snow was piling up our yard in winter I wore bathing trunks and tinted shades and walked around the house in bare feet. My mother called a doctor and the doctor was an African from Mozambique. I told him I was going for a swim. He said he'd join me. We drove up the hill together in his car to the hospital on the edge of town. Inside this hospital was a vat of goat's milk used for making cheese for diabetic patients. We stripped and dived in. It was great.' I thought then, if you believe hard enough things'll come true. The pearl diver's daughter was eighteen and had a womb like a vegetable garden. She said, 'I went with a boy for two years. He wouldn't touch me.' I licked her ears. She didn't move. She said, 'He was pure, you see. He was keeping himself pure for me. I told him, we don't have to hang on forever, luv. We're not bloody trapese artists. And he said something funny then. He said, sex is sacred.' I was warming her arse with my hands. I said, 'Did you fly out the window and shit on the Bishop's hat?' She pushed me away. She said, 'It's *true*!' She was hurt. She didn't kiss me. She said, 'You're foolin around.' I said, 'Fools inherit the earth because other people are too busy conjugating verbs.' She said, 'What's that?' All lies and stories. I found them easy. There was a drummer I knew called Rick Stanley, a Londoner working with a northern rock band. His attitude was simple. He was killing time before going to art school. He didn't care. None of them did. Paul Cowan, lead vocalist, spent half the gig insulting his audience and the other half insulting himself. 'Git off yo'r packasses, f'r Chrissake, let's get some *balls* up here!' he'd scream. 'I wanna see the whites o yo'r nippies, darlin! I wanna see you shake yo'rself outta yo'r socknaps right *here'n now*, squealin an cryin, baby! We're a

FUCK band! So WATCH AOUT!' The more outrageous they were the more successful they became. Record companies hassled for contracts, music paper journalists pleaded for interviews. Rick said, 'It's crazy when you think about it. Here we are shitting on the image, night after night, a parody, a living insult, man, and these cunts offer us the fuckin world.' They were unique and brilliant and yet cut no album and were seen in selected venues in the north. Rick told me the only lesson he'd learnt was never answer a straight question straight and never let them get at you because once they did you were dead and the whole dream factory went up in smoke. His style influenced me in the sense that I became less shy and hesitant. If he was serious about anything it was the waste of people's lives, how we strive for useless goals and worry about things that aren't important like money, morality and making it with authority. He said, 'Life's a fuckin joke, man. If we spend all our time wondering what it means we'll blow our sweet brains to hell. What's it for, man? What's fan clubs and squealing chicks and big deal promotion all about? Who wants it? *Christ!* Do *you* want it?' He made restraint feel like fear. He was so plausible. I was taught guitar by Brother Mark. It was another life, an ethnic nursery. We sat opposite each other on separate benches in the warehouse, he playing, I following. Occasionally he would stop, point out a mistake, make me go back, try again, but on the whole he didn't talk much. We played. He said, 'Music is a force.' I said, 'What kind of force?' He said, 'Like love is a force.' When he talked his hands shivered. I had a strong desire to hold them. Once I did. Their heat and energy were extraordinary. I let go, let them fall, turning away quickly in confusion. He said, 'Whatever you give comes back. Whatever you take you take forever. I'm giving you lessons in music. One day you'll play well and that'll give me pleasure. It comes back.' I spent more time at Brother Mark's than anywhere. He had a gramophone and a large collection of blues records and I sat there alone with the guitar and tried to follow the chords. No one bothered me. The others were going to the gym or painting scenery. Murdo, a small dark boy of my age, had written a play. He wanted me to compose music for it. I had never tried composing music. I said, 'No.' He said, 'Shakespeare was a

bloody poacher. He had to start somewhere.' In the end I wrote
eight songs. Murdo's play, 'Sweet Sally & The Dead Bear', was
a violent episodic story of Sweet Sally, daughter of the Rock
Café owner, and Black Bear, leader of a motorcycle gang, who
want to ride off into the country and escape everything that
ties them to the city. They don't make it because there's too
much going against them and Black Bear dies in a battle with
a rival gang and Sweet Sally walks out of the Rock Café at the
end and says, 'Whatever life is meant to be it's not meant to be
this', and her Dad says, 'What do you know about life?', and
then Sally sings the last song, 'Someone Tell Me Where The
Wild Flowers Grow', as the rest of the cast move up behind and
take up the chorus. Murdo played Black Bear and a chick called
Maggie Burns played Sally. Brother Mark was the father. I sat
on the edge with my guitar. It didn't matter that I wasn't in
the action. I walked out and stood close to whoever was singing.
We gave three performances. Murdo hugged Maggie and me
afterwards and said we really made it happen. I asked Maggie
whether she had liked it and she said she liked the songs. She
was sixteen and already had a strong bluesy gutter voice. She
was taller than Murdo and fat and when she came first to
try for the part Murdo said he wouldn't consider her. He
wanted a blonde sexy starlet type. Brother Mark said, 'The
tragedy's not only that Black Bear gets killed but also that
Sally's not going to find anyone else. When her father says,
what do you know about life, he's saying, you've got to accept
what you're given. In her case that means accepting who she is
and what she is. The audience must understand she's lost
everything.' Murdo said, 'People'll ask what sort of fella's this
Black Bear if he can't score a decent-looking chick?' Brother
Mark said, 'He's someone who recognizes character.' Murdo
said, 'The whole jive of Black Bear's gang is image. They don't
know anything about character.' Brother Mark said, 'Black
Bear is trying to escape, don't forget. He's found a girl he loves
and who loves him and she's nothing to do with this other life
and she changes him.' Brother Mark made the motives sound
sincere and serious. Murdo said, 'Okay.' I found the songs easy
because the story was there and the music came out of the story
quite naturally. I wrote *against* emotion. It was instinctive, un-

intentional. Brother Mark said that the slow numbers succeeded in the scenes at the gang meetings as much as Maggie's fast rock number in the Café when she's complaining about the waste of her youth and she's singing, 'Lordie, Lordie, won't the firestorm touch me/coz I paid m'money/an I need the light/an I don't find nothin/in this cold stone water/an I don't feel your arms, chil'/don't feel your love/no more.' But the best song was Murdo's in the Café with Maggie before going out to the fight. He sings 'Beat Down Boogie', a real rocker, and he's dancing too, and Murdo was good at that, and he's telling Maggie he's going to beat down the bully boys once and for all because he's ace, he's killer monkey. The songs were good. Brother Mark liked them. He encouraged me. But I knew it was Murdo's story that had done it and when I tried to write from my own experience I didn't know where to begin. Jack Field dropped by whenever he was in the area. He said, 'How's your sex life? Getting all those little girls into trouble?' I said, 'Every one.' He said, 'What are you going to do when it's over?' I said, 'I'm not staying here.' He said, 'Ambition's a funny thing. It's destructive and constructive at the same time.' I said, 'Why have ambition if you know it can't work?' He said, 'Kids don't have the experience to recognize what's coming and so make decisions that are going to affect the rest of their lives *blind*.' Four days after leaving school I packed my bag. I told my mother I had a job in Birmingham with a friend humping meat for a cold storage firm. My father said, 'You'll need something for the journey, lad.' He went to the kitchen dresser and counted £20 in single notes. He sealed them in an envelope. He said, 'Remember to write us where you are.' He put his hand in mine. I said, 'Okay, Dad.' I wanted to blow clean out of my skin. He said, 'God bless you.' My sister walked me to the bus. She asked, 'What's this job, then?' I said, 'Just a job.' She was working as a waitress and going to evening classes for shorthand typing. She said, 'You don't waste much time.' I said, 'They don't want me here.' She said, 'Who's fault's that?' I stopped. I put my bag down. I said, 'Not yours, that's for sure.' She said, 'Our Mum's crying her eyes out up in that house and you're taking *his* money.' It wasn't raining but it was that kind of night. I said, 'Would you go back if you could?' She said,

'Back where?' I said, 'To the country.' She said, 'Would you?'
She leaned against me, took my arm. I pulled away. The bus
arrived. I said, 'Goodbye.'

- What's been your most meaningful experience?
- Controlling my bowels.
- Are you naturally a shy person?
- I'm bloody terrified.
- Can you expound on that?
- Reporters and writers have a definite image in their minds.
  I don't. I'm changing all the time.
- That may not be important to you but it is to the fans who
  buy your records.
- They buy my records for their own reasons.
- Your work has progressed in a remarkable way, unlike the
  majority of your contemporaries. Now you're playing with
  a band.
- Yes.
- Were you influenced by the trend towards looser associa-
  tions between name artists and back-up groups, using hand-
  picked musicians for a particular session or album?
- I wasn't influenced. I'm not in touch with Top 100. Music
  isn't dependent on trends. Southern soul, blues, rock'n'roll
  hasn't changed that much over the years. What changes is
  the attitude of the kids.
- You say you're not in touch with Top 100. Do you think
  you're in touch with the public?
- How can I tell?
- By their response.
- Kids scream at anything. They don't discriminate any more.
  They used to. We played Long Beach early this tour and
  we were terrible. The mikes and PA weren't working
  properly and the sound was awful. I wanted to apologize
  because it's important to me that they get the right sound.
  But the kids went crazy despite everything. I wanted to tell
  them, for Christ's sake, we're not *worth* that kind of shit,
  take your money back.
- Has it been the same all along?
- Bad gigs?

– Audience reaction.
– Long Beach was the worst because we couldn't get it together. Some of the critics picked us up and were quite perceptive. That's another thing I've noticed, the wide gap between critics in the music papers and kids out front. Once concerts become an extension of the vibes emanating from the floor it's time to go back to the studio.

The doctor gives me an injection, sews me up, ties a bandage round my head.

"What about the stitches?" I ask.

"They won't go away," he says.

"They might need cutting."

"They dissolve."

"Inside?"

"Right."

Red Indians lay their dead on the mountains, let birds picnic on their bones. We hide, shivering under sheets in numbered rooms and die in pain, alone, in places like this.

Jane Alexander is at Reception.

"I feel raped," I say.

"The wonders of modern medicine," she says.

"You walk up to these guys with your guts hanging out and they say, hold it, old buddy, and lie you down on some table for two hours and then come back and cut your leg off because they can't remember who you are and can't see anything because they're stoned on pure oxygen having just laid the ward sister in Intensive Care and masturbated Matron with a greased stethoscope on the way through Terminal. No one knows what the next guy's talking about because he's some kind of specialist Dr Frankenstein. When I was a kid we had a human being doctor. He lived in the village. We knew his *name*. He had a wife who was real too. *She* had a name."

"Let's sit here and play Doctors and Nurses. We'll raid the drug cupboarl," Jane Alexander says. "He's done a fine job. You could pass for the Sheikh of Araby."

100

"If I pass anywhere it'll be out," I say.

"They'll have your liver on a dish in two flicks of a swab bag," she says.

A young nurse with hair tied in bunches glides through the glass doors. She has brought my bill.

"You pay at the office," she says, smiling.

"Mr Fischer will look after that," Jane Alexander says.

The nurse nods.

Jane Alexander signs "Maria Fischer" on the bill.

We leave.

"Do you do that often?" I ask.

"Not really," she says.

"Why do it now?"

"You were going to pay."

We reach the car. I look at my face in the mirror. I begin to unwind the bandage. Jane Alexander lights a cigarette.

"The nice doctor will be angry with you," she says.

"Not as angry as Maria Fischer."

She laughs.

"Max is gay," she says.

The bandage is falling around us. There is a lump of lint like a slab of cheese over the stitches. I take it off. The hair has been shaved in a circle. I replace the lint and hold it on with my hand. I close my eyes. I feel the blood beating.

"What are you doing in Las Vegas?" I ask.

"Wasting other people's money," she says.

"Why are you interested?"

"I've spent too long in the company of gamblers and gangsters. I prefer other vices for a change. You, for instance."

"I'm a capitalist."

"Does it get to you?"

"What?"

"The absurdity of making that kind of money."

"I don't see the money. It goes into a bank."

We sit in silence. Cigarette smoke in the car. Warmth. If she doesn't speak I'll float. Stitches begin to dissolve. I see lights, colours, moons collide. Lint soaked in LSD. I dig the sting.

"You look like the man who shot Liberty Vallance," Jane Alexander says.

101

"Who's Liberty Valance?"

"He's the bad guy."

"If I shot the bad guy I should be Mayor or something."

"You don't know you shot him. You're stupid with firearms."

"The dumb guy never gets the chick."

"There aren't any smart guys in this movie."

"Sounds like a box office smash. What time is it?"

"Time to eat."

She starts the car. I sit up.

"Hey!"

She has long wrists and fingers.

"I had better bandange you up," she says, switching off the engine.

My voice is megaphoned through buttermilk.

"I've got to get to the gig . . ."

I can't breathe. I reach for the handle, my body rippling like sailcloth. I open the door, stand in the wind, feel her arm across my shoulder, her bare arm across my neck. I'm *gasping*. She guides me. I am the blind soldier wounded as we stumble towards the lights of the hospital, my legs dancing although everything else is slow. She holds me. In her Park Avenue suit, she holds me. And we walk together. The wind is like soup. I stop, touch my skull. The field is full of cars. I am a soldier in a white garage. The red cars excite me. The blue cars appease me. She is standing at the centre. She kisses my cheek, my eyelid. Fear sinks slowly. Evaporates. I am aware of myself in a particular condition, in a particular place. It is no longer strange and terrifying. We walk round and round. I begin to wonder what it is that has happened, like at Chicago, speculation a wasted journey, thousand reasons for a single move. I feel close to my father now. He took nothing, accepted no charity. And yet I could not believe. I knelt with my sister at the edge of our bed and recited verses that meant as little as tossing cow dung at hens. I wanted a sign, looking up at the sky, thinking, that is the same sky above the whole world, above cities and green land, and it is wrong to accept desolation as emptiness because the sky enfolds us and protects us and the air is life. As my bones grew so did the trees, the leaves, the wild raspberries, the corn, the grass, the heather, the fish. Seasons were

102

the knowledge and love of God if anything was, if anything could be. Walking the hill or walking in the wood was to walk with God as part of Him, the senses alive to His continuing presence, spirits of dead land, dead forest, together as one, the lost and the found, as winter is with summer. My understanding of isolation changed. After school we climbed the glen or guddled trout in the burn or ambushed the girls and tied them to the trees and dared each other to kiss them. I hated that but did it because we all did it. When my sister was captured I had to kiss her too. I leaned forward, grinning. I saw that she was crying. I untied the rope. They attacked me, five boys, my friends. We were in the wood across the field. The ground was damp and mossy. They forced my face into the wet muddy moss. I thought, I'll die. Afterwards they said I was stupid and ugly. The girls spat at me. It was an indication of the spaces between us, the difference that would tear us apart. We lived separate lives. My father never went to the village on Friday nights or to the Saturday socials like everyone else. Mrs Pillansky at the grocery who married a Pole, and Jock Campbell, the butcher, and Mrs Grant, the baker's wife, sympathized with my mother. They were kind to her. They were kind people. Life was slow and ordered, full of gossip and the smell of fresh scones. I was the Baptist's boy who wrote rhymes. They knew everything. I wouldn't talk. I had visions. I was there, inside myself, in *me*. I was *there*. I wrote poems because the teacher encouraged me. I enjoyed it, the music of language. I read poetry too, even at the age of eight. The teacher said, 'Words are rocks with which to shape your land.' I understood that. The poet as artist. Now my songs are ruins on a blasted heath. I want to destroy false magic. I want to shout out loud. I want to tell them, I know how it feels to need hope and protection, I know how it feels to lose. There comes a time, as all time comes, when truth breaks our resistance and the world we're taught to honour is seen as a mechanized imitation manipulated by monsters where extortion, inequality, hate and deceit continue unabated and God is recognized at last as a symbol of servitude. Far off in the corners of another place I hear the wise old frogs complain that modern youth is too depressed, too dissatisfied, too obscured by unhappiness to see the bright flags flying above their heads. I want to tear down their walls and break into their rooms where once they fought and strove for the position they now enjoy. I want to ask, 'What would *you* do? How would *you* move the earth?' They would offer me a glass of port from the sideboard and say, 'One doesn't *move* the earth, dear boy, one moves *with* it, observes changes, indulges the profits of the same, and with one's new-found freedom one grows, one builds one's life, because one has the tools now, one has the time, a precious opportunity that mustn't be wasted or frittered away.' I tell them in reply that what hurts most is our weakness. Freedom without power is an illusion. They smile as if to say, you're moving along the right lines, lad. Beccy said, 'If you go on re-writing the Book of Genesis you'll explode.' We were sitting in her kitchen. Matthew was in the other room watching TV. Beccy leaned across the table and put her hands out, her long hair hanging loose on either side of her face, shading her eyes. I felt the warmth of her fingers on my neck. She sat back and lit a cigarette. She said, 'I was in love with a boy when I was fourteen. A big curly-haired Jewish boy at our school. I fancied him for a whole year. Followed him home. Stuff like that. I knew he had a girl in Hampstead because my friend, Stella Goodman, said she'd seen him up there Friday nights. I said, so what? Who cares? He doesn't know I exist. Which was true. I thought, I'll go and look anyway. And so one Friday after school I took a tube to Hampstead and waited. Nothing happened. I kept telling myself I was an idiot. What difference did it make if he had a girl or not? He wasn't going to look at me. And just as I'd decided to pack it in I saw him coming up the stairs. It was like a movie or something. There he was. BAZAM! But he was different. He didn't look the same. And being a movie you thought, *huh huh,* it's another bloke, and she's going to fall for it. He's the *real* hero, this new guy. But it *was* him. He was wearing tight pants and patent leathers and a skinny jacket with pockets all over the place and a great fat silver-buckled belt and a coloured shirt with buttons undone and something round his neck, some kind of cross. I followed him up the hill and, of course, it's obvious what happened. There wasn't a girl at all. There were fellas. I didn't believe it. I *wouldn't.* I told myself, he needs the bread. He needs it for his crippled mother.

104

But it made me ill. I was ill for months. I had dreamed so much about him. That's when I realized you can't be sure about people. It's wrong to make them so important. You shouldn't expect things to work out like they do in stories. Not with anyone. You shouldn't expect kids to know what they're doing because most of the time they're floating. Just catching the news. You know? I was flat chested as a kid. Still am. I didn't rely on that to get me through, didn't expect blokes to fall foaming in the street when I passed or sit around coffee bars in knee-high leather boots waiting for Antonioni to walk by and say, right, you're the one. When I met Matthew I'll admit I thought he was as flash as the rest. And he was. But that's just the varnish. The top shine. I'm like you, really. I don't pretend I'm anyone.' She sat smoking, smiling, watching to see how I would react. I said, 'Do you believe in things?' She said, 'Like what?' She flicked ash onto the floor. She had a funny way of holding her head on the side like a thrush. I said, 'We start off the same at the beginning. Being born. And then, depending on who we are, where we live, all those things, we change and become different. But as kids we believe things. As we grow older we stop believing. We understand the difference between truth and untruth although some people don't get that far. We believe in love. Or think we do. And that changes, like you were saying about movies, until there comes a point when we're left with nothing. The whole of life seems crazy. We laugh at it. We don't take it seriously anymore. People say we're sophisticated, we don't care. But we only appear like that because there's nothing inside. We believe in *nothing*. It's all lies. Everything. And then someone dies. Like a kid dies. Someone close. We realize, that was *real*. We start looking for handholds, something to cling onto. Believing in nothing doesn't appeal any more. Death's no joke. We cling to religion or the job or politics. It doesn't matter. We start inventing things to be important again so that we don't feel so scared. But we don't *really* believe in them. We *make* ourselves. We grow old clinging to these fake ideals until we die. That's it. We die and we're empty shells. They peel us off the bottom.'

The air is restful now, the lights of Las Vegas glowing beyond the buildings down the hill. Jane Alexander collects the bandage from the front seat of the car and winds it in a roll. She tells me to hold the lint and then ties the bandage like a bonnet under my chin and over my head.

We sit in the car again. It smells of cigarette smoke and new leather.

"You still tripping?" she asks.

"What?"

"You know what I mean."

Her body is tense. She has soft olive skin, a long clear face. Her eyes are shadowed lightly with mascara and blue pencil.

"I was thinking maybe you'd taken something," she says.

"No."

"You were acting so strange."

"You didn't seem scared."

"I was."

"I get blackouts. I crashed in Chicago last year. They flew me home on a stretcher."

"And it happened again? Right now?"

"If you hadn't been there."

"Why?"

"You held me together. You held onto me."

"I held onto you?"

"You kissed me."

"This is getting *weird*." She laughs nervously. "You say I *kissed* you?" She reaches for her bag, takes out a Filter King. "You wouldn't let me out the goddam *car*."

I look across at the white building of the hospital. Everything is quiet.

"You fell out the door," she says. "I came round to pick you up. I guess you had fainted or something. But you were okay. I said I'd drive you to the hotel. You shouted at me to stay inside. I made some kind of gesture about needing the bandage. I don't remember. You grabbed me and pushed me through the door. You said you'd cut my heart out. You said worse things."

I'm holding my fists on my knees, clenching, unclenching.

"A man drove up in a convertible and parked it back there. You didn't see him. I was trying to get the window up and you were pushing down on it and he ran over. He heard you screaming at me, I guess. But when he appeared you stopped. You

106

calmed right down. You told him we're having a disagreement, it's okay. He looked through the window and said, you all right, lady? I thought you were going to kill him. You had this look on your face."

"Where is he now?"

"He went into the hospital."

"What was he like?"

"I don't know. He was middle-aged."

I leave the car and walk back across the parking lot. She doesn't attempt to stop or follow me.

There is a different nurse at Reception. She's talking on the telephone.

I look for a chair. The hallway is empty. I sit on a padded bench. I try to think.

The nurse is speaking.

"Have you registered? Have you registered already?"

I walk over to the desk.

"I'm looking for someone who came in maybe fifteen minutes ago."

"Do you have a name?"

"He's middle-aged. That's all I know."

"Is he a patient? Can you tell me that?"

"Has anyone been through?"

"I'll make enquiries."

It seems ridiculous.

I leave through the swing doors, out across the parking lot again. The air is cooler now. Jane Alexander's car has gone. I search for a note, a message. There is nothing. I walk in a circle and return to the hospital and ask the nurse to call a cab. I stand outside. I wait. The cab arrives. I tell the driver to take me to the Convention Center. He begins to talk. He tells me the story of his war, how he was stationed in Essex ("Great people! Jeez!"), how he's planning to take the kids over next year just to teach them a bit of history, see the old folks, his friends in England, show Nance and Jo Jo and Chuck Jr, Piccadilly Circus, the Houses of Parliament, Saint Paul's Cathedral, Carnaby Street. I say nothing. His words are like plastic pansies on a polished vinyl sideboard in a suburban bungalow where crazed kids dream, if they dream at all, of free acid, San Francisco, naked bronze nymphets on the beach at Carmel, white skies, white gulls, sex, sea and sand, a life of peace, welfare cheques, brotherhood and food stamps, so different from the cramped, crabbing synthetics of this dusty arse-end of Magicland. The distance between us is like the distance between two planets. Nixon's silent majority and Humphrey's labour heavies skulk in shadow as ghetto blacks are gunned off the streets and guilt-sick rich kids rage against the cancer society, sharing bread with hustlers, seeking a new identity in destitution, cultivating grass because it's cool to fuck the law, buying expensive stereos and records, wearing cheap clothes like depressed farmers from the rural south whom they've never met outside of magazines. This man, this cab driver, rambling his sentiments around the arbours of my skull, drinks beer, smokes Luckies, watches ball games on TV, goes bowling with the wife Saturdays, reads the comic and sport pages, drives a hire cab for another guy, makes enough to cover payments and a bit more, thinks about retirement, fishing, living in Colorado although he comes from Decatur, Illinois, distrusts Jews, niggers, liberals and Kennedys, approves of US involvement in Vietnam because "we're fighting Commies". I don't carry his weight but know why he is. I can tell him nothing. He needs no answers. I was raised amongst such people, not complexed by ethnic hassles or Civil Rights, but entrenched in a class war that harped back to the '30s and beyond like no time had passed, suspicious of education and change, losing noticeably the ethics of the workers' movement as material luxuries came within reach.

We turn left off The Strip past a giant parking lot. The Convention Center is ahead, a low wide flat building, glass fronted and lit. I tell the driver to go round the back. I'm nervous now. I haven't eaten.

The high aluminium factory doors are shut. I get out. I bang on the doors. I can hear music in the distance. I keep hitting the aluminium until someone opens the flap. The cab driver is beside me, a porky fat man wearing dark slacks, blue golfing shirt and sneakers.

"Hey! Fantastic, man!"

It's Maxwell. He opens the small side door. Music roars out.

I hear Rain Fortune singing 'They Brought My Baby Home'.

"What happened to your head, man?"

"How long have they been on?"

Maxwell looks at his wrist although he's not wearing a watch.

"Twenty minutes maybe," he says.

I glance down the wide tunnel to the stage and see a crowd of kids and security cops on the steps.

"Have you any bread?"

Maxwell pulls up his T-shirt. He's wearing a money belt under the rim of tie dyed jeans.

"How much you need?"

"Five."

"Three sixty," the cab driver says.

Maxwell takes out a wad of notes and peels me a bill. I give it to the cab driver.

"Forget the change," I say.

He jerks a brown wallet from his hip pocket and pushes the note in. We shake hands.

"Good luck," he says.

I'm walking fast down the corridor, Maxwell almost running to keep up. We reach the dressing room without being seen. The door is locked. Maxwell's flustered, frightened. He starts feeling in his pockets. His flat boy's face is fuzzed with pale yellow hair. His eyes are pools of sky where birds don't swim, a child whose head was baked at birth and left on the sand to bleach, a white man's forgotten son, raised in Sacramento by a truck stop waitress who dreamed of being a dancer on the silver screen. He has no life but the life of those he's with and one day, like tomorrow, he'll think it fine to tell the chicks at the milk bar that I'm his friend, his real muddy buddy. Kids who get used by the whole world, greasing the cogs of big wheel syndicators, eating shit for pleasure, make me *fierce*.

"Ask Ken for the key," I say.

Maxwell hesitates, half turning in his rush to do what he's told.

"Ken?"

"On stage. Our roadie. You've seen the guy. Sitting at the back of the cabinets."

"Okay."

109

He knows nothing, but he goes, squeezing through the crowd on the steps into the light. A cop tries to stop him and I can see them arguing, Maxwell gesticulating, pointing back at me, the cop peering into the tunnel, Maxwell moving away to the right behind the cabinets. The song closes with Rain Fortune, Bella Prentice and Martha laying back on the chorus, repeating the last two lines, giving it a strong gospel inflection, and then Rain Fortune alone takes 'Dark clouds are blowin, child' to the end of the first verse again with only Patrick's guitar. The hall is hushed and quiet. The song ends almost on a whisper and although I can't see her I imagine Rain Fortune leaning over the mike, brushing it with my mouth, 'And they brought m'baby home so still', her body tuned to the tension of the sound as if controlling it by muscle alone. For a moment there is silence and then the applause washes over us. I hear Patrick pick at the strings, tuning, Charlie beating a short roll. The applause is loud and continuous. I have this feeling, this deep ache, almost envy, that the song works better with Rain Fortune than it does with me, that what I heard was a new rendering, a different shading altogether, and I'm reminded suddenly of that movie memoir classic when the young understudy takes over the lead because the star's on the booze or being blackmailed in an out of town motel and the understudy's so good he steals the show and next morning the workmen are up above the theatre taking the old guy's name down and the producer's saying, the kid's got talent, Mac, you should have seen him last night, and the old guy, the George Sanders figure who plays the star, exits into a windswept, snowswept street because it's always winter at times like that in those movies, and he bends down for the last time to stroke Irving, the theatre cat, or Sam's Boy, the black kid who sells programmes on opening night, and then shuffles off to the bar on the corner and you know, that's it, the bugger's done his number, confiding with Honest Joe, the heart of gold bartender, about *his* year on Broadway when every studio in Hollywood was bidding for him, but he wouldn't touch them, spurned them all to play Shylock in *Merchant* and save a small theatre at the back end of Shit Street because that's where he was given his break twenty years before, and as he's talking Joe tiptoes to the window and looks out and there's the

young understudy with his girl walking to the theatre and the
girl looks up at the lights above the building and squeezes the
young guy's arm and whispers, darling, I'm so *proud,* and the
young guy, inevitably the worst actor in the movie, smiles down
at her because he's walking on some constructed ramp to make
him look like Gary Cooper and says, did I tell you I rang Mama
and she's patched it up with Dad and they're coming to the
wedding after all?

Maxwell returns with Terry, waving the key. He unlocks the
door and we go in.

"Can you get some Cokes from the machine?" I ask.

"Sure," Maxwell says.

He jumps up and goes out swinging his arms.

"Lock it," I say.

Terry locks the door.

I find my case, take the guitar out, begin to tune it. Terry
says Matthew's meeting us tomorrow at St Louis.

"When did you hear?" I ask.

"He phoned the hotel," he says. "Patrick spoke to him. I
thought you were there."

I know why Matthew's come back. Beccy's dead. I don't
want to hear a single word. I don't want to listen now. I remember talking in the hall of someone's house the evening before we
left. Matthew said, 'She'll pull through. She's done it before.'
I said, 'She's sinking through the fucking floor, man!' He said,
'Once the new drug takes hold things will change.' I went out
into the garden. It was a clear warm night. There was a party
going on upstairs. I listened to the sound of laughter and music.
All I wanted was to give her what I had, sit and talk to her,
be with her. But I didn't. I didn't stop the tour. I didn't offer.
I did nothing. Next morning we flew to the States. Matthew
had a chick waiting in L.A. She travelled with us. A week later
when the news came through that Beccy was weaker Matthew
thought it best to stay with us because the chances were she'd
have improved by the time he reached England and then there
wouldn't be anything for him to do. I said, 'If you don't go,
I quit.' The chick was in his room smoking a joint. I wouldn't
speak to her. She made me hate Matthew, something I had
never done before. I kept hearing Beccy's voice that last time

111

as I laid my ear close. She said, 'Don't worry about me.' I kissed her goodbye. She said, 'Come home soon.' It was then in San Diego that Rain Fortune told me about her kid brother. She said, 'I stays in bed all day, not wantin to eat or anythin, an my Mama says, you no good to anyone like that, an I say, it don't matter to me, Mama, an she says, you give us a call when you left this world so's we can pack you up an give this bed to your cousin Huey or your cousin Belle Alline, an I say, don't give m'bed to m'cousin Belle Alline, an she says, Belle Alline's had a hard life an I reckon she need somewhere decent to live, an after about a while I says to myself, it ain't so smart makin room for Belle Alline, an I think, when someone dies like your own kid brother you think, that could have been me, man, an I tells God that time, you did a mean thing lettin him get hisself run down in the road there, you did a mean, mean thing, Lord, but what I was thinkin is, I'm livin an breathin an *I'm glad*.' She took me outside and showed me the wind in the palms, the cars on the highway beyond the scrub ground, the people walking in the patio. She said, 'That brings hope when you think on it, honey.' But what brought hope was the warmth of her body, the dark sweetness of her thighs.

Maxwell's back, knocking at the door.

"Don't let him in," I say.

The lights are bright, the floor covered with clothes, boots, open guitar cases, food. There's a mirror on the wall behind the basin. I wash my hands and face. I empty like a bottle. I pour myself away.

I carry the guitar out. Terry follows. We leave the dressing room and reach the crowd on the steps. I push through. Jug Meat are ending one of their own numbers. Charlie sees me, waves his sticks. Rain Fortune, Martha and Bella Prentice are at the far end beyond Steve's organ. Ken's sitting on a box behind the cabinet close to Charlie. The lights are full in our faces. I can't see the audience except on the tiered seats at the edge. I dodge around the cabinets. Ken looks up. I pass him, cross over the cables to the other side. Patrick lays down a heavy riff, standing in the spot. The audience is clapping as he comes over to the mike again, sings the last verse. He's taut, clean, hardly moving his body. I join Rain Fortune. She laughs when

112

she sees my bandage. I can't hear what she's saying. She hugs me, giggling. The song has ended, the audience applaud. Rain Fortune runs to Patrick. Patrick tells them I've arrived. I walk out with Martha and Bella Prentice. The kids are on their feet. I stand at the front and raise my arms. Terry's beside me fixing the guitar mikes. He works fast. The cheering subsides.

"I want to say it's kind of you to wait."

Howls, whistles.

"I didn't know there were so many kids in Las Vegas. All I see are these fat cats in the hotel playing ball games."

Cheers.

"I had a bit of trouble on the road. Walked into a Nazi patrol."

Cries of "Right on!" Feet stomping.

"They didn't like me having these ladies in the band. Thought maybe I was colour blind. I told them these ladies sing like angels."

Whistles. Screams.

"I thought Las Vegas was a holiday town."

Laughter.

"But you know that's not true."

Cheers.

"Wherever I go on this tour I hear talk of the Revolution. Like they've got the guns and we've got the music. You know what they say about the pen and the sword. This music's stronger."

I see faces, shiny and white, not too stoned.

"I wrote a song a few years ago about the hard things we have to do in our lives to keep believing it's going to be all right. It's called 'Moonshine Season'."

They know it. They cheer. I expect that. I play soft and slow, holding the guitar close to the mike, bending forward. Lee Young is below me at the control box, guarded on either side by Firefly and Duke. My mind is on the music now, the sound coming back through the monitors at my feet. I keep my eyes straight ahead. The sound is good. I am relaxed and confident. Afterwards Jug Meat return and we continue the set. We play 'Child In The Water' and 'Wonder Of The Universe' and two others from the new album and then bring Rain

113

Fortune forward to do 'I Love To See You Smile'. We finish with 'Sky's On Fire', a hard blues rocker. The kids are clapping and shouting unlike anything I had expected here. At the end they're up, stomping at the edge of the stage. We go off, down the steps into the tunnel, and wait. My head is thumping. The applause goes on and on, gaining in power. We climb back. The kids yell at us, arms stretching to touch us. A few have scrambled along the sides onto the stage itself. Terry's trying to persuade them to get down again. I know that if I leave it Ken'll move out from behind the cabinets and throw them off physically. I tell Terry, "It's okay. They'll be all right." Terry stays with them. They squat on the boards, cross legged. Sweat is running down my face. I think it's blood. I wipe my cheeks. The bandage is loose and damp. Patrick plays the opening bars of 'Jesus Was a Junkie'. The hall is hushed now. Quiet. The song has a slow deceptive opening, rising higher and higher, louder and louder, until it cuts suddenly at the last verse which I sing like the first alone with acoustic, allowing the rhythm to return slowly on the final chorus which is repeated and repeated as more sound is added until the air pulsates, ending in a storm. We leave quickly. The house lights come up. The audience is left to itself. The roadies begin taking mikes off, unplugging wires. Afterwards I feel drained, sitting in the dressing room, the anticlimactic stillness creating a detachment, a sense of loss. Kids push through the crowd and stand, embarrassed, in front of me, their eyes sick with anticipation. They say it was beautiful. I say something hard. I don't feel safe now.

I hear Maxwell's voice.

"You were a gas," he says.

"Gas kills," Patrick says.

I put my guitar into its case and take it with me, take it outside. Terry has backed the van down the tunnel. He's filling it with amp boxes. Others help. Ken stands at the side watching them work. I give him my guitar.

"How are we getting back?" I ask.

"There's room in the van," he says.

I don't answer.

I walk across the empty stage. One of the kids helping Terry offers me a joint.

114

"I don't smoke," I say.

He has faded patched jeans and a blue working shirt, bare feet.

"What do you do?" I ask.

"Like now?" he says.

"Yes."

"I move around." He waves his arms in the air. "Like it's free, you know?"

He's smiling all the time.

"What are you doing in Vegas?" I ask.

"I don't live in Vegas, man." He laughs. "I mean, no one *lives* here."

"Did you like the concert?"

He mimes a bomb exploding in his head.

"Saw you in San Diego a few weeks back," he says. "But this time you reely got it on. I dig the crazy Bandaid. That's something else."

"You notice changes since San Diego?"

"Yeh."

"What?"

"Like you got it more shaped, you know? It's a tight group thing. It's very together. San Diego's a whole other fucker, man. A real asshole."

"We did all right there."

"I had these friends driving down from L.A. Right? When you played Long Beach they missed out and they dig it, you know? They dig your music. But they never showed for the concert that night. I had the tickets but no one came. So I called next day to find out what it was and this chick answers. She's acting crazy on the phone you know? I say, isn't there anyone else up there I can talk to? This guy comes on and asks me my name, where I live, stuff like that. I hung up so fast, man. I hitch a ride to L.A. and find this chick. She says they were busted. Highway patrol stopped them at the city limits, took them right out there on the road and tore that car to fuckin bits. Came back with a stash of dope that was never in there, man."

He's shaking his head.

"Where are you going now?" I ask.

115

He shrugs.

"I'll hustle a ride with you guys, maybe," he says.

"Talk to Ken."

"Who's he?"

"Hates San Diego as much as you."

"Is that right?"

"Hates most things. Keeps piranha fish in the bath."

"No shit!"

"He has this theory that Hitler was a blood freak. He's working on it himself. He's into black magic."

Patrick comes across and says the cars are waiting. We move away.

"Hey!" The barefoot kid shouts. "You carry albums in that van?"

"Ask Ken."

He waves.

On the way out I tell Ken that the kid fancies him. Ken scowls.

We climb down the steps and along the tunnel.

"What were you talking about?" Patrick asks.

"He offered me a joint."

"What do you do when you're offered a joint?"

"Nothing. I don't take it."

Patrick smiles.

"You sat in that dressing room like we'd bombed the worst gig in history and then bawled out those chicks for walking over the instruments when all they wanted was a can of Coke, for Christ's sake."

"What chicks?"

"I don't understand how you change."

I stop at the door. The cars are outside.

"Half the day you're avoiding having to talk to anyone," Patrick says, "and the other half you're bullshitting some kid who thinks you're Leonard Cohen."

"Everyone thinks I'm Leonard Cohen. *I* think I'm Leonard Cohen. In fact I might sue Leonard Cohen for being Leonard Cohen."

"Let's not start that again."

"Start what again?"

116

We duck out the door.

"You're Donovan's mother," he says. "Don't forget."

"I *knew* it!"

I jump on him. He squirms away and runs, leaps into the back seat of the nearest car beside Martha. I cross to the other. Steve, Charlie, Bobby and Bernie are already there. The front nearside door opens. I climb in next to Maxwell. He starts the motor. We circle the parking lot.

"Join the party," Bobby says, her blonde curls breaking loose around her neck. Steve pulls her closer.

"You're outta sight about *me*, babe," he says.

"She's a generous girl," I say.

"She's got a beautiful fanny," Steve says. "Have you seen her fanny?"

Bobby struggles. Steve holds her arms.

"Don't encourage him," I say.

"I've got bigger things to think about," Steve says. "Getting bigger all the time, darlin."

Bobby giggles.

"How's it going, Charlie?" I ask.

"D'you want to feel my cock?" Steve says, unzipping his fly.

"For Christ's sake!" Charlie says.

"Leave her alone," I tell Steve.

"She's the original Virginia Water, mate," he says. "Wet on the outside, dry in the cracks."

Bernie turns on him.

"You think you're some smart prick," she says. "Charlie's a *sensitive* person."

Steve howls.

"Fu-u-uckin mothers!"

Bernie leans forward.

"What's wrong with him?" she asks.

"He's a sex maniac," I say.

"Is that all?"

"He's a dope fiend and a petty thief."

"What about you?"

"I'm celibate."

"What's that?"

"I don't take showers."

"You mean you don't wash?"

"I'm scared of athlete's foot."

"What do you do about it?"

"Powder twice a day."

"Some kind of workout, huh?"

"Preventative medicine."

"Like quit-smoking classes?"

I nudge Charlie.

"Keep an eye on this chick. She's intelligent."

Steve's hand is deep inside Bobby's T-shirt. Maxwell doesn't speak, watches the road. The bandage is slipping. I let it. Bernie's tits squash on the plastic cover as she bends forward.

"What do you do when you're not waiting for the next rock concert?" I ask.

"We hike out to the desert," she says. "A whole group of guys. Bobby comes. It's a kinda nice thing to do. You reely get to understand about yourself, you know? When the sun's coming up across the mountains before it gets real hot in the morning. It's like there's no one else anywhere in the world, you know?"

Maxwell drives along The Strip. Lights flashing. Simulation of explosion. White and coloured neon. Enormous animated cartoons radiating excitement a hundred miles high. I try to visualize Bernie in the desert dawn, wishfully delicate, riding the dust roads back on the pillion of a Harley Davidson.

"What do you think will happen?" I ask.

"What do I *think*?"

"Do you believe in the future?"

She understands her body. She understands the motion of the car. She has slept with more boys than she can remember and yet remains alone, hoping to find Jesus in a sand dune so that he can tell her the way it's going to be and what she must do to seek salvation and when she asks, what do you mean by salvation, Jesus says, the mystery of the universe, and when she asks, what must I do to uncover the mystery of the universe, Jesus says, be generous of heart and gentle of spirit, and when she says, I give what I can, Jesus says, you must expect nothing, hope for nothing, empty your mind of selfishness and desire, live in the realization of poverty and oppression, become like a crawling sewer rat licking effluence from the pipes because

118

without pain there is no joy, without war there is no peace, without betrayal there is no honour.

"Sure, I believe in the future."

"What will happen?"

"I don't know."

"Will you marry and live in Arizona?"

"I don't reckon on marrying anyone."

"Charlie wants some chick to wash his socks. He won't bring his mother on tour. Marry Charlie and wash his socks."

"I like Charlie. I don't want to marry him."

"Can't you wash?"

"Sure, I can wash."

"He's worn those socks for a month. Things are growing on them. What can he do?"

"Take them to the laundry."

"Charlie doesn't like laundries. They're full of Chinese guys. Charlie thinks China is a Communist country."

"That's crazy."

"Not as crazy as walking around with fungus in your shoes. I tell him they have machines over here that change people into cabbages. They have these vans that drive around disguised as hippie love bugs with smelly sock detectors inside. When they find a guy with mushrooms in his boots they grab him and drive him to the forest farms and give him the treatment. Out in the farms they have these enormous places like cleared areas no one sees where giant cabbages grow. These are those guys who didn't have chicks to wash their socks which is why Women's Lib is going to destroy America. Women's Lib say chicks shouldn't do any more washing for smelly guys. It's not their job. All over America these machines are working and these guys are changing into cabbages. I think you should have pity on Charlie and marry him before he's taken out and planted."

We arrive at the hotel. Bernie pulls Bobby away and asks her to find out from Steve whether it's really true what I've said. Steve overhears them, grips his crotch and howls.

"She's so dumb she thinks Liverpool is an island off the coast of London," Charlie says.

Sometimes I wonder whether I believe half the stories. Catherine used to play a game with her brothers at home in which they made up scenes and characters and took parts and other kids who weren't playing tried to guess who they were and what they were doing. She asked whether I had played. I said, 'Always.' She said, 'It's a *game*.' I said, 'I know it's a game. I'm very good at it.' She said, 'You can't play with two.' I said, 'I play with myself.'

I go upstairs and lie on the bed. I ring Room Service and ask for plaster and a bottle of aspirin. I wait. I ring again.

"Can you bring it yourself," I say.

"Bring what?" A voice answers.

I repeat the request. I'm talking to someone else now. Fifteen minutes later a man dressed as a bellhop appears with a tin of Bandaid.

"Haven't you anything bigger?"

"Huh?"

"Could you bring lint?"

"I'll get onto Medical."

"I've tried."

"I better go check that one out."

He leaves.

I lie under the blankets, fully clothed. Things are moving. No sound but the brain roaring through ether. A thousand miles of open track with villages dazing in a pass. The sparkle of summer. Blue lakes through trees. All the movies of Canadian mountain railways coming back. Rushing through. My body soaked with the slime of slugs from green garden grass piled in heaps under a wall sweetened by moss like the places I love best, walls without roofs, fields overgrown. I hear bees in the honeysuckle hedge behind the school at the side of the field where we sat, where we built fires and the girls jumped calling the names of the boys they loved. I turn and run. I find the hive in a hollow and plunder it. A golden bird flies over the farms, over my father's house. The sky is like a blue sea. I want to soar into the distance until I am gone. This desire is a desire for death. I am prisoner in the bird's flesh. I feel the weight of its wings like the weight of dew on the petal of a flower. I cannot alter the upward flight, being locked inside. The bird says, if you kill me we'll both die. I tell the bird, let me out and I won't kill you. The bird opens its body and I fall. As I fall I awake. There are women standing above me. I think they must be angels.

"I want to look at you," one of them says.

She has stiff airplane hair. She's wearing a uniform. The other is Jane Alexander.

"I had to get back," Jane Alexander says.

The one with the uniform tells me to lie still. I feel her hand across my forehead. She cuts a strip of lint from a roll. She packs the lint on my wound and begins to wind the bandage. Her breasts are moulded into armour plating. She smells of cod liver oil.

"This should hold quite safely," she says.

"I'm having hallucinations."

She fixes a safety pin, collects the scissors and slips them into a small blue holdall.

"Shall I leave you with sleeping tablets?" she asks.

"Just leave me."

She places a bottle of white pills on the table, walks to the door, opens it and goes out.

"What are you going to tell them?" Jane Alexander asks.

"Tell who?"

"The Press."

"You're the Press."

"I'm not."

"Who are you?"

"I work for the hotel."

"You said you lived in New York."

"I live in the hotel. I work here."

She flips open a pack of Winstons, crosses to the window, comes back with an ashtray.

"There was going to be bad publicity," she says. "You must appreciate that."

I close my eyes.

"Do you feel like resting?" she asks.

"I don't feel like anything."

Her fingers touch my throat and then her lips. She's a woman of sensitivity, older than Beccy. She wears perfume and scarlet nail varnish.

"I won't ask you to understand," she whispers.

121

NEW YORK

We flew into St Louis late in the morning. Matthew was waiting at the airport. I was tired although I had slept on the plane. Matthew said, 'You look awful.' He was talking to the others, joking. Ken bitched about the hassles at Las Vegas concerning the weight of the equipment and how much bread was needed to bribe the airline authorities. Steve looked along the flat chromium Arrivals Hall and said, 'Where the fuck are they?' Meaning the chicks. Matthew said, 'The cars are outside.' Rain Fortune said, 'I haven't eaten.' Matthew said, 'We'll eat at the motel.' Rain Fortune said, 'What kind of welcome's that?' Matthew said, 'Let's collect the bags.' I said, 'What's up?' Matthew said, 'How have you been?' I said, 'How have *you* been?' Matthew said, 'Bloody miserable.'

Driving from the airport Patrick kept talking about the greenness of the grass. Rain Fortune said, 'It's like pennies from heaven.' I said, 'Why?' Rain Fortune said, 'All that food on the ground.' Patrick said, 'What food?' Rain Fortune said, 'They lay cookie traps to catch poor whites and niggers.' Patrick asked, 'Why do a thing like that?' Rain Fortune said, 'They pollute the landscape with their poverty.' I said, *'For Christ's sake!'* Rain Fortune said, 'Do you believe in Brer Rabbit?' I said, 'No.' Rain Fortune said, 'Brer Rabbit was the original

125

smartass nigger.' I said, 'Why's he so smart?' Rain Fortune said, 'He wouldn't get stuck in any cookie trap.' I said, 'He got stuck in the tar baby.' Rain Fortune said, 'Brer Rabbit digs soul food.' I said, 'Brer Rabbit was a rabbit.' Rain Fortune said, 'That don't make him crazy.' I said, 'Doesn't make him black either.' Rain Fortune said, 'Ever heard of black rabbits?' I said, 'I've heard of white hares.'

The motel was on the edge of the city, low and flat with grey concrete walls. We took the stuff out of the cars. Matthew told us to wait. The cars left. We went inside. The man at the desk was chewing a dead cigar. Matthew said, 'I am sure you are not responsible for what appears to be a misunderstanding on the part of our agency but we would like to rectify the situation as these people have been on an aeroplane for four hours and are very hungry.' The man pulled the cigar away from his face. He said, 'You wanna meal? Burgers and beans?' Matthew said, 'What we need are decent rooms, hot water and a four-course luncheon.' The man said, 'It's all here.' Matthew came round to the back of the desk. The man said, 'Let me talk to Mrs Solihaltz.' There was a telephone next to the key rack. Beside it was the number of a local taxi service. Matthew began dialling. The man hesitated. No one spoke. The man disappeared through a door marked FIRE EXIT. Matthew ordered a taxi.

Ken and Terry arrived with the gear in a hired Hertz. Matthew said, 'Put the bags into the van. We're not staying.' We put them in. Terry said, 'What the fuck is this?' Ken didn't move. The man behind the desk returned with a small middle-aged lady who introduced herself as Mrs Soltz. Matthew said, 'This is not what we were led to expect.' Mrs Soltz said, 'The rooms have been booked. That's all I know about it. A booking's a booking.' Matthew said, 'It is indeed.' Mrs Soltz said, 'You made the reservations?' Matthew said, 'A booking is a booking.' Mrs Soltz said, 'That's right.'

A taxi drove up and parked beside the Hertz. The driver looked over and asked, 'Which of you guys is Shaw?' Matthew snapped a wallet out of his breast pocket and hung it in the air. The driver waited, slowly opening the cab door. He was large and heavy with a crew cut and fresh white T-shirt. He came over to Mrs Soltz and asked, 'Are these people causing trouble, Mollie?' She said, 'They won't pay their rooms, Henry.' The driver said, 'Is that right?' Matthew said, 'A great deal depends on whether she is willing to help us find alternative accommodation although I fail to see why the economics of such a transaction should concern you.' The driver said, 'Maybe you need eyeglasses, Mister.' We stood together, leaning against the van, knowing what was going to happen. Mrs Soltz touched the driver's arm. She turned to Matthew. She said, 'Shall we arrange the reservations?' Matthew said, 'How many can your friend accommodate?' The driver said, 'I don't *accommodate* nobody.' He walked across to the cab, leant in to switch off the clock, took a notebook from under the dash and wrote something in it. He said, 'That's five dollars ninety.' Matthew said, 'You seem incapable of comprehending that I'm asking you to leave.' The driver said, 'You made a call from the motel under the name Shaw, right?' Matthew said, 'The cost of my conversation is a matter between me and the company who installed the machine.' The driver said, 'There's five dollars ninety on the clock.' Matthew said, 'If you choose to stand about wasting everybody's time that's your business. Don't expect me or anyone else to finance it.' The driver slid the notebook into his back pocket and said, 'You won't find it easy to get yourself a ride, Mister.' Matthew said, 'Is that a threat?' The driver said, 'No sir. That's a fact.'

Mrs Soltz stood at the door of the motel. The driver spoke to her. I said to Terry, 'Get the bags out.' Terry took the key off his belt and fitted it into the padlock. Ken jumped down from the front. I told him to carry the bags into the motel. He said, 'You a superstar or something?' He stood watching as Terry handed the bags down to me. Matthew appeared. He said, 'We're not staying.' I said, 'I am.' He told Terry to put the bags back again. I heard the taxi drive away. Matthew said, 'I'm calling the promoters.' I picked up my suitcase and carried it towards the motel. Matthew ran up behind me and forced it out of my hand. I kept walking. It was dark inside the lobby. I recognized dim figures against the grey wall. I said, 'Can I talk to you?' Mrs Soltz said, 'Yes.' I said, 'In private.' She said, 'If you like.' She took me along a corridor to a sliding partition marked OFFICE EQUIPMENT. We went through. The space beyond was cramped, a table in the corner covered with newspapers, dirty plates, knives, forks, empty bottles of beer. There was a calendar above the desk with a nude girl astride a motor bike wearing a jockey cap. Mrs Soltz said, 'This is my husband's room.' I said, 'Where is your husband?' She had a hard grained face and black hair. She was not thin. She said, 'What is it you want to talk to me about?' I said, 'I'm sorry about what happened.' She held her hands close to her chin. She said, 'I don't understand why your friend is so difficult. That person who drives the cab is an associate of my husband's. He is a good man but he can make trouble. I don't understand why your friend wants to make trouble.' I said, 'My friend believes that the right way to gain respect in this country is to make more noise and be more difficult than anyone else.' She had gold in her teeth. It spoiled her face. She said, 'He is back to front, I think.'

LETTER TO MY SISTER

I am staying over. Did Matthew mention it? I can work better here.

Patrick may call. I gave him our number.

Things feel different this time. I don't know why. It could be Nixon or the behaviour of the police. It could be drugs. There's no sense of restraint now, great talk of the Revolution. I can't be serious about it and yet the kids are. They speak a different language.

I'm living on the north side of the park. I find it restful. I go for walks most afternoons and wander down to a movie or a meal somewhere in the evening. I don't eat here except for breakfast sent up to the room. American breakfasts are (as Matthew would say) "ace". Otherwise hotel food is dull and expensive.

Description of city: holes in the road, streets breaking up, taxis with bulletproof windows, apartment blocks protected by armed guards and steel doors treble locked, kids on $100 habits stealing $500 a day. I wear the uniform of nomadic tribes –

denim, rough leather boots. It's okay. I feel safe. There's an air of desperate negligence. I like that. I have a good growth of hair on my face. I look like a student.

I am writing again. I have come to certain conclusions which differ little from yours although I have taken longer to accept them. What you never understood is how easily confidence can be destroyed. One day we die. All of us. We disappear. No one notices. No one remembers. The desire to remain a solid object surrounded by other solid objects is the strongest single force.

I must have been mad as a kid. I think unhappiness is a kind of madness. I can't explain why music mattered, how I got involved with the library, read all those books, why I stole stuff. Everything was a reaction, a feeling of having been betrayed. You slipped under their wing. Your reaction, if it existed, was against me, not them. Mam said I ruined Dad's health. I said he ruined his own.

Next morning.

So much of what the kids are into scares me now – astrology, horoscopes, fate, worship of unknown forces, instinct representing the subconscious, the subconscious representing essential truth. By freeing their actions of personal responsibility they lay themselves open to the powers of evil. The new philosophy says that evil is a figment of repressive Christian dogma. All forces must be recognized because all energy is relevant. Who has the right to judge? Jesus? They say Jesus was a hip revolutionary who had this logic flash. Mao's into a similar trip. There is no morality but the morality of life. We do not kill because it is against our nature to kill. We do not seduce our neighbour's wife (without permission) because it is against our nature to do so. We do not steal because we realize that material things are not of the spirit. I say, bullshit! They say, you have not washed in the waters of enlightenment. I say, man is an aggressive marauding killer with the instincts of a bitch bison. They say, are not apes gentle creatures of the forest? I say, we're not fucking apes.

I equate the new philosophy with psychedelic drugs. Acid exposes the mind to irrational experience of such intensity that beliefs based on rational thought appear restrictive and contained. This is the true freedom, they say, the threshold of astral possibility. And yet because it is so hard to describe the wonders of the starship galaxy in language of the known world other dreams take shape and become real. The crackpot ravers of

129

earlier generations, prophets and mystics, return as teachers of the New Revelation. Reality is no longer the relationship between man and man, man and object, object and object, but the spirit that moves in the void, the senses that lie beyond the sea, the forces that spin the stars.

What is sad is that kids who have lived in fifteen different cities, five different States, with step-parents, real parents, uncles and aunts, been educated in twenty different schools by hundreds of assorted teachers, have no lines left, no directions home, only addresses, houses, rooms, women in kitchens, sometimes their mothers, sun blazing on sprinkled lawns, neat clipped hedges leading to streets, colour TVs, fridges bulging with cartoned yoghurt/beer/half a cow. One bright morning they open their eyes and look out and it's all unreal. It's a fake. And so they leave, pack up, very brave and strong. But after they've done it they find they need protection and security all over again and so wrap themselves around some transient life style, have heroes who become like gods because they can't handle themselves alone. What's lacking is love, their parents so desperate for happiness, no time to stop, no time for the kids, and so love is something they want to find, something they need, not having known it outside the movies, thinking it's soft and calm like slow-motion runs through the edge of waves on some lonely white beach, and so grow older and more ignorant, playing games like they think they should, too crippled and crazed to understand the real causes of change, heads hurting from half-digested psychology. When things begin to slide they stop, sit down and analyse it like it isn't happening to them, like it's happening to someone else. They distance themselves from it. If they feel bad they say so. If they feel bored they discuss it. Part of the freedom message is commitment and confrontation. They become surgical zombie doctors rapping every shift and shudder in every hour of every day together, cutting their moods into cause and effect, action and reaction, slicing their hearts' meat like warm turnips.

Next morning.

I hate flattery. I hate those honeydew chicks. 'I dig your music, man,' You know? 'Wow, man!' I know about the music. I understand it. Emotive response is wetting your knickers. A medical disorder. Nothing personal. But if newspapermen or TV interviewers mention intellect, intuition, the ability to converse in more than two-syllable words, I fall off my seat with

130

gratitude. I KNOW these guys. I know what they're doing. It's called SUCKING THE SAP. They'll say "an interesting point of view" or "I hadn't thought of it that way" and every time it happens I think, maybe he's right, and dig him because he appreciates me on another level. But what do I know of other levels? I don't even know what I mean.

After this tour I told myself I wanted a rest, at least for six weeks, to be away from everyone.

There's a certain song that indulges these feelings and succeeds every time it's used. Half the kids in the world have the same fantasy. It's the story of a chick who wanders in from the midnight train and meets an innocent country boy and says, "I've been searching all my life for a place to lie down", and so they lie down together and the boy says, "You make me feel whole", and the chicks says, "Don't leave me", and the boy says, "You'll never be alone again", and the chick says, "Be gentle with me", and the boy says, "There's straw in your hair", and the chick says, "I've lost my travellin shoes", and the boy says, "You've come home."

It's so deep at the core of the American myth. What they do in the story is build themselves a cabin in the woods and break out a bit of land and have babies and believe in love and peace, the soul's white daisy circle, hearts as fresh as baked apple pie, the flag flying high above them, Old Glory Peep Peep, bring out the red guitar and sing us a blueberry lullabye, the sun's over the mountain and the child's a'wakin. I want to set it down like root and tree — THIS is true, this is NOT true. Romance says nothing for the sexual abattoir. Unless we see what's happening we'll be washed out of sight on a five star luxury liner. Life is hard. There's so much to know and discover starting right here, with me. Older guys who've compromised in order to retain a reasonable degree of sanity say, "Dollars and cents is what it's all about, boy." The younger kids are turned off. They're looking for something else. Fundamentals don't change. The Jews understand this. The Mafioso understand this. The American Negroes when they're not brainwashed into thinking white understand this. I don't. Or didn't. I thought there was some kind of mystery.

The desire for family is stronger than the desire for escape. After rejecting their own, kids invent others (communes are doing little else) and the urban ideal of village life (conservationists' trip right now) becomes a romanticized family thing with the community interrelated. Bushmen, Abos, lost tribes of

131

the Andes, have been rediscovered as having something "meaningful" to say to affluent North Americans. Idealism based on absolute conviction is a dangerous force. Absolutes of any kind are dangerous. The history of Christianity is bloody and vicious. The Spaniards raped Aztec culture in the name of Jesus. Missionaries in Africa did the same. Absolute conviction makes war.

What destroys family is money. Status becomes more than material pleasure. It's the way you look, the way you behave, the way your kids behave. You buy expensive things and want to protect them. You join protection societies. You join clubs. You become aggressive towards people whom you suspect want to steal your things and then you become aggressive towards people who don't want to steal your things because you think they don't like them enough and so surround yourself with associates who have the same wealth because it makes you feel safer and better and more powerful, but deep down inside you're scared of the day the crowds in the street are going to come and kill you because you know, even as they're doing it, that they're right.

Kids have won their independence but don't know what to do with it. They're cut off. So am I. At a different level. I've lost what they've lost. But I'm lucky. Most of the time I have a sense of self. Their expectations are high. Mine, at their age, were nothing. Vague squeals.

I was hired to perform the cabaret at a debutante ball. That was three years ago, the first time I met Catherine. On arrival at the hotel the commissionaire stopped me. I was wearing jeans and jacket. I showed him the letter of confirmation from the Ball Committee addressed to Matthew. He glanced at it briefly and asked, 'You Mr Shaw?' I said, 'Does it matter?' He said, 'No.' A girl with red cheeks and yellow curls advanced towards us. The commissionaire handed me back my letter. The girl interrupted. She smelt of lemon juice. She said, 'I'm looking for someone quite tall with short fuzzy hair and rather horrid buckled shoes.' The commissionaire said, 'Except for the occasional rumble of discontent from the public at large,

132

Miss, we've been relatively quiet on departures.' She looked at me and noticed the guitar case. She said, 'You must be the cabaret.' I said, 'Yes.' She said, 'I'm Laura.' The commissionaire stepped between us. Laura said, 'It's all right.' The commissionaire said, 'Not by me, Miss.' Laura galloped off, calling over her shoulder, 'Stay put. It's crucial.'

The commissionaire was over sixty. He wore a braided uniform with ribbons. I asked, 'Do you enjoy your job?' His teeth were false. He held himself straight. He said, 'I don't presume.' He stood with his arms behind him. At ease. He did not look at me. He looked at the wall opposite. Laura's mother swooped round the curve of the corridor like a winged sheep. The commissionaire turned, his face a doormat. Laura's mother ignored him. She asked me, 'Did you bring a change suit?'

I picked up the guitar case and followed her to a room at the back of the dancing area. She said, 'I'll have someone inspect the cold table.' She left, closing the door behind her. The room had minimal furniture, a two-bar electric fire, a bed, odd chairs.

Catherine entered with a bottle of champagne, a glass and a plate of smoked salmon sandwiches. Her hair was thick black, almost oily, her eyes like grey-green stones. She said, 'The aspic chicken tasted of junket so I brought you this instead.' I said, 'Thanks.' She asked, 'Do you want strawberries or raspberries?' I said, 'Pardon?' She said, 'Laura's mother found me in the loo and told me to fill you up.'

The champagne tickled my nose. I sneezed. A silver-haired man like an Italian actor with a silk handkerchief falling out of the top pocket of his white tuxedo arrived. He introduced himself as the leader of the band. We shook hands. He lit a black cigarette from a square box and sat down on one of the chairs. Catherine was eating the sandwiches. I passed her my glass. She looked at it and offered me the plate. I accepted. The bandleader watched Catherine closely. He said, 'Your face is distinctive.' Catherine grinned. She began rolling her shoulders and lifting her head and letting her mouth fall open, sitting on the bed with her legs crossed. The bandleader asked whether I had any sheets. I said, 'I'm not staying the night.' He said, 'What are you going to give us?' I said, 'I'll think about it.' He looked across at Catherine who was tearing the last sandwich in half.

She laid a piece on the back of her tongue, curled it, let her eyes flicker. The bread dropped off, out of her mouth, onto the floor.

Laura burst into the room, followed by her mother. She said, 'We're about to make the announcement.' Catherine nudged me. The bandleader leant over and offered her his black box of Russian cigarettes. She took one. Laura's mother said, 'I think we must do something about the clothes, don't you?' Laura said, 'What's wrong with the clothes?' Her mother said, 'Ask Johnny to rush back to the flat and bring some things.' Laura said, 'What about the cabaret?' Her mother said, 'That can wait.' Laura told Catherine to find Johnny. She said, 'He'll be in the night club with Pug.' Catherine stopped in front of me on the way out. She said, *'Hasta la vista!'* Laura's mother asked, 'Are you ready for pudding?' I said, 'I don't think so.' The bandleader left with Laura's mother and Catherine. Laura stayed. She shut the door. I took the guitar out of its case. I was nervous now. I said, 'Shouldn't you be dancing?' She said, 'I suppose so.' I said, 'Do they have whisky?' She said, 'Do you want some?' I said, 'Yes.' She said, 'I'll go and have a search.' I lay on the bed. Talking to Laura's mother was like talking to someone who was talking to someone else at the same time about something completely different. It was a manner, a way of speaking, through the nose, an instinctive acceptance of place and duty, subconscious reflex of the ruling classes, and yet it wasn't that either, too dramatic, too emphatic, the heart conditioned like an engine to avoid contamination from outside sources. She would have walked through the centre of the Indian Independence massacres, slapping crazed Hindus over the face with her brolly and talking afterwards about a spot of bother in the High Street. Confidence was no hassle with these people. They were born with it.

I didn't see Catherine again until after the set. Johnny appeared with Laura's mother, Pug and a suitcase full of clothes. He was tall and fair and soft. Later I met others like him, twenty-year-old virgins with girlish complexions, Catherine's brothers' friends, who had that same passivity and innocence, that same shy nervous naivety.

Laura's mother insisted that I chose something from the suitcase. She said, 'You would be doing us a great service.'

134

A fierce argument ensued in which Johnny took my side against Laura's mother and Pug. I sat on the bed, listening. Laura's mother accused Johnny of pretending to admire qualities in the lower classes that were abhorrent to him. Johnny shouted, 'It's *nothing* to do with *me*!' Pug told him, 'You're talking through your hat, Johnno.' He ignored her and shouted, 'It's to do with *integrity*!' Laura arrived with a thin balding middle-aged man who wore delicate tortoiseshell spectacles. He said, 'Isn't it time we moved the troops, Marge?' Laura looked at the suitcase and then at me. Outside I heard slow handclapping. The man addressed me. He said, 'I'm the one who signs the cheques.' He smiled and added, 'Sounds like they're anxious to make your acquaintance.' His manner was courteous and friendly. I disliked whatever it was inside me that reacted against him.

The suitcase was closed. Johnny, Pug and Laura's mother left the room. At the door Johnny looked back, grinned and raised his thumb. I nodded. Laura asked, 'Who's going to do the introduction?' I said, 'Is there a bathroom I can use?' The clapping grew louder. The man with the tortoiseshell spectacles said, 'I doubt if there's time for the full rub-a-dub-dub.' Laura said, 'We'll go round the back to the loo at the lifts.' The man patted her shoulder. He said, 'Don't forget there's more champers in the bucket if you need it.' Laura said, 'Thanks, Daddy.'

We hurried down the corridor. Laura pointed to a door. I opened it. She said, 'See you out there.' I said, 'Okay.' She waved. I pushed through the door and closed it, locked it. I sat on the can. They weren't *interested,* any of them, not even Catherine. I was an object, *the cabaret,* to be dressed and un-dressed.

No one talked of hype in those days. It wasn't an issue. Cornfed substitutes were ritualistically defiled. Life became stylized in concrete and aluminium, the imagery reflecting new consciousness of neorealistic cinema, a boy waiting for a bus in the rain at six o'clock in the morning in a dirty northern town with a dose of clap, no regular chick and a fouled-up job he couldn't quit. This was fashion reversed. I learned to suspect it as I suspected middle-class intellectuals rolling to the rhythm of regional dialects. Matthew had publicity handouts prepared in which I was portrayed as the child of a labouring peasant family, suffering formative years in the degrading hell of a city slum. I told him, 'My father wasn't a peasant. He was a farmer.' Matthew said, 'Don't split hairs. We're talking about liner notes.' I said, 'You may be. I'm talking about what's true.'

I walked along the corridor, carrying my guitar. I found the ballroom. The lights were dimmed except for a circle in the centre. Everyone sat on the floor or stood against the walls. A man was telling a story about how he lost Don Bradman's cricket bag in Cairo during the war. I searched for Laura in the crowd. All the faces were turned towards the storyteller. They weren't like kids in clubs. They were giraffes. I returned to the room. It was empty. I sat on the bed and tuned the guitar. I began worrying about my clothes. It seemed wrong suddenly, almost shocking, to be wearing jeans and boots when everyone else was in black ties and patent leathers.

Laura appeared. She said, 'Come *on*!' I said, 'I couldn't find you.' She said, 'We're late.' I followed her. We entered the darkened ballroom together. I had to step over bodies to reach the circle at the centre, still holding the guitar. There was a brief introduction. I said, 'I want to start with an old blues.' My voice was high and nervous. I heard them moving in the dimness as I played, calling for cigarettes, calling each other's names. Afterwards the applause was polite. I began using the space. I played 'Moon Rock Deliver' which sounded thin without backing. Many of them recognized it. The laugher stopped. I played 'Shout A Night'. I said, 'This is a love song about a blind chick who can't see her guy's cheating her.' They giggled. They thought that funny. I didn't change my style to suit them. I didn't care enough. I sang five songs and then left, climbing over bodies that began to rise and cheer. They wouldn't let me go, demanding another, an encore, *shouting*. I thought, there's only one song heavy enough to bring them down, 'Jesus Sat At The Dancing Wheel', a slow, bitter blues, twelve and a half minutes of tense political music. I sang it loud. There was no mistaking their reaction. The passion frightened them. They were embarrassed.

I had no illusions. I believed love to be fantasy, a myth. I thought, if life is such a fearful thing we shall return to Christ because his teaching contains some element of hope. Beccy talked of hope often, the need to face the future. I asked, 'Are you thinking of Jesus?' She shook her head. She said, 'Jesus sat at the dancing wheel.' I said, 'What's that?' She said, 'A symbol of decadence.' Brother Mark said, 'God's possessions are sacred.' He meant the soul. I told him, 'If He's there, if He exists, He owns everything, *my* dirty socks *and* my sister's orange pullover, but if He's not there, if He *doesn't* exist, He owns nothing.' Brother Mark said, 'God didn't make your socks. He made animals and trees and nature. He made you. He didn't make refuse dumps and rubbish tips and skyscrapers and amusement arcades. That's us.' I said, 'Man is sacred then?' He said, 'Yes.' I said, 'Murderers and sadists and child molesters?' He said, 'Yes.' I said, 'What else?' He said, 'The human form and the human mind.' I said, 'If I am sacred and my sister's sacred who is the most sacred?' He said, 'You are the same. You are equal.' I said, 'Why is the body of a man sacred when the body of a bull is just the body of a bull?' He put an arm across my shoulder. He did that often. He said, 'Jesus touches us with his blessing.' I said, 'I can pretend the wind is God's kisses or I can pretend it's angels farting, but I *know,* I know all the time, it's only *air.*' He said, 'Put out your hands.' I put them out. He said, 'Stretch your fingers wide.' I stretched them wide. He touched the tips of my fingers with his and then brought the palms of our hands together. He asked, 'What do you feel?' The power was strong. I said, 'I feel hot.' He said, 'Do you embrace your father and mother?' He wanted me to say how their bodies were like stone while his was fire.

Faced with the truth Joe Fitzburg, Jr, shot his wife, Linda, through the head, slashed his baby girls, Mandy and Paula, with a razor and telephoned the police. When they arrived he was lying on the living room floor, dying of gunshot wounds. Father Pat Murphy, a neighbour and friend of the family, said that Joe was stricken by the fate of children orphaned as a result of United States involvement in South-East Asia and felt unable to accept responsibility for atrocities committed in the name of peace and freedom. He was an idealist. He believed in the American way.

Such an act would be dismissed in England as typical of the diseased state of a troubled psyche.

I write my fourteenth song in ten days and call it 'Ballad Of A Patriot'.

The story of Joe Fitzburg, Jr, is the tragedy of one man's belief in the propaganda of his time. Americans want Christian ethics to succeed and yet every day, every hour, violate them.

I hate deception. I hate style as affectation. Rain Fortune and Catherine have natural style. Matthew doesn't.

The trouble with isolation is the amount of time wasted in reflection. A singer should be instinctive.

I leave the room. The door locks automatically. I walk along the corridor to the elevator and press the button. A lady with tinted hair and check tweed suit appears.

"Did you?"

She points at the button.

I nod.

I am affected by the way others look at me. As a result I cannot eat in the hotel dining room or drink at the bar. Safety in sameness is exposed too often as soft centred. Sooner or later I'm going to find myself stranded in the hallway with a Mothers For Vietnam Reunion. I cannot escape prejudice or madness. Life becomes increasingly irrational. Western culture has reached a period of sophistication so far from the roots of nature that trees fall in their own good time and no one remembers. Morality is Catholic nerve gas. God fucks. Everyone does. Fine thoughts about sex being the expression of wonder is advertising copy. I'll show you movies and live shows in which sex is an act of war. Love sells washing machines. Jesus digs natural cotton. It's all on TV.

The elevator door slides open. The lady in the tweed suit walks through into the cage. Her arm rises to the panel, finger touches, pushes. She takes a step back, stands, looks at me, makes no motion. The elevator door closes. I squat on the carpet with my back against the wall. I expect she'll return

138

once she discovers I'm not there. I wait. I feel the density of the building around me, strangers locked in cells like the lady who was glad to be alone, away from me. Is it possible to make love to a university graduate without knowing the name of her favourite film director? Children hide nothing which is why they are dangerous. As they grow up they begin to forget and when they are completely grown they have forgotten completely, existing in a regulated, regimented capsule. Unless we recognize our weakness we have no strength. Can I look at myself and admit that my feelings are always reasonable? Can I disassociate my stage personality from my real personality?

I sit on the floor, take a note pad and pencil from the inside of my jacket.

I write : "Past thought, future thought, does not affect present thought. The moment IS. Existence IS. You appear and I see you. Your thought is inside your head. I imagine what it is. I do not KNOW. I look at you. Things you are wearing remind me of other places, other people. You have made yourself an actress. We begin to perform a play that is written as we speak. Inside, protected by the role, is the body. In a false world truth has no substance. The lady in the tweed suit has become someone else now. A girl. An imaginary beautiful girl. The idea is formed. The girl is not being herself because she does not understand or like herself and so invents another self, based on someone who lived, a white girl walking in a garden."

Always it is a garden. I don't recognize the horticultural imagery and yet forever find myself involved with it.

I continue : "A white girl walked beside the gasworks."

The lyric must express the incompleteness of arrival and meeting, how the actors play out the ritual of conversation and yet have genuine fears and passions inside. I want this girl to imagine herself as Greta Garbo and the boy to imagine himself as Gary Cooper. They walk through a public park talking in cinematic clichés and at the end Gary Cooper says, 'Let's make the earth move', and Greta Garbo says, 'I don't have any songs left to sing.' The girl arrives. The boy is there. The girl says, 'Will you escort me?' The boy says, 'I don't have an automobile.' The girls says, 'I live in Scarsdale.' The boy says, 'If we hurry we can walk it by morning.'

139

I write: "She wonders why his mouth changes when he smiles. She wonders why his eyes watch the high windows as they walk. She tells him her mother is a countess. He says, 'My father is a pig breeder.' She says, 'That's interesting.' He says, 'Believe me, it's not.' "

The elevator doors opens again. A man comes out carrying a miniature poodle. He sees me sitting on the floor against the wall. He lets the dog down.

"Are you making a protest?" he asks.

I have my note pad and pencil in my hand.

"No," I say.

He holds the dog by its leather lead.

"Take it easy," he says.

"I will," I say.

He walks past me and then stops at the corner and looks back.

"Want to walk the dog?"

"Where would I do that?"

"Take it into the elevator, down to the ground floor and out into the street. Stand where the traffic's heaviest and then let it off the hook."

"I couldn't do that."

He has brown eyes, hair the colour of chocolate nougat, flat ground teeth and purple lips.

"What's wrong with my dog?" he asks.

He moves closer.

"I don't like it," I say.

"I'll throw the sonofabitch out the window."

He looks at me suspiciously.

"You don't give a goddam, do you?" he says.

I find it hard to respond. I walk away from him. I return to my room. The guitar is on the bed. I place the note pad on the table and sit down. I read what I have written, thinking of the man with the dog, wondering why he had to talk to me like that, why he had to talk to me at all.

I write: "The human FACE. Nakedness. What we fear is ourselves. Expression of the naked face."

By remaining alone in New York I am attempting to consolidate energy in order to discover my true position.

140

I write: "REAL. What we know. What we have seen. What we have felt. Reality IS. Reality is fantasy. I AM because I AM. I exist. I breathe. Enter a young girl. I see her. She is wearing clothes in a certain style which represents to me the way that she wishes to be recognized. Deep inside is her real self. I cannot reach that far."

The man with the dog did not exist. I imagined him. I am beginning to doubt everything. He came out of the elevator carrying a monkey. He saw me sitting on the floor against the wall and asked whether I was all right, thinking that I had fallen and was hurt. I told him, 'Yes. I'm all right.' He said, 'That's good.' He left, carrying the monkey like a handbag.

The attack on humour begins again.

I write: "Life is a joke, a cruelty, a journey, an expedition into the unknown, an important exercise, an unimportant game, a reaching into the self, a race, a celebration, a war, a gathering together, a throwing away, a sea cruise, a survival, a reaction. Humour releases the pressure. Safety valve. What IS humour? Knocking at the serious things? Are they important? What are they? Is my life serious? YOUR life? How we lead our lives? Is THAT serious?"

My father is a serious man. He has been destroyed. Do I care that he has been destroyed? Yes, I do. Why? Because he is an honourable man. Do I consider it important to be an honourable man? I think it is foolish to be an honourable man. Why? Because it's too hard. Do I believe that everything that is too hard must therefore be foolish? No. Why not? A hard life is more valuable than a soft life. Why's it foolish to be an honourable man if a hard life is more valuable than a soft life? It is foolish only when it fails.

I am laughing. Even as I write I am laughing.

I conclude: "Is it foolish to be serious?"

Beccy said that everyone, sooner or later, reaches the point of asking the one indefinable question. The answer is always the same. It's nothing.

Sometimes I wonder whether my brain developed. My mother talked of having a nice start to the day. Our house was always clean, smelling of table polish and floor wax. My room was an arcade. I felt no affinity towards the world. I was afraid of it and yet not afraid of it. My mother said, 'If you look tidy you'll feel tidy.' I said, 'I'll feel like a clown.' Brother Mark said, 'You know how you feel. You know it's right.' I said, 'I don't.' He said, 'You know *yourself*.' I said, 'I'm walking out of school and I see this girl I want to talk to because I like her although I've never talked to her before and I think, I'm going to talk to her now and I'm going to ask her out, and then I think, what can I say to her that she hasn't heard from everyone else, and so I don't talk to her and she doesn't notice me and that's another day gone, another chance wasted.'

I recognized in Catherine different levels. Brother Mark wasn't there. I couldn't ask why. I saw her almost every day for two weeks before daring to kiss her. Finally she said, 'I thought you didn't like me.' I said, 'I can't explain it.' There are areas of our lives that exist simultaneously and yet there are people in the world who remain always locked along a single line. I was reckless. I knew evil. I sensed it. I said, 'I've seen kids skin kittens alive.' She said, 'I don't believe you.' I said, 'It's worse to allow families to live in condemned houses.' She said, 'Yes, I know.' But she didn't. She *wanted* to know. Brother Mark said, 'Evil is man's inhumanity to man.' I said, 'Do you believe in hell?' He said, 'Hell is life itself.' I said, 'How can you say that when you believe God is good and makes us happy?' He said, 'God doesn't make us happy. We make ourselves happy.' I moved away. Catherine didn't know how close we were to the influences of evil, didn't recognize despair or the sickness of defeated spirits, hadn't witnessed my father rocking in his chair in the dark cold of our clean front room, nor watched tears shine in the eyes of grown men. The influence of my father and mother meant nothing to me. I could walk out and leave them. They would remain always. I asked my sister, 'How are they?' She said, 'They don't change.' That's all the family I had. When I left I left everything. I closed the door. Catherine had cousins, aunts, uncles, friends of family, friends of friends. She was surrounded and protected. She had another skin.

I write: "Girl recognizes what she needs. Boy recognizes what he needs. In the context of their own lives they exist together. Immunity. Enclosure. Their love is real only to them.

142

Outside they are judged, discarded, mocked, envied, misunderstood. Love IS isolation. The island myth. All I need is you. All you need is me. She strengthens his weakness. He fills her empty spaces. Why do we change? Why does happiness fade?"

I pick up the guitar. There is something important I want to say in this song that remains, in my mind, a song of distances, the bringing together out of space and time the truth of one person towards another, the fact, existing within it, that love is many-sided, multicoloured, inexplicably frail.

Catherine was a creature of impulse, her strangeness balancing the vulnerability of her innocence. When we met again after the debutante ball I was walking down Oxford Street in London. She hooted at me. I looked over the traffic and saw her waving from a white sports car. I didn't recognize her. She jumped out and ran across the street. She said, 'I'll give you a lift.' The cars nearest to us had begun to move. Those behind couldn't. I said, 'I'd rather walk.' She held my arm. We dashed across the street. She opened the door of the car for me. I climbed in. It smelt of stale cigars. Her face was pale with a hint of mascara at the eyes, hair curling over the front of a white jersey, this very black hair against white wool. She drove fast down Park Lane, dodging in and out. She said, 'I should have had it back by twelve.' She meant the car. It was five to one. I asked, 'Where are we going?' She said, 'Two minutes.' I recognized her then as someone I had seen somewhere. I couldn't remember exactly. I was flattered, not afraid. I said, 'Do you smoke cigars?' She said, 'Only on my birthday.' She was impatient. I kept looking behind watching for police. She asked, 'How old are you?' I said, 'Older than you.' She stopped the car suddenly in a wide street to the north of Victoria and jumped out. I followed. She shouted, 'Wait here.' She ran up the steps of one of the houses and rang the bell. A man dressed as a butler opened the door. She went in. The door closed. I waited. I tried to think where I had seen her, surprised that I couldn't remember. The voice was unusual. And the eyes. She came out again and ran down the steps. She said, 'They want you to stay for lunch. Do you mind?' I said, 'Who are they?' She said, 'My cousin, Charles, and the cook.' She made me feel that I would be letting her down if I refused and yet I saw no reason

143

to accept. She said, 'I'll look after you, don't worry.' The door of the house was open. There was another man standing there, watching us. We went inside. The man at the door was her cousin. She called him Charlie. He was my age. He wore grey flannel trousers and the kind of sweater you see skiers wear in cigarette ads. His hair was blond and short, brushed close to the head and parted on the left. He said, 'I'm Charles Dumfrey. Catherine tells me you're a famous pop singer.' His voice was condescending. I said, 'I'm not famous.' He said, 'I'm stupid about these things.' The house was large. There were modern pictures on the walls and fitted carpets on the floor. Catherine ran ahead up the stairs. Charles said, 'I'm going to clue in kitchen life. Tell Bowles to open another bottle of champagne.' I hesitated. He said, 'I'll see you in the drawing room. Have a look through the records. You might find something you like.' I walked up the stairs slowly. Catherine had disappeared. I didn't know what I was doing there. It seemed unreal. I met the butler on the landing. He was wearing a striped apron, white shirt, stiff collar, dark trousers. He said, 'Lady Catherine is in the drawing room, sir.' I couldn't look him in the face. I almost laughed. He said, 'Let me show you.' He walked along the landing. I said, 'Can I wash my hands?' He stopped, turned, led me to a door at the other end. He said, 'This is the bath-room, sir.' I said, 'Thanks.' The bathroom was the size of my flat. I locked the door. There were framed pictures of horses jumping into ponds and red velvet curtains and a thick white carpet. I thought, I'd better not use the soap in case I ruin it. I looked into the mirror. I hadn't shaved for two days and my hair wasn't combed. I went to the window. By standing on the ledge I could reach the branch of a lime tree in the garden. I ran water into the basin and washed my hands. I used the soap. It was aqua green and scented. I washed my face, dried it on the warm towel, dried the soap. I went out onto the land-ing again. I could hear music. I went into the drawing room. Catherine was dancing alone in front of the window. She stopped when she saw me. She said, 'Come and have some champagne.' She handed me a glass and then poured the cham-pagne into it from a big bottle. She said, 'Charlie's my first cousin.' I said, 'Is he?' She said, 'Do you like him?' I said,

144

'I don't know him.' She said, 'Do you think he looks like me?'
I said, 'No.' She said, 'I don't think so either.' We ate in a
panelled dining room downstairs. Bowles, the butler, waited on
us. Catherine laughed at my discomfort and Charles told her she
was a pig for doing so. Catherine said, 'Why don't we eat in
the kitchen next time with Mrs K?' They were childish together.
Charles said he was writing a book about Victorian miniatures.
Catherine said, 'Last week it was Royal French chefs.' Charles
said, 'I'm doing that as well.' They talked as if it didn't matter
whether it was chefs, miniatures or the first thing that came into
their heads. I asked, 'Do you pay rent for living here?' Charles
said, 'The house belongs to my mother, actually.' We drank
brandy in huge tulip-shaped glasses. Coffee was carried upstairs
into the drawing room. We flopped on the sofas and listened to
old 78s, taking it in turns to change the records. Catherine
would complain about Charles' choice and Charles would groan
at Catherine's but whatever I put on they liked. I said, 'Do you
do this every day?' Catherine looked at Charles. He said, 'I'm
four years older than this idiot child and for my sins – or lack
of them – have been given the job of looking after her during
the Season which means spending afternoons in the cinema which
I hate and evenings at those appalling hoolies which I hate
even more. All because her exceptionally intelligent parents
can't be bothered, quite rightly. They think my mother's doing
it which she isn't. She's in Persia being cultivated by some of
the Shah's less presentable *aides de champignon*.' He lit a cigar
and put his feet up on the cushions. When Bowles came in to
clear the coffee tray he didn't move. Bowles asked, 'Will you be
taking tea today, m'lord?' Charles nodded at Catherine.
Catherine looked at me. Charles said, 'I think that would be
very nice, Bowles. Please thank Mrs K for a delicious meal.'
Bowles stood holding the tray in both hands. He said, 'Thank
you, m'lord.' He left the room. Catherine was struggling to contain herself, stuffing fingers into her mouth. Charles said, 'Shut
up! You're drunk.' I said, 'I've got to go now.' Charles said,
'You *mustn't*! It's not dark yet.' I tried to think of something
important I was supposed to be doing, but couldn't. I stayed.
We talked. Charles appeared to take nothing seriously. He said,
'Life is a conspiracy.' I agreed. I said, 'Workers have been con-

145

ditioned into accepting the necessity of labour.' Charles said, 'One has to waste whole *mornings* in the London Library confusing inquisitive relatives who suffer an irrational misconception that idleness is bad for one.' Catherine was more interested in me. She wondered what it was like having girls pull off my pants. I said, 'They don't.' She said, 'I've seen them.' I said, 'There's nothing magic about it.' Charles said, 'Don't let modesty undo the traces, old man.' Catherine lay on the carpet in front of the fire. The day passed. She drove me home. She said, 'I'm not doing anything tomorrow.' It was an easy and natural beginning. She told me that Charles had been a scholar at school. I said, 'I hadn't noticed.' She said, 'You don't with really clever people.' I met him again only once, after the summer in Spain when I was preparing the album with Jug Meat. He telephoned the office and left a message to meet him for lunch at an Hungarian restaurant in Soho. I was suspicious. That afternoon in his house had had a strange effect on me, like opening a door in a wall and revealing a secret world. At the time I was flattered that they had accepted me as if I was always welcome and would come again. But I never did despite the fact that Catherine lived there. Once she told me that Charles was a Jekyll and Hyde. I said, 'What do you mean?' She wouldn't tell me. She said, 'His father died of drink and his mother never sees him.' Often I wondered why I couldn't return to the house, why Catherine insisted on going home in taxis, why we met at my flat or in places away from the house. She said he was jealous. I didn't believe her. I decided to go to Soho anyway, to see him. It would have been wrong to refuse. The restaurant was a long thin room with tables close together covered with white linen. Charles was sitting by himself near the end on the left. He raised his hand and smiled. I was wearing a brown velvet suit, open-neck shirt and suede boots. Charles was fatter in the face, pinker. He had grown his hair to the edge of his collar. I sat down. He said, 'I read in the paper that you'd been ill.' I said, 'Yes.' He said, 'Why?' I said, 'I don't eat enough and don't sleep.' He seemed interested. He said, 'You must be hungry then?' I was envious of his style, so effortless and affectionate. I wondered what his life was really like, what Catherine had meant by Jekyll and Hyde. He said, 'I'm a great admirer

146

of yours. Did Catherine tell you?' I said, 'I never let her talk like that.' He approved. He said, 'I wish I could be of help.' I said, 'You've got your own things.' He said, 'I have a particular talent for avoiding my own things.' I looked at him. I said, 'Have you heard from Catherine?' He said, 'She's back in England. She wants to talk to you.' I felt uneasy. He said, 'Will you see her?' I couldn't answer. I said, 'I don't know.' He said, 'Can you remain friends?' I wasn't sure what he was trying to make me do. I said, 'We are friends.' I wanted to leave. The last weeks in Spain had been bad. I was incapable of love. The fantasy fazed into areas of definite reality. My life was here. Her life was there. I saw the earlier months unconnected with a need to exist in the outer world. She said, 'I love you more.' She kissed my neck. She held me against her with her arms around me, the balance of embrace controlled by hands, toes, lips. She told me stories, how she wanted to be free. I thought, yes, I know, I feel that too. But it wasn't the same. She could always go back. She had that behind her, that knowledge. I had nothing. I imagined the world as a jungle of warring factions in which a single body was too easily crushed. I understood the desolation of the spirit, why people gathered in pubs and churches, why God was beautiful being invisible, why reactionary politics was more acceptable in countries that feared for their future, why security bred revolt. Catherine suffered guilt because of the privilege of her childhood but that was different from *knowing* the realities. She said, 'I feel so ignorant.' I said, 'That's why you're lucky.' She said, 'Lucky as a mouse.' I said, 'I'm ignorant too.' She said, 'You're not. You write songs.' I said, 'Anyone can write songs like anyone can paint pictures. It's a trick.' She said, 'Let's pretend we're clever.' I said, 'Let's pretend we ran away to an island in the Pacific.' She said, 'Let's do that.' I said, 'It wouldn't be clever.' She said, 'It would be nice.' I said, 'Only until we discovered how incredibly ignorant we were.' She said, 'We'd die of delight.' I said, 'We'd die lonely.' She said, 'Dark deeds follow dark thoughts.' I said, 'Are you afraid?' She said, 'All my dreams are sweet. Even my nightmares.' As talk lapsed there were no more games. We had each other. I felt constricted by a responsibility that belonged in her mind. I resented it. I said, 'What

147

we make of our lives matters more than who we sleep with.' She tried to understand her inability to control my happiness or be the inspiration of my work. She wanted to know me as a brother *and* a lover. I resisted. I said, 'There are pieces inside I can't share with anyone.' She wanted those too. She said, 'You don't trust me.' I said, 'I do.' She said, 'You don't tell me things. You don't tell me why you love me.'

LETTER TO PATRICK

I hear that Matthew is rushing you into the glass booth without a second to recycle. Be careful. He's tripping. (What's the ultimate high? SUCCESS!!) Beccy was the saviour. I didn't realize how much. She slapped him down whenever he cut the string. His reaction to Miami was typical. He dug the publicity and then locked me in my room until I agreed to do the New York gigs. I was in a bad state as you no doubt recall. He kept shouting, "Be a realist! Be a realist!", and I thought he was saying, "Be a racist! Be a racist!"

Don't let him rush you. It's important. Make this album YOURS. It's too easy to strike while the iron is hot. Good music's going to rise and be noticed no matter what the timing. Matthew thinks you're ready for the States on your own. He freaks out his friends with the crit of the Las Vegas gig where that chick raved on about the band and how tight it was. She didn't throw shit at me, just happened to think you were "something else". I was "right on" but you were "too much". She wrote Rain Fortune a love poem. Did you see it?

I find I work best when I'm alone. The recovery principle is DON'T LET THE COLOURED LIGHTS THROW YOU. I can't evaluate yet how much was gained from the tour, whether we helped each other. I feel I gained something, possibly at your expense. I hope the experiment was worth it although acting as backup isn't everybody's bag. I didn't think of it like that. I felt as much part of Jug Meat as Steve and Charlie. Perhaps I shouldn't.

The new songs are very different. Two or three could be given weight but on the whole they're acoustic. The simplicity excites me. You'll hear them when I come.

Today is Friday. Or Saturday. This room is costing money. It's not the Chelsea Hotel but there's no better place to be right now. The porters are pimps and the waiters gay. I'm the only one with hair. I'm going to ground. Isolation drains me. I feel the juices flow to the roots.

Insecurity is a definition. I expect little else considering the way it's been. Fame is a false religion. It doesn't change anything. I see myself through others' eyes. I am your mirror. You are mine.

Fillmore East was the last gig of the tour. Martha and Bella Prentice had gone. I hadn't heard a word from Rain Fortune. The idea of the Fillmore excited Patrick. It was known as the Mecca of East Coast rock. I said, 'There isn't such a thing. There's only Bill Graham hoping you'll think there is.' He said, 'I want to believe in magic.' I said, 'The only magic is you and me.'

We rehearsed in the afternoon. The theatre was empty except for a stage crew who wandered in and out and a chick called Maybelle asking for Matthew. I said, 'Why do you want to know?' She said, 'I'm a friend of his.' I said, 'So's his wife.' She said, 'Why make waves?' I said, 'We're trying to rehearse this thing.' She said, 'Fuck you.' I walked away from her. Patrick said, 'Who was that?' She stood in the shadows under the steps leading to the dressing rooms. I told Steve to go and cheer her up. He looked at her for a moment, this skinny chick with hair half-way down her back, wearing tight flared jeans, brown sweater and red velvet jacket. He said, 'No meat on the bone.' I said, 'Talk to her, that's all.' He said, 'You jokin?'

We climbed the steps along a narrow corridor to the dressing room. It was bare and grubby, decorated with graffiti and faded yellow paint. We sat on a broken sofa and discussed whether to go out and eat or send Terry to the hamburger bar across the road. We had two hours before the gig. They decided to stay. I returned alone to the hotel. I didn't eat. I had a bath. I lay in the warm water until Matthew called from the theatre. He

149

said, 'What the hell are you doing?' I said, 'I'm coming.' I changed, left the room, took the elevator down to the foyer, dropped my keys at the desk and walked out into the street. A cab passed almost immediately. I told the driver, 'Fillmore East.' I watched the other cars, watched people in the street, shapes of buildings, shadows, bright neon signs on shop fronts. When we arrived there was a large crowd thronging and milling outside. I told the driver to go round the back to the stage door. We turned into a cul-de-sac. I gave him a five dollar bill. I said, 'Keep it.' I couldn't move. The stage door was closed. There were kids sitting on the step, smoking. I asked the driver, 'Could you knock on that door and tell them I'm here?' He said, 'You okay?' I said, 'Yeh.' He left the cab. He walked to the door and knocked on it. The kids sitting on the step shouted at him. The door opened. The kids on the step jumped up. They began crowding in. The door closed again. The driver pushed the kids away and walked back to the cab. He climbed into the front seat, flicked down the window. He said, 'They're sending someone out.' I said, 'Thanks.' He said, 'They're crazy those kids.' I said, 'What are they doing?' He said, 'It's always like this.' I said, 'Do you come here yourself?' He said, 'You mean to the concerts?' He had short hair and a woollen ski beret. He said, 'I listen to classical records. I enjoy opera.' I asked how long he had been a cab driver. He said, 'Five years.' I said, 'What else do you do?' He said, 'I'm studying night school. Except for me it's day school.' I said, 'Why?' He said, 'I want to write good novels.' I said, 'Who do you like?' He said, 'The Russians.' I said, 'What about the Americans?' He said, 'Whitman, Eliot, Henry James.' I said, 'Don't you find Henry James pedantic?' He grinned. He said, 'You read the guy?' I said, 'Yeh.' He said, 'You don't dig him?' I said, 'Not as much as Hemingway.' He said, 'For Chrissake! You're talking about stuff we threw out in high school.' I said, 'What about Richard Brautigan?' He said, 'What about him?' I said, 'Good writer.' He drove the cab to the bottom of the cul-de-sac and parked it. I said, 'Hemingway had a profound influence on American literature.' He said, 'It's a public disgrace.' He switched off the engine, climbed out and opened my door. He said, 'Think you can brave the mountain air?' We walked up the street. He was small and heavy. I said, 'I've never read *Don Quixote.*' He said, 'I like to hear you say that, brother. Neither have I.' As we approached the group sitting on the step the stage door opened and Ken appeared. He saw us and waited. I pushed quickly through the crowd. Ken held them off as I went in under his arm. The cab driver tried to follow. Ken stopped him. I said, 'He's with me.' Ken said, 'You're in enough shit as it is.' The cab driver said, 'Cool your head, brother.' Ken grabbed him by the coat and flung him down the steps. He ducked back through the door and closed it fast. I said, 'What the fuck's wrong with you?' Ken ignored me, walked away down a passage to the rear of the stage. I heard Patrick playing our first number. Ken turned. He shouted, 'You think you're some fuckin Hollywood *actress!*' I said, 'I'm a *star,* baby.' I walked behind the backdrop curtain to the far side where the steps led up to the dressing rooms. Matthew stopped me. He had my guitar. He said, 'Forget the clothes.' I was wearing baseball shoes, red T-shirt, a short-sleeved Fair Isle jumper. I said, 'I need my boots.' He gripped the fleshy part of my arm. There were three men at the curtain break, watching. Terry was on the other side. He grinned. I recognized one of the men from the rehearsal. Matthew said, 'You're stoned.' I said, 'I had a *bath.*' Patrick finished the song. I ducked into the light, aware of Charlie, Steve, kids shouting, cheering, the position of mikes, wires, PA columns. In the early days I was sensitive to every phrase and chord, the lyric meaning as much as what I said or did on stage. Beginning nowhere I had nowhere to fall. Now expectations were high. Energy flowed both ways. I had won before I started. All I could do was lose. Confidence is the bounty of success. Or so I'm told. Confidence in the knowledge that what has been can be again, what worked in Tucson, Arizona, will work in New York City. I don't believe that. Success is built on false assumptions. To care so much in a business that values quality in terms of currency is a delusion. Catherine said, 'Life is too serious to be taken seriously.' I said, 'Who told you that?' None of her friends were serious. When I complained of this she laughed. She said, 'What is serious?' I wasn't sure. I said, 'Caring about the purpose of existence.' She said, 'What's that?' I said, 'Knowing where you're going and why you're going.' She said, 'My brother sells computers to illiterate Africans. He admits he wants to make a million before he's thirty. My father tells him there is no morality in a society built on the profit incentive. My brother says you get rich first and worry about ethics later. You can't be poor *and* have morals. That's a contradiction in terms.' I said, 'Do you agree?' She said, 'He does.' I said, 'There is a time when possibility outweighs impossibility, when the spirit soars with the knowledge that there is no limit, that the barriers existing around the towers built for the protection of the rich are papier-maché and that whatever we want we can have and that all of us are capable of changing the shape of people's lives because the faith we have inside is stronger than the powers that want to kill us. We stand in our shoes like ten-year-old kids and tell the lame to walk and the lame fall down, tell the sky to rain and the sky blows away, tell the rivers to run red with wine and the rivers roar and tumble as before. We think, the power's gone, the magic's died, we're screwed to the floor, that's it! We get a job with a good pension, marry the wrong girl because she's there, file taxes, dig gardens, bitch at niggers and long-haired fairies, switch on TV and go to bed. In our sleep we dream we're leading great multitudes into a chasm of extraordinary depth and beauty. The wife says, you were shouting and screaming all night! We say, I dreamed I was a leader. The wife says, that's *truly* frightening. And we know, forgetting how to stop the process of thought, that once we believed there was a way, that life was never meant to be like this, that all the juice has dried, all the guts gone, all the wonder of youth faded, all the opportunities passed, all the days and nights from now until death repeated and repeated, and we know also that hope was a candle burning in the corner of a room and one day, years past, a woman – or was it a bear? – brushed too close in a flowing skirt and knocked that candle down, and we know at last, as we know all things too late, that once there was a faith that failed for lack of trying as once there was a boy who had a vision and he changed too and became a man. I want to catch these kids when their hopes are high. I want to tell them, you can do it, you can *do* it! Wash your minds of fear and dread. The great black future storms are blowing. The great black winter fades to spring. The soft light mountain morning glows golden in reflections of blood and fire. Violence ceases as the wind calms. The whole country is alive to the coming of summer. I want to say, there's still time, hold on.'

LETTER TO MATTHEW

Whenever I go to the office Bonnie Welk, that chick who works there, says, "I have a message from Mr Shaw. Will you accept it?" I have accepted four messages in two weeks. The answer to every one is NO. Please understand. I am STAYING HERE. The fact that my sister was surprised to receive a letter from me is no reason to suggest I'm ill. She may have found it "confused". That's her privilege/interpretation. SHE may be confused. She knows me well enough. In the old days that letter would have been written to Beccy. Why's it strange? I can't talk to walls.

Your insistence on my returning for the Albert Hall gig is irrelevant. I know about these free concerts. The degree of media hype is directly proportional to the loss of sincerity, a sad fact you may or may not accept. If they need TV to persuade half decent bands to appear what does that say for their organization?

Cancel the exclusive. I'm working fast and have a considerable amount of new material, none of which I want to discuss. The European tour is booked. You keep reminding me. Hartford was an exception. I don't blow gigs.

Whether we take Jug Meat is a matter between you and Patrick. We'll need replacements for Rain Fortune & Co. That won't be easy, especially in England.

Patrick tells me they're back in the studio. You push your luck. Why not give them more time? How many original cuts can they get together? You treat them like bubblegum.

NO MESSAGES!

I'll be back with a tape in time for the Paris gig. That's all. Bonnie Welk says I should see an analyst. I love these chicks. They're so far out they've dropped off the edge. She says I've got this motivation crisis. I say, "What's a motivation crisis?" She says If I knew that I wouldn't have one. I see her twice a week. I go up the stairs to the apartment expecting to find Derek. There's music playing. Bonnie Welk sits at a desk in the living room wearing groove outfits and different hair every day, waiting for the telephone to ring. She opens a drawer, looks through a pile of letters and gives me mine. I say, "Thanks." Then I leave. Last week she comes up with this shit about my identification problem. I say, "I'm never here for more than three minutes." She says, "That's it." I say, "What?" She says, "You take off so fast I get the impression you've something against me. Then I rationalize that for a while and reckon it's nothing to do with me as an INDIVIDUAL but what I represent as a BOLSTER IMAGE." I say, "I'm not into that stuff." She says, "You're not sure what you're into." I say, "Is anyone?" She says, "Psychoanalysis turns you on to yourself." I say, "So does acid." She perks up. "YOU DROP ACID???"

I know that Rain Fortune is suing. It seems like a conspiracy over here, lawyers getting together and agreeing to delay as long as possible. I suppose she had to attack someone. Lucky it wasn't us – not that we're any less responsible. It's crazy when you look at it. Students don't have that kind of bread. If her agent's advising (he must be) he's doing it for the publicity. I had a letter from an attorney called P. Friers Buck (I'm having a sticker printed : SUCK BUCK). He wants a statement. I told him I've made a statement already. The police have it. I'm not making another. I heard that Martha laid the finger on me in an interview the other day. She said it was the way I acted on stage. She meant the way I LOOKED. I rang Bella Prentice. She said, "She hasn't said a word." Meaning Rain Fortune. I asked, "Is that bad?" She said, "It's bad right now but they say things will change." I said, "I'll send money." She said, "She won't take it." I asked, "Does she blame me?" She said, "She doesn't talk." I don't know what to believe. I'm thinking of flying to Chicago. I want to discuss this with Derek. He must have contacts there. Perhaps they can make discreet inquiries like they used to in Raymond Chandler movies. Where the hell IS Derek? I don't want to sit and wait in his office. That could take days. Bonnie Welk knows nothing. She says, "He's out." I ask, "Where?" She says, "Buying drinks." I ask, "Why?" She says, "He's a sociable man." I ask, "What do you do then?" She says, "I look after the office." I say, "You call this an office?" She says, "What do you call it?" I say, "It's someone's flat." She says, "APARTMENT!" I say, "Okay, APARTMENT!"

She says, "You're getting to me." I say, "I'm getting nowhere." She says, "You're repressing the metabolism." I say, "What do you suggest?" She says, "Let it all hang out."

Could you write to Derek. Or call him. Arrange for us to meet.

Working with Jug Meat has overcome many of my fears. I want to get back on the road. The change is considerable, not simply a question of confidence. You like to translate music into definite areas for exploitation. You can't see things as objects in their own right. The next album won't fit your head although it fits mine. There's a feeling of release, returning to basics without any of the hangups that marred some of the earlier work. I'm excited!

Letters have become self-analysis. (BONNIE WELK LIVES!) I hope you will accept them as such and not assume the worst.

I have this image of a hermit in his cave. God's voice comes blowing on the morning breeze, "Get up, you lazy sod!" The hermit says, "I'm a hermit and hermits live alone." God says, "I'm giving you an order." The hermit rolls over and goes to sleep again. God sends thunderbolts to smash the mountain. The cave is destroyed. The hermit stands in the ruins with his beard covering his body. God says, "Loosen your loins, old fucker." The hermit says, "I live here." God says, "From now on you're a prophet." The hermit leaves the mountain and begins to preach to the people. He becomes a famous person and when he dies is remembered as the prophet who came to that country with messages from God. No one asks, "What was he doing all those years before he arrived?" They say, "He was holy, man", and write stories about him.

I feel like that guy. The thunderbolts have been. I'm standing in the snow freezing my balls off and God's saying, "Get thee to yon Albert Hall, son." I say, "Hang on, God. Give us a vest and a woolly jumper." God says, "Sign here and all shall be provided."

I believe progression counts for more than repetition. Record company executives (that's you) study the galaxy from glass domed observatories and dictate directives to their lay pupils on earth. New capsules are lobbed into orbit, computerized to a formula of carbonized reproduction. Nothing happens.

"The ego," I was informed by a learned professor of Manic Depression at Berkeley, "is your mother." I said, "My mother would disagree." He said, "Ego is the maternal instinct." I said, "We're fairly bad friends." He said, "You have no maternal instinct?" I said, "I have a mother." He said, "Whom you dislike?" I said, "Who dislikes me." He said, "Your symptoms are classic schizophrenia." I said, "Eh?" He said, "The desire to retain the love of your mother whom you believe has rejected you and an equally strong desire to disown her love as a symbolic act of emulation." I said, "You're nuts, Doc." He said, "On the contrary."

Once I had a dream that I saw my mother naked. She was standing in the kitchen of our farm house plucking a goose. Her body was fat and heavy with great brown freckles like paw marks down her back. I was terrified. She took the innards, stomach and liver of the goose and asked me to rub them into the blemishes on her skin. I threw them outside. A fierce wind began to blow. She knelt on the floor and kissed my feet and wept. She said I was Jesus.

I won't tell you what Dr Bonnie Freud said.

We arrived in the early evening. Beyond the station it was dark and raining. The journey had been long, I stepped onto the platform, wearing my new shoes. My mother said, 'Mind where you're putting your feet.' The shoes hurt. My sister was carrying a holdall. I carried nothing. The station smelt of soot. Sounds echoed around its roof like the sounds in an underground factory. The lights were dim. My father said to my mother, 'Keep a hand on the bairns.' He was wearing Sunday clothes. He looked clean and washed with his head shaved beneath the cap, his black boots shined. My mother wore the coat she had been given for her wedding. It was still too loose. She had brought honey and jam sandwiches, fresh mince pies, a raisin cake, a thermos of vegetable soup and a tin of plain biscuits. The twine on the basket reminded me of thistles in the corn stooks. I held my mother's sleeve. The train was empty now. Soon it would move out, going north, and there would be nothing left but the dark rails in the ditch.

My father was pulling the suitcases and boxes out of the guard's van. I climbed up and joined him. There were three men inside wearing porters' uniform, standing together with their hands in their pockets. My father told me to push the suitcases to the door. They were heavy and wouldn't slide. One of the men helped me. He carried the suitcases across to my father who lifted them down. My father said, 'We need a cart.' The man said, 'You'll need a bus more like it.' My father said, 'Where can I find one?' The man said, 'The depot's round the corner.' My father said, 'Have the porters gone for their tea?' The man said, 'They'll be busy with other passengers.' My father said, 'Are you a porter?' The man said he was. My father said, 'Will you accept our luggage?' The man said, 'I could accept it but can't do anything with it.'

I noticed there were feathers on the floor, soft fluffy chicken feathers. My mother and my sister were sitting on the suitcases. The man who had helped us returned to where the others were standing. He pulled a packet of Capstan from his trousers. He offered it to each of them in turn and then to me. I shook my head. He smiled. My father had gone. I jumped down onto the platform. My mother said, 'What you got there?' I said, 'Feathers.' She said, 'Take them out.' I opened my hand. The feathers stuck to my palm. I blew them off. They floated like yellow leaves. I asked, 'Any pies left, Mam?' My mother said, 'We'll look in a while.' I said, 'I'm starved to death.' She said, 'Wait till we get to the house.' A porter passed through the gates at the end of the platform driving an electric buggy pulling three trolley carts. He stopped beside us. We began to lift the suitcases out of his way when the three men in the guard's van came and helped us. My mother said, 'That's very kind.' One of them asked the porter on the buggy whether he had space in the back for our stuff. The porter said, 'Yes.' They stacked the suitcases on the last of the three trolley carts and then unloaded parcels and mail bags from the train. My father had not returned. I wondered what he would say when he saw our things being driven off. He had warned us on the journey that people who lived in the city weren't like those at home. He said, 'There's dishonest folk about.'

The mail bags and parcels were loaded. My mother took some money from her purse and brought it over to the three men. She tried to give them the money but they wouldn't take it. They asked how long she was staying in the city. She said, 'We've flitted.' The oldest one said, 'Kiddies'll miss the country, won't they?' I asked my sister, 'Why's she give them money?' My sister said, 'It's for their dinner.' The porter driving the buggy said, 'Will you be wanting a taxi?' My mother said, 'Yes.' He told her he would bring the bags over once he had delivered the mail to the sorting office. My mother thanked him. He turned in a tight circle and drove slowly towards the gates. I tugged my mother's coat. I whispered, 'He'll steal our clothes.' She said, 'He'll do no such thing.' She was angry. She said, 'You've no trust.' We walked together along the deserted platform and stopped at the barrier. My sister wanted to buy a comic at the bookstall. My mother said, 'Wait here.' My sister said, 'I won't get lost.'

My father came back and my mother told him our luggage was safe. We walked through the station, out under an archway to where the taxis arrived. There was a queue. My father asked a man in a brown overcoat whether this was the right one. The man said he thought so. My father showed him the address of our house and asked whether he knew the name of the street. The man said he was a stranger. My father said, 'On holiday?' The man said, 'I wouldn't naturally choose this place.' My father nodded. I noticed he didn't like the way the man spoke. The porter appeared with the luggage. My father showed him the address and the porter said yes, he knew it. My father asked, 'How far?' The porter said, 'Cost you a quid.' This worried my father. He told my mother that we should have taken a bus. She was embarrassed in front of the stranger and the porter. She told him, 'It's done now.'

When our taxi arrived the porter who had waited all that time piled the cases and boxes in. My father stood and watched. Afterwards he gave the man a shilling. The porter looked at my father and then at the shilling. He said nothing. He tossed the coin into the gutter and marched off. My mother said, 'How much did you give him?' My father said, 'What was right.' He collected the shilling from where the porter had thrown it. My mother climbed into the taxi. My father told the driver where to go. My sister was sobbing quietly. My mother hugged her. My father slammed the door from the inside and sat opposite my bucket seat. He didn't talk to me. He said, 'Bring the bairn

158

here between us.' But my mother wouldn't let him touch her. The taxi moved away from the station. I stared out of the window at the shops, the black buildings, the huge coloured hoardings on the walls. I wondered why the porter had thrown the shilling away. We sat in silence. The city was bigger than all the farms on the hill stuck together. We turned and twisted through narrow streets. Nothing felt familiar, not even the way people talked. My father sat with his knees against mine. He said, 'You'll learn to like it once you get to know it.'

The taxi stopped in a quiet street. I saw a line of terraced houses with fenced patches of ground out front, lights in the windows, curtains drawn, a feeling of enclosure as if the place was protected. My father and the taxi driver carried the cases onto the pavement. My mother and my sister walked up the path to the door of the house. It had a blue knocker. They stood there and waited. They didn't go in. The rain had stopped but the wind was blowing. Our garden was of grass with a border of straggling roses. The grass was the colour of seaweed. I thought, if you live in cities you shouldn't have grass like that, you should have concrete. Everywhere, on either side, beyond and beyond, buildings stretched forever. I imagined people rushing suddenly from their front doors and filling the road. I said to my mother, 'I hate it.' She said, 'Be quiet!' I said, 'I'm cold.' She said, 'Where's your coat?' I said, 'I left it on the train.'

My father was carrying two suitcases up the path. He put them down and produced a key from his pocket. He unlocked the door and switched on the light in the narrow passage that led to the back room. We walked inside. My father said, 'Give us a hand with the bags, son.' I went with him to the street and began dragging the suitcases. He said, 'We'll be done in a minute.' I knew we wouldn't. He lied. We lined the suitcases along the wall in the passage. My sister came down the stairs. She said, 'Your room's half-way up. Mine's at the top.' My mother cooked beans and eggs. We sat at the table in front of the fireplace. My mother said, 'I don't like the gas.' My father said, 'It's well built. It's strong.' He thumped the walls with his fist. He said, 'It's good construction.' My mother said, 'We'll need coal, Dad.' He nodded. She said, 'I never liked coal although we had it when I was a youngster.' He said, 'Couldn't burn sticks on that fire, Mam.' She said, 'No.'

It was the beginning of a change that would close me like a knife. My room was empty, the sky a wall of purple above the breathing city. I thought, creatures who live here are zoo creatures and people who live with them are zoo people. Wildness is freedom. Nothing else belongs.

I knew that the pressure to conform would be stronger than the pressure to resist. Human nature is nastier than animal nature and so a code of morality is created to curb our craving for cruelty. God's existence excuses plagues, earthquakes, tidal waves, impossible feats of evolution, the sun and the moon, the four seasons, all mysteries except the bad ones which are passed on to Bell Zee, the Satanic goat, who is closer to man's true self anyway. Jesus stayed with the people. He wasn't tamed by temptation. He stayed wild. I liked that best about him. The fact that the Church became a power was not his fault. He preached unrefined Communism related to The Magic Father because people were superstitious then and needed facts wrapped in prophecy. Once science killed God a whole area of the mind withered. Men walked on the moon. It wasn't enough to be good. After beauty came anti-beauty, the admiration of dirt and the recognition of dirt's essential truth, the admiration of the real as against the admiration of the artifice, the breakdown of manners, tradition, ritual, the loss of the wild state with its extrasensory perception, the arrival of instant culture as the new religion, instant success, instant excitement, the age of reaction outstretching the age of reason, love floundering in a morass of TV nightly Vietnam, slogans shaping the intellectual void, giving words to feelings and feelings to words. Nature is dying. There is no communion. Kids in T-shirts and tennis shoes wave banners proclaiming support for survival. Saving trees in San Fernando Valley means as much as the quality of Muzak in Disneyland. Ecology takes the sting out of Civil Rights. On the coast migrant grape pickers organize to strike for better conditions and in South America whole tribes are massacred to make way for the exploitation of ancestral hunting grounds. Anger is not enough. Protest is not enough. It goes on. Only when the land is destroyed and the mines dry, when kids

160

suffocate in the streets of Los Angeles and the beaches of Santa Monica are bathed in oil will anyone of importance stand up and fight. It's always at the end after the last whale has been gutted and the last tiger shot that we remember how much we loved them. A senseless repetition of political rhetoric continues to spew from the mouths of madmen and demons as we stand at the foothills powerless to defend crimes committed in the name of progress, discovering at the heart a field of blood so wide and deep that no one dares tell of it. What happened to those kids born under the shadow of Nazi torture? How did they mend their minds? What happens to American kids now? The guru meditates on silken cushions in a curtained room at the top of the Hilton Hotel, his body shaped like a steam pudding, circled by the daughters of democracy dressed in gypsy linen. As the search for the mystic continues the re-emergence of magic follows the struggle for recognition in this land of racist fire. Freedom breeds dissatisfaction. Dissatisfaction breeds death.

Everything changed. My father discovered he was working class and as such shared a history of exploitation stretching back to the Industrial Revolution. He said, 'What happened a hundred and fifty years ago doesn't affect my ability to do a job.' He refused to join the union, believing it to be undemocratic and non-Christian, encouraging a block vote mentality that was narrow and iconoclastic. I said, 'What's iconoclastic?' He said, 'Breaking the images in the temple.' I said, 'Jesus did that.' He said, 'In the name of his Father.' I said, 'It's different for them. They've never been on a farm.' He said, 'The spattering of agricultural knowledge doesn't affect a man's view of the world.' I said, 'We're not like that. We never will be.' He said, 'All men are equal under heaven.' I said, 'They may be equal but they're not the same.' A year later I slashed my forehead with a razor and bled for a whole day. I thought, if God cares He'll let me die.

The centre holds. Nothing exists except repetition, the selfless and selfish together, fusing into a solid state which, when examined, becomes pitted with contradiction. My mother blamed me for my father's breakdown. I rejected his struggle. I was barren. My heart ached for peace. I had visions of lying in a field with another girl. We would touch each other on the arms

161

and face. I would kiss her neck. She would kiss my mouth. The gentleness would heal me. But these dreams had no value because they were dreams. The girl lay in the field like no one I had ever known. I wanted the emotion to contain a quality of stillness that was mechanical in its predictability. Everyone is alone. We cling together because we are afraid. Love is the art of communication.

I said, 'You believe God's in all of us. There isn't anyone who loses.' Brother Mark said, 'That's what we hope, isn't it?' I said, 'Do you think He knows what's happening?' He said, 'I can't imagine it quite in those terms.' I said, 'How do you imagine it?' He said, 'I see Him as a power for good and yet we talk of Him as a person.' I said, 'Only because we're taught.' He stopped me. He said, 'Teaching and feeling are not always the same. How would you describe love?' I said, 'I wouldn't.' He said, 'Try.' I said, 'I can't.' He said, 'You *know* it. You *understand* it.' I said, 'I don't feel it.' He said, 'You feel it more than most.'

I expect instant conversion to leave me frothy and shining on Damascus Road, mouthing Apo's Acts in some white mental wash house, seeing visions. That would be justice! A beautiful six-colour slogan across four blocks: HE FREAKED FOR JESUS. My father weeping in his woollies. My mother on her knees scrubbing the church steps. My sister writing letters to *Melody Maker* explaining the true meaning of my early lyrics. Brother Mark discounted mysticism as irrelevant. He said, 'Christ's miracles were exaggerated parlour tricks.'

I sense vibrations across a cosmic globe. Animals attune to a whole range of galactic forces. Man adapts so wilfully in the opposite direction that everything organic is explained by chemical formulae and everything inorganic by mathematical equations. Love remains the last frontier of scientific exploration.

Thoughts of mortality, immortality, are disrupted by the arrival at the drug store counter of Sweet Fanny Adams and Joe Crow. I say to Joe, 'What's your scene with Sweet Fanny?' Joe says, 'She grooves.' I say, 'Have you reached a conclusion?' Joe says, 'I live by the days.' I say, 'Don't you wonder why it's happening like this?' Joe says, 'Makes no difference to me.' I say, 'If you can't understand yourself how can you understand others?' Joe says, 'That's horse shit, man.' I say, 'What do you think people mean by the quality of life?' Joe says, 'Whatever turns them on.' I say, 'Do you believe in motivation?' Joe says, 'I eat when I'm hungry.' I say, 'What do you feel about good and evil?' Joe says, 'They're nice people.' I say, 'Do you believe in right and wrong?' Joe says, 'It's wrong to do things you don't want to do.' I say, 'What if you wanted to kill someone?' Joe says, 'That's unconstructive, man.' I ask Sweet Fanny, 'What do *you* think?' Sweet Fanny says, 'I think he's great.' I say, 'How long have you been with Joe?' Sweet Fanny says, 'Longer than anyone, I guess. Six months maybe.' I say, 'Do you believe in the institution of marriage?' Sweet Fanny says, 'I don't know about institutions.' I say, 'What about politics?' Sweet Fanny says, 'I read horoscopes.' I say, 'What do you enjoy most?' Sweet Fanny says, 'Balling.' I say, 'Anything else?' Sweet Fanny says, 'Dope.' I say, 'You dope a lot?' Sweet Fanny says, 'I guess so.' I say, 'Do you worry about the future?' Sweet Fanny says, 'Yeah.' I say, 'What about pollution? Do you worry about that?' Sweet Fanny says, 'They killed the buffalo, didn't they?' I say, 'Do you go to church?' Sweet Fanny says, 'Going to church and having religion ain't the same thing.' I say, 'Do you listen to music?' Sweet Fanny says, 'I listen to jukebox music.' I say, 'What makes you happy?' Sweet Fanny says, 'Joe.' I say, 'What does Joe do to make you happy?' Sweet Fanny says, 'It's what he don't do that makes me happy. He don't have high expectations.'

We reached Miami at 3.30 in the afternoon. I had slept on the flight. I felt hot and dazed. The hostesses stood at the exit door, saying, 'Gladtohaveyouaboard.' They wore red uniforms and red button hats pinned to their lacquered hair. They smiled. They were dolls. I staggered into the aisle carrying my jacket. They watched me. One of them came forward. She said, 'Sure of your hand luggage, sir?' Her voice was metallic tannoy. She said, 'Shall we lookit?' We returned to where I had been sitting. In the rack, above my seat, was Matthew's briefcase. She stretched on tiptoe, her skirt rising up her thighs. She said, 'Did you have a pleasant sleep?' I said, 'Bone dry.' She said, 'Hope you have a pleasant stay.' I said, 'Hope so too.' The other hostess joined us. She was younger. She said, 'Playing a concert?' I said, 'Yes.' The older one said, 'What's the name of your group?' I said, 'Flash Harry & The Windbreakers.' She said, 'Should I know you?' I said, 'We used to be called Old Kentucky Soup Kitchen.' She said, 'I've heard of them.' The younger one said, 'Where you playing?' I said, 'No one tells us until we get there.' She said, 'We could drop by, huh?' I said, 'It's a mystery tour.' She said, 'You mean you just go and maybe find some place you like?' I said, 'We expected Honolulu this morning. Now I believe we're in Pennsylvania.' She said, 'This is Miami, Florida.' I said, 'No kidding!' She touched my hand. I said, 'That's nice.' She said, 'D'you think you could sign an album for us?' I said, 'I don't have an album.' She took off one of her shoes. I could see Matthew coming out of the airport building, looking across at the aeroplane. She flicked a pen from the inside of her coat. I wrote TAKE CARE on her shoe and signed it. She said, 'Good luck.' I said, 'I'll remember.'

Students drove us to the hotel. They talked of the other bands that had arrived. They asked, 'How's your tour goin?' We said, 'Fine.' I hadn't realized this was another outdoor gig. The thought depressed me. Rain Fortune said, 'We're movin back into the jungle.' The kid who was driving said, 'I had a friend who was thrown through the plate glass of a truck-stop window couple of nights ago.' I said, 'What for?' He said, 'They had a notice up: NO HIPPIES! NO NIGGERS!' I said, 'Which was he?' He said, 'His Daddy owns real estate out on the peninsula. He's a rich sonofabitch, wears hair like longer than Tricia Nixon.' I said, 'Couldn't he read?' He said, 'Sure he can read. He's 250 pounds and a college boxer. He figured he could teach those goons.' I said, 'He didn't do too well.' He said, 'Sure as shit not!'

When we arrived at the hotel Matthew was arguing with the desk clerk. Our student driver, Rasp Morton, stayed. We sat in the lobby. Charlie was there with Rain Fortune and Martha. Rasp Morton wore a revolutionary red headband, jeans, Levi jacket and field boots. He had wire glasses. He said, 'Hotels turn me right around, man.' Rain Fortune said, 'What's the problem?' Rasp Morton said, 'I don't give a fuck for those cocksuckers.' He nodded towards the desk. He said, 'When they allocate rooms you'll be out back in some holed-off broom cupboard with no bath and an unlit firewalk stairway.' Rain Fortune said, 'Why's that?' Rasp Morton said, 'This is Florida, ma'am.' Patrick joined us. Rasp Morton said, 'You with The Jug Band?' Patrick said, 'I pass the hat.' Rasp Morton said, 'You pass the *what*?' Patrick said, 'There's an honoured tradition in English vaudeville akin to that of the Christian Church whereby a gentleman, in this case myself, goes amongst the congregation with a tin tray and receives offerings.' Rasp Morton frowned. He said, 'Where I come from they call that panhandlin.'

The rooms, when we reached them, had the bare necessities, TV, beds, chair, bathroom, windows, door. Rasp Morton said he'd come by in an hour and take us to the gig. I said, 'Right on!' Patrick said, 'Far much, man!' We gave him the V-sign. He gave us the clenched fist salute. Rain Fortune said, 'I'm sick 'n' tired of these political rap artists posin as Mister Fidel *Ass*hole.' We sang 'Rave On The Raving Rascals' and rang down for food. I took a shower. Patrick turned on the TV. Rain Fortune went to call Martha.

Patrick was on the bed. The food arrived. I said, 'Put it there.' The waiter put it there. I dressed and went out to find Rain Fortune. Matthew was leaving the elevator. I said, 'Where's Martha's room?' He said, 'Are you coming?' I said, 'We're eating.' He said, 'Now?' I said, 'That guy's picking us up.' He said, 'When?' I said, 'In a while.' He said, 'Okay.' I said, 'Where's Martha?' He said, 'I'm looking for Patrick.' I said, 'Patrick's in my room.' He said, 'I haven't seen Martha.' I went down and asked the desk clerk for Martha's room number. He gave it to me. The elevator had gone. I pressed the button. A crowd surged through the swing doors, Rasp Morton with them. He saw me and came running over. He said, 'Rooms okay?' I said, 'Fine.' The others joined him. They wore Californian tassled suede jackets and stiff leather hats. There were five, three with Commander Cody beards and long curling

165

hair, one tall Negro dressed in cowhide and knee-length country boots, and a stumpy dwarf with dark glasses called Fat Monk. The Negro was the singer. He was Texan. He said, 'I'm Slider, man.' He was smashed. One of the Buffalo Bills said they caught our gig in 'Frisco and *reely* dug it. I said, 'Great!' He said, 'We're in from Georgia. Had a roadie shot on the highway. Fuckin real bullets, man.' I said, 'We've been lucky.' Rasp said, 'When Jim Morrison jerked off on stage they arrested the sonofabitch.' One of them said, 'Shit man. That's heavy.' The elevator arrived. The doors opened. I walked in. Slider said, 'Stay cool.'

I went to Martha's room. Bella Prentice was there. I said, 'Where's Rain Fortune?' Bella Prentice said, 'She's lookin for you.' I said, 'Okay.' Rain Fortune and Martha were in my room. Martha was eating my steak. She said, 'It's Patrick's, honey.' I said, 'What's Patrick eating?' She said, 'He went out.' I collected the other plate from the tray and sat down on Patrick's bed. We talked about the gig. The steak was cold. I ate the salad. I said, 'A freak band caught me in the lobby.' Rain Fortune said, 'What you do? Run up the stairs?' I said, 'They had this black Texan who kept rolling his eyes and saying, yeaahhh man I dig it, you know? He was wiped out.' Patrick returned. He said Matthew had been talking about a new stage lineup. I said, 'Why the fuck didn't he talk to me?' Patrick said, 'He didn't think you'd go for it.' I said, 'Why didn't he think I'd go for it?' He said, 'I didn't ask.' I said, 'What's he want?' He said, 'You out front for a start.' I said, 'Sod that.' He said, 'I told him we'd worked it together. It wasn't just us or you. It was a joint decision.' I said, 'We'll bring everyone forward. That'll screw him.' I lay on the bed. Patrick rang room service. He ordered another steak and a pot of coffee. Rain Fortune said, 'Get some of that fruit salad, honey. It's good.' I said, 'Che Guevara's on the stairs. Watch it.' Patrick said, 'Lock the door.' I said, 'Okay.'

Rasp Morton rang from the lobby. He asked, 'How's it coming?' I said, 'You must be mistaken.' He said, 'Room 205?' I said, 'This is Sir Archibald MacIntyre's suite.' He said, 'I guess they got it wrong.' I said, 'Sorry about that.' I dropped the receiver. I said, 'Let's split.' Patrick said, 'What about the food?'

Rain Fortune said, 'How do we get to the gig?' I said, 'We'll
ask around.' Rain Fortune said, 'Where? We've got to go
sometime.' There was a knock on the door. Patrick said, 'It's
the food.' I said, 'It's the fucking revolution.' Martha, Rain
Fortune and I hid in the bathroom. Patrick opened the door.
He said, 'Hello.' We heard Rasp Morton's voice talking about
the car. He introduced someone else. He said, 'This is Abe
Funzey. He's with Blacktop Express.' Buffalo Bill's voice said,
'You all together, man?' Patrick said, 'The others are in the
sauna.' Buffalo said, 'I dig that.' Rasp Morton said, 'We're
going to have to leave now.' Patrick said, 'What's the rush?'
Rasp Morton said, 'You're scheduled for 7.30.' Patrick said,
'We'll be there.' Rasp Morton said, 'Without a car?' Buffalo
said, 'Do you smoke?' Patrick said, 'Not now.' Rasp Morton
said, 'There's a guy out here with a tray.' Sound of shuffling
feet, bodies. Buffalo said, 'Can I order one of those, man?' The
voice of the bellhop said, 'Room Service or Restaurant?' Buffalo
said, 'Wha??' The bellhop said, 'This your number?' Rasp
Morton said, '205.' Buffalo said, 'Got it?' Patrick said, 'Take
this one.' Buffalo said, 'That's yours, man.' Patrick said, 'I have
to go.' The bellhop said, 'Do you *want* another order?' Patrick
said, 'Cancel it.' Rasp Morton said, 'We're wasting time.'
Buffalo said, 'Fuck the mobile, man.' Patrick said, 'Who *is* this
guy?' Rasp Morton said, 'For *Chrissake*!' Patrick said, 'If you
want to eat my food do it somewhere else.' Buffalo said, 'Up
your ass!' Slider's voice could be heard in the corridor, 'Who's
havin a party?' Buffalo said, 'You make it with those chicks,
man?' Slider said, 'Dustier'n a dirt road, brother.' Buffalo said,
'You missin the action?' Slider said, 'Jonah's teasin tit right
now.' Buffalo said, 'The redhead?' Slider said, 'The *whale,*
man.' They laughed. Rasp Morton said, 'I wanna take you
guys to the fuckin gig.' Slider said, 'Got any stuff?' Buffalo said,
'They don't use it.' Slider said, 'You with a band?' Patrick said,
'Yes.' Rasp Morton said, 'Can we get the fuck outta here?'
Slider said, 'Got any stuff, Abe?' Buffalo said, 'Sure.' There was
a muffled sound. Buffalo said, 'I'm eatin *m'food,* man!' Patrick
said, 'This happens to be our room.' Buffalo said, 'Who says
so?' Slider said, 'You *speak,* or somethin?' Rasp Morton said,
'We're playing a *gig,* for Chrissake, not some fuckin *movie*!'

Slider said, 'Is that right?' Buffalo said, 'There's chicks in the other room, man.' Rasp Morton said, 'If you're not at that fuckin park in thirty minutes, man, we cancel you *out*.' Slider said, 'There's nothin about intimidation in the contract, muthafucker.' Buffalo laughed. Rasp Morton said, 'Okay, I dig it.' Buffalo said, 'Where you *goin*, man? I wanna take a piss.' Patrick said, 'In *your* room, if you don't mind.' Slider said, 'You *get* to me, babe. D'ye know that? You get to me like my *ass*.' Patrick said, 'If he wants to take a piss he can take it in his own bloody room.' Slider said, 'Piss on the bed, Abe.' Buffalo said, 'That's mighty inhospitable after what they done for us here.' Slider said, 'What they done for us, man?' Buffalo said, 'They're letting us stay, man; they're movin. Ain't that right, boy?' Rain Fortune was through the bathroom door so fast I couldn't touch her, bursting into the room. Slider shouted, 'Holy shit!' Rain Fortune screamed, 'Git outa here!' Slider said, 'Cool it, baby.' Rain Fortune said, 'I don't give nothin for yo'r black ass, nigger, or yo'r *high* opinion of yo'self!' Slider said, 'No chick talks t'me like that.' I was in the room now. Patrick stood over Buffalo on the bed. Slider wrestled Rain Fortune. I grabbed his arms from behind. Rain Fortune clawed and kicked, scratched his face. He was strong. Patrick held him from the other side and together we pulled him into the corridor. Buffalo followed. Patrick and I jumped back into the room. I closed the door. I locked it. No one spoke. Rain Fortune sat on the bed. I thought she was crying. Rasp Morton wasn't there. He must have run when the fighting started. Patrick's velvet trousers were torn. He took them off. Martha watched him. I returned to the bathroom and ran hot water into the basin. I looked at my eyes. There was blood in them. I washed my hands and face. I brushed my teeth. I returned to the bedroom. Patrick was sitting in his underpants. Martha and Rain Fortune had gone. I said, 'Where are they?' Patrick said, 'Sewing my trousers.' I turned off the TV. I said, 'We'd better go.' Patrick said, 'I've got to eat.' I said, 'Get something in the coffee shop.' I sat in the chair and put my boots up on the bed end. I said, 'Why did they do that?' Patrick said, 'To give us the needle.' I said, 'He would have *killed* her.' Patrick said, 'It was a giggle. He was *laughing*.' The door opened and Steve

168

walked in. Patrick said, 'I thought you were at the gig.' Steve said, 'Matthew's fucked it up again.' I said, 'How?' Steve said, 'We're not going on unless they do something about the PA.' Rain Fortune returned with the stitched trousers. We waited. Rasp Morton came back. He said, 'The PA's fixed.' I said, 'What was wrong with it?' He said, 'Nothing.' Rain Fortune said, 'You guys encourage us, man. The sound's okay so you change it.' Rasp Morton said, 'We didn't want to lose you, darlin.' Rain Fortune said, 'Maybe we want to lose *you*, man. Maybe this whole thing's runnin wild all over, like we make a big push in this direction or that direction until you say, we don't need any of this, we got enough trouble already, right?' Rasp Morton looked at me. Rain Fortune said, 'I'm *talkin* to you, man!' Rasp Morton said, 'I heard you, lady.' Rain Fortune said, 'You got this notion that nails b'n hammered into ma skull when I'm a kid to keep ma brains from fallin over the floor, right? You got friends who come into our room now an eat our food an *insult* us, man. Some tame nigger you bring to hassle us, man. *Why* you do *that*?' Patrick stood up. Rasp Morton said, 'What's gettin to her?' I said, 'She thinks Castro's a racist.' Rasp Morton said, 'Maybe Nixon's mother's Chinese. That don't make me buy a fuckin .22 and drill the sonofabitch.' Rain Fortune walked out the door. Rasp Morton whistled through his teeth. Patrick said, 'She can smell Capricorn a mile off.' Rasp Morton said, 'I'm the Crab. What's that supposed to mean?' Patrick said, 'She can smell the Crab too.' Rasp Morton said, 'Are we going to play *music*? Or *what*?' We moved out. Rasp Morton said, 'Tell that chick to get her tail in the car.' I walked along the corridor to Martha's room. Rain Fortune was pouring bourbon into a plastic cup. She said, 'When I was six years old I wouldn't go to school. I kicked and fought like a crazy kid. Mama said I'd be taken to another place, a prison house with bars on the windows, an they'd make me work for them, scrub their floors an cook their food an maybe other things too, things I wasn't meant to know about. I said, I'll go to that school, Mama, if you promise it won't ever happen to me, any of those things. Mama took a Bible off the shelf an put her hands on it and promised an I believed her man, I *believed* her. Now I gets us to Miami, Florida, man,

169

an the *driver* of the *car* comes over with heavy rap like I'm from Cottontown, Mississippi, man. Honey, when I was six years old I had *dreams,* like no kid *anywhere* had such dreams.' She drank the bourbon. She said, 'You scared, honey? You know you ain't the person no more like you thought you was. You're a *type* of a person, right? You get *classified.* When you're a kid you *know.* It's only later you get busted, learnin they got rules an walls keepin you away from the other side. I ask, why can't we go over like everyone else, man? They say, 'cause you're coloured, girl. I say, what you mean, man? They say, you're black, honey. I say, yeah, sure, okay. They say, that's why. I say, it don't matter, why's it matter, man? They don't explain. They don't talk no more. They walk off like it's all gone an finished. The sun's up the sky. Day's passin. We get these white dude liberal cats dressed in workin clothes, drivin beat up jalopies, come tell us how wrong it is we're livin in pig sheds, that we got discrimination, that we're all brothers under the skin like I'm his brother an he's my brother an we're goin to fight together to bring justice back to this country. I say, don't lay your troubles on me, man. We're through with all that. Don't tell me we're brothers, man, 'cause I *know* who *my* brothers are.'

Rasp Morton drove us to the gig. The stage was built on the edge of a small park with a seven-foot wire-mesh fence fronting it below the musicians' level. A band was playing. I saw Terry with two chicks leaning against the side of the Hertz. I stayed in the car. Rasp Morton said he'd check out the promoter. Ken joined us. I rolled down the window. I said, 'How many more bands after this?' He said, 'Three.' I said, 'Where's Matthew?' He said, 'Doing his Colonel Parker for the Girl Guides.' I was nervous. There were so many people behind the stage. Rasp Morton returned with a short-haired kid in a white suit. He said, 'This is Dave.' I said, 'Hello.' Dave said, 'You're on after Blacktop Express.' I said, 'When's that?' He said, 'Nine o'clock.' Rasp Morton said, 'I'll show you to the trailer.' Dave left. I said, 'Are the guitars in the van?' Ken said, 'We flogged 'em.' I said, 'I need mine.' He said, 'Who's responsible if they get nicked?' Patrick said, 'I'll get them.' Ken said, 'Want a job?' We walked to the van. I went to the front and glanced through the window. Terry was half sitting, half lying on the seat, head against the door, shirt high around his chest. There was a chick kneeling between his legs. Ken had the back down. Amps and drum boxes and PA cabinets were piled to the roof. Tucked into the side were the guitar cases. I took mine and Patrick's. A mike stand fell off the pile. Ken picked it up and pushed it in again. He closed the doors and locked them. Terry appeared. He said, 'Gettin the gear out?' He grinned. We walked towards the trailers, carrying the guitars. I asked, 'Seen Matthew?' Terry said, 'Haven't been looking.' I asked whether he remembered to lock the door. He said, 'What door?' I said, 'The door of the van.' He laughed. I said, 'Chicks always find you, don't they?' He said, 'They know what's good for them.'

The trailer smelt of new lino and chemical acids. Rasp Morton dragged a crate of beer from under one of the seats. Terry took a can, shook it and pulled the tab. Beer exploded over the ceiling and walls. He said, 'Vietcong whisky, man!' Rasp Morton opened the door and spat. Terry peeled off his shirt. Rain Fortune arrived. She looked at his brown chest and arms. She said, 'You got such *bones* on your body, honey.'

I watched hares dance believing them to be the spirits of dead children.

Are we changed by what others think of us? Like my father telling my sister I didn't have the will to work? Or my mother saying it was the fault of my associations?

I was found in the bullrushes beside an old mill house by a sexy lady called Emma Unction who was married to an artist called Fred Glucose who sat in a hut at the bottom of the garden being sick into a bucket and beating his head against a broken stove because he couldn't finish whatever it was he was doing and Emma Unction would walk down the path through the garden on lazy summer afternoons and stroke his balls with a feather boa and recite Emily Brontë in a Yorkshire accent. Fred Glucose was a moody man. He believed that all artists were tortured and tormented and so became tortured and tormented himself when naturally he was a fool and should have been working on the railways like his Dad. Emma Unction brought me home in a wicker cradle and nursed me and let me run free in the garden. When I was nine I went to school. I learnt how to fight. I became a different child. One day Emma Unction walked into the forest and met a stranger. Always she had dreamed of it. Fred Glucose left his hut to search for her. I escaped. The stranger was Death. I came to a town and lived there. I learnt to play the harmonica.

That's the story I like best. Sometimes I believe it's true.

Slider shouted, 'Git it on, man!' He gave a Panther salute. We pushed up the steps to the stage, Rain Fortune behind, the nut knuckle of her nipples hard against the seat of my pants. It was dark now, the arc lights full. Patrick, Charlie and Steve were moving on stage. Hidden figures beyond the mesh wire seemed restless and noisy. Bella Prentice and Martha waited for Rain Fortune. We went out together. Patrick was tuning his Gibson. The lights exposed every muscle, every false step. I walked to the front, introduced Jug Meat as I did at every gig. I began without them. A quiet acoustic number. 'The Mountains Are Broken'. The kids knew it. They cheered. I felt safer. Rain Fortune, Martha and Bella Prentice joined at the first chorus. I wasn't hearing the monitors. I beckoned to Terry. He ran across, knelt to check the wires as we went into the second song, Jug Meat leading. I could see kids at the barrier clapping their hands and swaying. I moved away. Rain Fortune sang the middle section alone. I gave Ken my acoustic, took the Les Paul, plugged it in. I noticed people at the back, squatting on the boards. I asked Ken, 'What are they doing?' He didn't know. I said, 'They're too close.' Patrick was positioned at stage centre. I joined him, stepping forward to the mike and repeating the first verse alone. The monitors were coming up clear now. I shouted, 'Right! That's right!' We did 'Blues At River Ending' and 'Lucy Wilder' and then Rain Fortune took my place at the front for her solo, 'Reap What You Sow'. I heard a crashing behind me. I saw a kid in denim shorts wade through the drum kit. Ken lunged at him, missed. Terry moved to intercept. He was kicked in the groin. Patrick and I continued playing, instinctively locked to the music. Rain Fortune turned. The kid slashed her across the face with a barbershop razor. She went, 'Oh!' He slashed again and again. Slider hurled himself across stage, wrestled the kid, dragged him to the floor. Rain Fortune collapsed sideways over the monitor boxes. Figures surrounded us, the crowd in the park shocked and still, not certain what it was they had seen. We carried Rain Fortune back. I heard Rasp Morton asking for a doctor over the PA. He said, 'She's okay, she's okay, she's gonna be okay.' The skin above her left eye wouldn't close. We laid her beside the drum cases. She was shivering. I tried to warm her. Matthew said, 'We can handle it.' Slider said, 'You can handle *fuck*!' I said, 'Where's the cloth?' Slider said, 'I should have killed that muthafucker.' I said, 'What happened?' Slider said, 'People tried to get the crowd off the stage behind the boxes down the steps there. Kids were hasslin them, givin them a bad time. An then this dude comes out of nowhere an just does it, man. Like he walks straight out there.' A wet cloth was handed to us. We wiped the wounds. I heard Matthew and the short-haired student promoter discussing what they were going to do. Martha was crying. Blood and water oozed from holes in Rain Fortune's face. Matthew said, 'The ambulance is on its way.' I waited. My ears were buzzing. A kid with a flashlight camera began taking pictures. Slider shouted, 'What you *doin,* man?' The kid wore a scarred leather jerkin. He looked very young. He tried to answer. The words dried in his mouth. He unfolded the film and gave it to Slider. Two men in white jackets arrived with a stretcher. They laid it down, lifted Rain Fortune, wrapped her in blankets and tied the straps. I said, 'Can I stay with her?' One of them shook his head. They carried her to the car. I said to Matthew, 'Has Ken taken the guitars?' Matthew put his hand on my arm. He said, 'Don't worry about a thing.'

173

I said, 'I want to go to the hospital.' He said, 'We'll ring from the hotel. She'll be okay.'

I didn't get there until after midnight. I went with Martha. The doctors had gone. It was too late. I asked, 'Can we see her?' The nurse said, 'She's heavily sedated.' We returned to the hotel. I talked to Matthew in his room. I said, 'I'm not going to Hartford.' He said, 'She's not dead, for God's sake.' He spoke of my responsibility as a performer. It was 2.30 in the morning. I walked out. I went to my room. Patrick asked, 'How is she?' I said, 'I don't know.' I lay on the bed. All the time I was thinking of when that kid came through, how perfect she was. He must have cut her as she turned, slashed at the neck, the vocal cords, and as she struggled, struck again, at the eyes. Once Catherine had described how pheasants were driven out of woods by beaters and gunned down at the very moment they felt they were free. It was like that.

I stayed in Miami four days. Matthew cancelled the Hartford gig. Rain Fortune's father travelled from Chicago to bring her home. Martha moved out of the hotel and went with him to another place in another part of town. I told him I was proud to have worked with Rain Fortune. He wouldn't look me in the face. He wouldn't acknowledge me. Bella Prentice waited. We talked. She said, 'We knew one thing for sure, right from the very start, she was goin to be a star. Dressed in clothes that were like Billie Holiday clothes, singin South Side clubs as kids, we formed ourselves around her, Martha and me. She wanted herself a hard time, she wanted pain to give whatever it needed, an one day found herself a kid as crazy as she an they hung out together for a whole while. This kid stole from car lots an broke into stores an put money together to buy guns. We asked, what you gonna do with those guns, man? He said, you look out for *yourself*, sister. Rain Fortune told us he was makin ready for the Revolution. We said, what revolution's that, honey? She didn't know. She didn't say. She went with him for two years before he got himself killed. I guess she knew it all along. Maybe that's why she stayed. One mornin they broke into his room. She's there, asleep. He's there too. They start shoutin, hittin the furniture with their sticks. He don't respond. He's cool. He stays cool. He says not one word. They tell her, you get yourself dressed, honey.

174

She wants to go out into the hall, not likin to do it in front of them. They tell her, you do it right *here*. She's holdin the blankets aroun herself when this big cop comes an pulls them away an turns to one of the others an says the worst things in his mind, the worst things he can think of to insult her. Then this kid who's stood silent all that time goes wild. That's what they wanted. An they beat him. They beat him an beat him. Even after he's fallen they beat him. An when it's over they take him to the hospital where he lies in a coma for two weeks. Rain Fortune don't speak, don't testify, don't say a word. Brothers come to her an plead with her. It's like her throat is closed. After he dies she gets up an goes to find his people. But they've gone. It's finished. An then she says to me, Billie Holiday knew nothin, honey, I took it *all* myself.'

We went to the hospital again. They let us look through a glass window. Rain Fortune's face was bandaged, one eye completely covered. I asked the nurse to let me in. I said, 'I'm leaving today.' Bella Prentice waited outside. I sat on a chair beside the bed. Rain Fortune lay still. I told her that the kid who attacked her was from Jacksonville. He worked at a gas station. I said, 'I'll call in a couple of days.' She made no movement.

Capitalism crumbles in a drug-dazed euphoric skyquake beyond which another country exists, the country of the poor. The energy of that first great immigration dissipates into inevitable meaningless prosperity as life in the suburbs suffers the neurosis of a consumer society eating itself alive.

I trust my feelings but feelings change. Writing doesn't come easy. Always the lines have held. Now they're broken.

This story ends with a walk to Central Station. I'm going to Chicago to see Rain Fortune again. I meet a crowd of young Puerto Ricans who tell me to lie on the ground. It's a busy street. I think they're playing games and so I lie on the ground. They kick my teeth in. I jump up and shout, 'Fuckin hell what you doin?' They stick a rag in my mouth. It tastes of kerosene. My arms are tied. They stop a soldier on his way to Saigon and ask him for a light. The soldier strikes a match. He brings it to my face. I breathe fire into my lungs. At the hospital I hear Raymond Massey saying, 'He'll never sing again.' And then I die. The experience is interesting. I float into a pink cushion which grows and grows until the whole of consciousness is pink and soft. In it are the feelings and emotions I could never find on earth. These feelings smother me. I become a tingling sense of wonder and light.

I wasn't important enough at the beginning to be taken seriously by music critics. That came later. I tried to be good. I cared about how the kids reacted. I wanted them to like me and when they did I liked them. The machinery of promotion began selling my product to a specialist market. I couldn't believe in it. Straight chicks brought their poems back stage. They wanted to sleep with me. I asked, 'Why?' They said, 'You have a beautiful soul.' I said, 'What's that?' They said, 'You have a loving aura.' Sometimes I couldn't fuck them unless I hated them. That's when I stopped. I smoked dope, dropped pills, attempting to overcome feelings of alienation, being outside myself, existing as an image I knew to be unreal. I tried to alleviate the boredom and loneliness. I tried to make sense of what I was doing. English bands I met, especially in the States, indulged in pantomimes of destruction, pouring liquor over furniture, smashing TVs. I couldn't do that. I needed privacy and distance.

Matthew asked whether Beccy had given me the standard lecture on the misuse of drugs. I said, 'She never leaves it alone.' He rolled a joint. We were gigging out of London at the time. He offered me the joint. I refused. He said, 'She's got through.' I said, 'Maybe.' In the office he trusted himself. At home he was uncertain. He admired Beccy's strength and yet despised it.

On the first tour of the States I saw a different side to him, posed in his Californian leathers, wide black hat, Denver boots. He said that Beccy wasn't interested in sex although couldn't have enough of it before they were married. I didn't want to know.

Beccy said, 'Matthew hates himself.' I said, 'He's too arrogant to do that.' She said, 'It's all reaction.' I said, 'Against what?' She said, 'He has to prove he's made it. He has to prove it all the time. To everyone.' I said, 'He *has* made it.' She said, 'I remember when he started. He had this girl, Janice, on the switchboard. The office was no bigger than my kitchen with a partition between his room and hers. Janice was hired because she had sexy legs and wore mini skirts and was the first person you saw as you walked in, her and a sort of padded bench with curly ends. When a visitor arrived Janice said, Mr Shaw's engaged at present, do you mind waiting? The man said, no. He sat on the bench and looked up her knickers. Matthew was on the other side of the partition, hearing everything. Janice flashed her knees and offered coffee. Finally Matthew came through with a sheaf of papers. He saw the man sitting there. He said, hello, come in, sorry to keep you. He passed the papers to Janice, saying, these are contracts for the States, can you handle them? Of course they were nothing, scrap. The man went into Matthew's office. He was made to sit on a very modern, very low chair, almost on the floor, with Matthew looming over him on the other side of a desk. They started to talk. Matthew had a sign with Janice, tapping the partition with a pencil or something, at which she rang his telephone. He picked it up and had a fictitious conversation with California or New York. The man in the chair, flat down on the floor, began to feel that he was into some big deal enterprise.'

Matthew's insecurity was something I couldn't understand. Pulling chicks at gigs was part of it, the insatiable hunger of the ego. I asked Beccy, 'What's missing?' She said, 'It's artificial.' I said, 'The music's not artificial.' She said, 'Everything is.' I asked, 'What's genuine?' She said, 'The kids are genuine. Their *feelings*.' I said, 'That doesn't change the performance.' She said, 'The scenery's fake.' I said, 'There isn't any scenery.' She said, 'What are those big boxes?' I said, 'You can't pretend

177

they're not necessary.' She said, 'You're just an actor.' I said, 'What's wrong with being an actor?' She said, 'It's artificial.' I said, 'That's your opinion.' She said, 'If I go to the movies I know what I'm doing. I don't pretend it's real. I can't *touch* those people. You're trying to *make* it real. You come on stage like a real person in real clothes. You make the kids go with you. You make them listen. You believe in it. Or I assume you believe in it. The way you make them go with you is the quality of your performance. It's still artificial. Like the best movie in the world is nothing more than the best movie in the world.' I said, 'I'm confused.' She said, 'Everyone is.' I said, 'You're not.' She said, 'Why do you think I married Matthew?' I said, 'You loved him.' She said, 'Girls are very nervous about themselves.'

She died of diseased blood. She spoke of it like a birthday. She said, 'I'll be twenty-three years old.' Matthew wouldn't listen. It was unbearable. She lay in fine cotton sheets. She said, 'We have no right to expect good to come out of life.' I said, 'You mustn't believe that.' She said, 'We shouldn't ask for anything more than to be allowed to grow in our own time, in our own way.' I said, 'Why?' She said, 'We torture children and force them into schools. We can't teach them love.' She began to cry. I held her hands. She cried for a long time. She said, 'You'd better go. It's no use.' She was weak and exhausted. I wiped her cheeks with paper tissue. She said, 'You're such a baby. You do everything right.' I felt the warmth of the room around me. I said, 'Will you sleep?' She said, 'It's so *stupid*.' I thought of her and Matthew in bed together, his body like a coffin enclosing her, his mouth sucking life from her lungs.

The artist exists on the edge, his language the language of sky. The earth under his feet is made of leaves. He floats, floats in air, *is* air. He comes back. The thread that ties him to the ground has frayed.

Brother Mark said, 'There's no such thing as a cultivated man. By the nature of their existence specialists are narrow and inadequate.' The basis of his belief was visionary. He said, 'We shut out whole areas of experience because they are too difficult or too bitter and yet all of us are capable, all of us creative.' He believed we should use what we had. We told him, 'We have nothing.' He said, 'Use that.' I said, 'The Church is based on the concept of guilt.' He said, 'Ethics are the natural laws.' Few of us worried. I did. I had been taught the meaning of right and wrong since I was old enough to walk. Blasphemy didn't hurt. I was damned anyway. I thought heaven must be boring and pious and empty of anger. I didn't care. I told my father I wouldn't make friends up there. He said, 'You'll be with your mother.' I said, 'I'm with her now.' He said, 'You should be grateful.' I said, 'I didn't ask to be born.' He said, 'Shut up!' I said, 'May the Lord forgive you.' He hit me. I laughed in his face. I said, 'God saw that, you old bugger.' He said, 'Get out!' I said, 'You've shat yourself now, Dad. You're fucked.' He attacked me. I ran out the door. If pain is the Devil's spunk I'm the Devil's child. I cannot condone what I did. He was drowning, that man. My sister understood. It was she who told me how much I hurt him. When it rained I said, 'God's pissing again, Dad.' He tried not to listen. He sat in his chair in the back room ignoring me. I said, 'He'll piss on you if you walk outside, Dad. It's all the same to Him, saints or sinners.' I invented a story that Jesus was a chick and they changed it in the books because no one would have listened if they'd known although the first Pope was given the word one night when God was drunk which explains all that Catholic stuff about the Virgin Mary who isn't the mother of all because VM stands for Verily Mistaken but then I couldn't decide about the Crucifixion because they nailed him nude and so I said he was queer because he'd never had it off with Mary Magdalene. My father didn't attempt to argue. After hitting me that time he was apologetic and ashamed. I told him, 'It doesn't matter what you do, Dad. I don't notice.' He said, 'I lost my temper.' I said, 'Lose your balls for all I care.' He said, 'I'm sorry, son.' I had my own feelings about the nature of life. They didn't involve participation. I was suspicious and defensive. I thought, God's so old He can't function. A voice spoke to me out of darkness, 'Perhaps He forgives you.' It wasn't easy to live then.

I come downstairs and deposit my key with the porter at the desk. The porter gives me a letter. I take it outside and read it in the street, in the sunlight. The letter terrifies me. I go back into the hotel and ask the porter, 'Who left this?' The porter says, 'A young man not unlike yourself.' I say, 'Did he go out afterwards?' The porter shakes his head. I look for the man in the lobby. There is no one. I return to the desk and ask for my key. The porter says he doesn't have it. I say, 'I gave it to you a few minutes ago.' He says, 'I don't remember.' I ask to speak to the hotel detective. A small, fat, bald man appears. He introduces himself. I say, 'There's someone in my room.' He asks, 'Do you have a description?' I say, 'He looks like me.' He says, 'That's difficult.' We go upstairs. He stops twice to take off his trousers. Each time there is another pair of trousers underneath. When we reach my room he takes off his jacket. There is another jacket underneath. He takes off the second jacket. There is another under that. I say, 'Are you quite finished?' He says, 'Yes.' I tell him to wait in the corridor until I shout. He nods. I open the door of my room. I go inside. Everything is upside down, the tables and chairs broken, the curtains torn. A man is standing with his back to me hunched over a figure on the bed. He is naked. He turns to look at me. His stomach and chest are covered with blood. I know that the figure on the bed is Rain Fortune. I see maggots and frogs squirm and swim inside her belly. The man says, *'Lap it up.'* His face is hidden in a strange misty haze. He has a huge erection. He picks up a shotgun and points it at me. I stare at Rain Fortune's wound, at the frogs eating the maggots, at the red lake of blood. The man comes closer. I don't move. He slips the barrel of the gun into my mouth. I suck the cold steel. I hear a sound like rushing wind. He is on me. I scream. I see the detective at the door with a long tubular weapon. I shout, *'No!'* He fires. The man's head falls off his body like a football. It is me. My head! My face! I hear Rain Fortune weeping. The detective ties my wrists behind my neck. I open my mouth.

It is filled with vomit. I cannot breathe. I am choking. The bedclothes are on the floor, sheets tangled and hot. I switch on the light. I lie in my sweat for a long time, trying not to sleep again.

Later I ring Bella Prentice in Chicago. She isn't there. Her sister says that she is staying with her brother's family in Detroit. I ask if she knows Rain Fortune.

"Sure I know her," she says. "She's my cousin."

"Do you know *of* her?"

"Yeah."

"Is she still in hospital?"

'Yeah."

"Which one?"

"I don't recall."

I ring Rain Fortune's number hoping to find Martha. A young male black voice answers.

"Is Martha there?" I ask.

"Who's that?"

I tell him.

"Shit, man, what you want?"

"Talk to Martha."

"She's in L.A."

"How is Rain Fortune?"

"I don't under*stand* you, man."

"Where is she?"

"Don't you *listen* good?"

He hangs up.

It is a bright cold afternoon. I walk through Central Park. There are children playing.

I like New York. I like its contrasts and its tensions. I like its age. There's nothing artificial about holes in the road. There's nothing safe about them either.

I find a barber's shop in a side alley. I have my beard shaved. The barber is Italian. He tells me how his kids were attacked at school, how his sister was raped, how a relative of his mother's uncle was run over by a train.

"Why do you tell me these things?" I ask.

"Whatever happens to you won't be as bad as what happened to me," he says. "Maybe you feel better. Maybe you go out into the street and talk to the people.'

He asks what I'm doing in New York.

"Travelling," I say.

"You're lucky," he says. "I don't envy you."

He tells me a story of one of his mother's brothers, Carlo, who left Milan to find a girl he had heard about from a friend. This girl lived in northern France. She was very beautiful. When Carlo arrived in the village where the girl lived he had spent all his money. He found himself a job as assistant to a baker at the patisserie. After arranging his lodgings and settling his affairs he began sending little boxes of cakes to the girl's house. In return he received pressed flowers wrapped in coloured silk. But he never met her. Whenever he went to the house the girl's mother said that she was ill or gone to the country or was staying with an aunt in Paris. Carlo had to leave. After many months he grew impatient and so one night told the baker that he was sick and couldn't work. He went to the house and climbed a wall onto a low roof leading to an upstairs window. He squeezed through and searched the empty bedrooms until, finally, he came to one that was locked. He called the girl's name. A voice answered. He asked whether she knew how to unlock the door. She said that her mother kept the key tied to her apron string. He tiptoed downstairs. The mother was sitting at the kitchen table. Beside her were squares of coloured silk and a box of pressed flowers. He could see the key hanging from her apron string. He hid in the shadows behind the door and watched. The mother wrapped the flowers in the coloured squares of silk and laid them out in rows. There were so many. Carlo counted fifteen. He waited. When she went upstairs he crept into the kitchen. He untied the little silk squares and read the names, 'My beloved Jacques', 'My longed-for Pierre', 'My dearest Paul'. He determined to confront the mother immediately. As he climbed the stairs he noticed that the door to the girl's room was open. He heard voices. He went closer and

182

peered through the crack of the door. The mother was sitting on the side of a big brass bed washing the face of the most beautiful girl he had ever seen. His heart melted with love. But as he watched he realized that her body was bandaged in cheesecloth. She had no arms nor legs. Next day he left the village and returned to Milan. He sought his friend to ask why he had played such a trick on him. His friend was not there. They said he had married and was living in Rome. He asked, 'Whom did he marry?' They said, 'Claudia, your childhood sweetheart.'

"No one tells stories like that anymore," I say.

"Once I told it to the son of a rich Jewish customer," the barber says. "He was enormously impressed by the friend's cunning."

"It is a very sad story," I say.

I take off my clothes. I go into the bathroom and run the taps. Tomorrow I return to London. Next week I record my sixth album. Next month I begin a European tour. I'm almost thirty.

Loneliness is the mist that gathers at the heart. I feel a long way from life. The Greeks, Egyptians, Persians had a better understanding of civilization. Art is the mirror of expectation. Or should be. Illusion and truth fight for possession. Drugs exist as the ultimate in space travel. We have no confidence in continuity. Science creates weapons that can destroy us a thousand times and thoughts of cosmic catastrophe drive our children mad.

Nostalgia glues the soul. I hate its stench. I have not released the past, nor lost sight of origin. Reputation cannot save me. Next year's kids won't need this year's heroes' style. Changes are swelling and rising, running under the surface of sanity. Something has come into me that belongs outside, almost evil, a terror, but worse, a climbing and a flowering, so far away, so deep inside that I doubt the memory of my own actions, the reality of my own memory.

I was afraid of everything, Catherine leaving, staying, wanting me, not wanting me. I said, 'When I'm working I become absorbed.' She said, 'It's like there's never been any true emotion.' The trees were granite, symbols of a phallic god. I said, 'I'm writing a song about these stone trees.' She was a child on Moroccan cushions. She said, 'Can I hear it?' I played the opening chords. I said, 'Shall we swim?' She said, 'I want to hear more.' I laid the guitar down. I said, 'It's too hot.'

She was wrapped and tissued like the porcelain figures in her mother's travelling case. She had friends she had known since she was young and whatever they did, wherever they went, they would remain her friends. I had people I went with, people I knew, Brother Mark, Jack Field, chicks I had loved at a distance, never loved in the flesh, memories of faces passing, club band guitarists, rock'n'roll singers, innocent budding groupies dying of dreams. There was no pattern. Friends changed. I changed. I moved up and out, bringing nothing with me, wanting nothing.

We met again only once. I asked how she had been. We talked of small things. She said she was working in a flower shop with a friend called Susan Rose. I said, 'Why isn't Susan Rose called Sue or Rosie?' She said, 'She's like Anne Marie or Jean Claude.' I said, 'Who are they?' We sat in a dark room with candles, picking at food. She looked pale and ill. She said, 'You remember?' Our hands touched across the table. She pulled hers back. She said, 'I never wanted to tell you this. I didn't want to hurt you. I've felt such bitterness.' She looked away, kept her eyes from me, down, as if ashamed. 'You don't know what it is, this love, this gift I have which is yours. You don't understand its value or its sensitivity. It frightens you. You're like a child. Even now you can't imagine what you've lost.' I watched her. I said nothing. 'I loved you more than you'll ever know, probably more than anyone. When you forced me away there was nothing. I was hollow. I didn't care about living. I wanted *you*. Later when I came home and thought about it again I tried to understand what it was. You never inflicted yourself upon me. It was not like that. It was a sweetness, something you don't know or want to talk about, allowing the dream to exist, encouraging it. And yet when you sing you become like another person. You have a tension that *radiates* on stage. It is very strong. You don't have it in life. You have the opposite, a lack of commitment that is extraordinary, a shyness that is part of your nature.' She spread her hands flat on the table. 'There is something else too, something I didn't realize at the beginning, a kind of self-destroying angel forcing you to hate the loving qualities and sour the sweetness. This angel becomes a devil. You don't deny it. You can't. You think it's your true self, the one you hide. But it isn't. Your true self is someone infinitely more precious and good. You fight this war inside yourself and it's other people who get hurt like I was hurt. All I wanted was to beat the devil and all you felt was me cutting your creative life. I would never do that. I was trying to make you recognize the goodness, *believe* in it.' She looked at me. 'It's *that* I cherished. Don't you see?' I nodded. 'I wonder whether you're aware of what I have to offer. I'll always love you. I know that. It's worse now to hear you talk like you do. I think the goodness is dying and the other thing coming up and killing you. I can't bear it. I loved my child life and you allowed me to live longer with it than I should. I am grateful. But I've had to change so much. Things have fallen. I've grown older. Whether that's good or not, I don't know. I'm not the same anymore.'

Beccy said, 'Write what you feel.' I said, 'I wrote a song called "No One Asked Me To The Party". Who's interested in that?' She said, 'None of us were asked to the party.' I laughed. She said, 'We believe what we want to believe.' I said, 'We have eyes. We can *look*.' She said, 'Matthew tells me I'm his base, his security, and yet discards my feelings whenever it suits him.' She had a habit of sitting in chairs with her knees up, looking sideways at me, her hair falling across her face, very girlish and vulnerable, smoking thin white cigarettes. She said, 'You live in your own world which is why you'll succeed. You're untouched by what destroys most of us.' I said, 'I'm not.' She said, 'It would be nice to sleep with you.' I said, 'Yes.' She laid her head back on the chair. She said, 'You *know* it would be terrible.' I felt the veins in my wrists, the blood in my stomach. I said, 'Why?' She said, 'We have friendships and we have lovers. They aren't the same.' I said, 'Do you have lovers?' She lifted her head and looked at me. She said, 'What do you think?' I said, 'Yes.' She said, 'Yes what?' I said, 'Yes, you do.' She said, 'Why won't I sleep with you then?' I said, 'Because of Matthew.' She said, 'Don't be stupid.' I said, 'Wouldn't he mind?' She said, 'He'd be destroyed if he knew but he wouldn't know. That's what's so ridiculous. Men treat their wives like pieces of furniture and suddenly when they discover someone else sitting in their seat they go mad.' I said, 'It's the same with you.' She said, 'Sexual liberation doesn't suit men unless it works in their favour. What they want is simple direct confrontation. Women don't. They're intrigued by complexity and subtlety.'

Rain Fortune, in the damp soft heat of a southern night, said, 'We ain't had our babies rest out in fields, man. We ain't had our daughters ravished right there in the cotton. It's b'n a long while. The only respect whites understand is the respect of the gun. That's how they live. That's how they've always lived. Rich dudes buy protection an their kids go hitch a ride to some place where the weather's cool, say Martin Luther King was a great American who acted an behaved like a white man, told everyone we want no blood in the streets which is what rich kids need to know 'cause they're scared in their ass, man, not only them, a whole mess all over, scared of the day black brothers come out of the ghettoes demandin retribution. Suddenly from the south where it all began there's this nigger, this great buck preacher, sayin, we can do it with the Lord's help, we can do it without killing, sayin, yassum boss, yassum boss, an

186

puttin his hands deep down in their pockets an callin the price. White dudes say, okay Mister Marty, we'll ask you up to the house for cocktails some night an give you this big fat Nobel Peace Award that means nothin an everyone's goin to love you an feel proud of you an we'll let you do yo'r own thing jes as long as you remember we don't want no action, man, we don't want trouble. But Mister Marty has a dream. He sees hi'self crowned Prince Of The World. He comes over strong with his Bible talk. He tells the people, *feel* it an we'll *dig* it, man. The people think, maybe that's not the real story, maybe he sold out after all. Mister Marty's friends say, there was this Indian cat called Gandhi who made it all happen. But the brothers who know America shake their heads an smile an say, India's a *civilized* country, man, an that's a whole different thing.'

The basis of control is hypocrisy as the basis of rules is political, the rich exploiting the poor, the strong enslaving the weak. Once right and wrong have been eliminated kids slide wild across the fields of ice that are the fields of their youth and if someone offers glue for their shoes they take it no matter what the cost. Men of will, whether Manson or the Maharishi, become heroic leaders by the very nature of their conviction. The medium is the message, McLuhan says, and he's right, not in history but now, understanding the desire for solidity in the death black freeze where every step cracks your arse.

Kids see it clearly, being young and unrestrained, material-istic consumer society equating middle-class ideals, shaped by the capitalistic dogma of the freedom of individuals to sell their souls to mortgage brokers, living off a need for social accept-ance. Kids rebel, break free, dress in rags, live rough, emulate the superficialities of poverty with the zeal of religious converts, misunderstanding the true hunger of the poor which is a hunger of the spirit, a feeling of hopelessness that is born in them like blackness is born in Negroes and can't be changed by sending flowers.

I remember after the Fillmore gig in San Francisco going to

187

a party at someone's house and sitting by the window looking out across the bay when a large bearded man wearing shabby clothes and old tennis shoes came up and talked to me. He said he was born in San Francisco and lived on welfare. He had a slow lazy way of speaking. I wondered what he was doing there, surrounded by beach boys in soft leather pants and doe-skin boots. He asked my opinion of the concert. I told him it was too frenetic. He asked, 'Why?' I said, 'I like an audience to listen.' We talked about California and it was obvious we were talking of two different worlds. He said, 'L.A. is a good place to be. Food's cheap and you can find anything you want. People are friendlier than in 'Frisco where they're more into their own thing.' I said, 'The cult of eccentricity's reached a crazy level, freaks outfreaking each other, gays tripping in drag like they're high on chocolate malts.' He said, 'You've been looking from the outside, man, you haven't come through the *door*.'

Afterwards I thought it strange to be so wrong. The isolation of the singer goes beyond the isolation of the stage. Roots are deeper than I know, cold wind blowing from the west, rain in the corn, my mother scrubbing blueberry juice from my mouth, my father reading aloud from the Bible, dog barking in the night from the shed in the yard, barking at shadows, my mother walking to school that first morning, leaving me at the step.

If I am lost it is because childhood never grew away from its own sense of uniqueness, never passed the period of myth and legend. I was plucked from the land and tossed into a spiritless city where factual things were mechanical or electronic. The history of stones and mountains may be geological but my stones contained the secret of the universe and my mountains hung misty with ghosts. Men cannot believe the miracle of spring. They call it *natural*. Animals know. It's their only strength. Sometimes I think instinct is the voice of God and the less we listen the closer we move towards oblivion.

188

The sky's stillness invites me. Everyone is asleep. I stare out
the window at the sun lying beyond the curve of the earth as
we fly suspended between present and future, chasing the dawn.
There are things I know, things I don't have to question. Space
is infinite. Singers are imitators or creators. Rain Fortune said,
'Either you got soul or you got music. If you got soul you die
young. If you got music you get rich.' Fear blows from both
sides now. Catherine never sensed it, living all her life indoors.
Beccy knew. I became her ally. She could have healed me but
forgot. Loving her I recognized nothing. It makes no difference.
Death comes like a curtain drawn across the world, its folds
containing chinks of light. I fix my eyes there and believe I
am still alive. We are responsible for every action, every defeat.
Beccy wept in desolation. I cannot pretend it is not so.

I listen to the drone of the engines. There must be a reason.
A beginning. Love shelters us. The lonely body dies of cold.
The lonely child has many friends. Often they are animals.
Grown men cannot accept weakness or senility, cannot live without hope. I have tried to remain true to a conception of self.
Truth eludes me. Catherine said, 'You think you're the only
one and that's right, you are, but so am I, so are we all.' I am
creator and created, both. The son *and* the father. I am John.
I am Magdalene. I am killer and victim, executioner and
criminal. My head lies against the wall. Vibrations ripple.
Future is a storm of darkness beyond which galaxies of decayed
stars orbit in a void. The sky sucks. The wind squeezes. I am
a bird flying over the school house, the golden bird of my
dreams. Inside us are secrets we never uncover, countries and
oceans and phantoms of war. The world won't acknowledge
them, this world we have made. Truth is denied, withheld,
destroyed in asylum hospitals. Jesus recognized it. He came
down from the mountain. He preached the laws of God which
were his laws. He said, 'Happiness is not the accumulation
of money or a belief in status or a philosophy of sexual indulg-
ence. It is sacrifice.' He created an ideal of heaven which gave
meaning to suffering. He lied to save us. Always I hated his
certainty. Truth is The Word and The Word is God. Now I
know it isn't. It's camouflage disguising God. He was a rene-
gade, a rebel, a believer in the honesty of deception. He invented

189

a system for love to grow in arid wastes and did it with conviction, understanding our desire for reassurance. I am his brother, I have tasted fire. I have seen the lip of the abyss crawling with disease. I have laboured and fought in the wilderness, discovered truth at the moment when death crept in under my jacket. Truth is terrible. I am relieved. Jesus smiles behind his cloak. He's won me. He climbs off the cross. We stand together in the evening. I ask, 'How did you do it, you old bugger?' He says, 'I was tough. I didn't waste time.'

A hand touches my shoulder. I open my eyes. A woman bends over me.

"Fasten your seat belt, please."

Outside, below us, I see features of matchbox houses through a scum of cloud. It's the same as it was, as it always will be, row after row of dark wet roofs, silent and grey as graves.

HÄGAR

Who Dares Wins

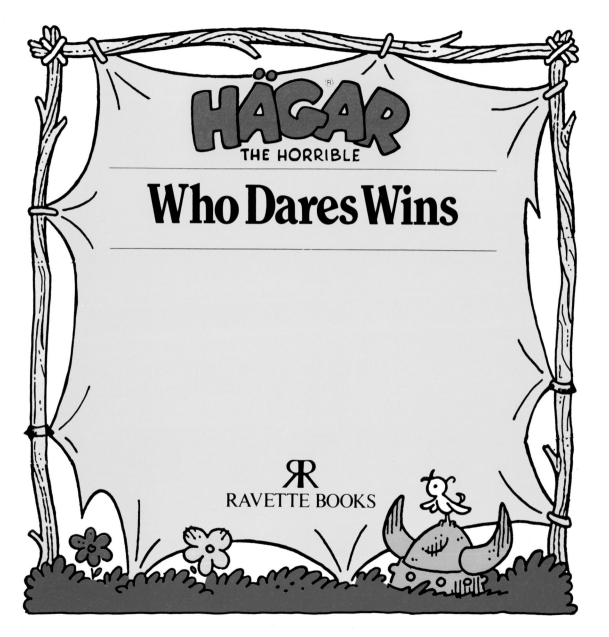

Printed and Bound in Great Britain
for Ravette Books Limited,
3 Glenside Estate, Star Road, Partridge Green,
Horsham, West Sussex RH13 8RA
by Ebenezer Baylis, Worcester

ISBN: 1 85304 238 2

OKAY, OKAY!

GOOD MORNING, WORLD!

ANOTHER DAY FULL OF CHALLENGES TO BE MET, NEW WORLDS TO CONQUER...

BATTLES TO BE WON... FAME AND GLORY TO BE GAINED...

DRAGONS TO BE SLAIN... BILLS TO BE PAID... ARGUMENTS TO BE SETTLED... COMPLAINTS...

DIK BROWNE

DIK BROWNE

YOU GOT A NICE TOWN, HÄGAR

WE LIKE IT

BUT DON'T YOU WORRY ABOUT INVADERS?

NAW! VIKINGS DON'T WORRY

AREN'T YOU AFRAID THE HUNS WILL ATTACK YOUR VILLAGE?

NOT WITH OUR EARLY WARNING SYSTEM

AT THE FIRST SIGN OF DANGER ALL LUCKY EDDIE HAS TO DO IS PULL THAT CHAIN

IT DROPS 10 BIG LEAD BALLS ON A BIG BASS DRUM WITH A NOISE LOUD ENOUGH TO WAKE UP THE WHOLE TOWN!

BAM BOOM BAM BOOM

BUT TO MAKE SURE — IT WAKES UP 12 SQUEAKING GEESE AND KNOCKS OVER 20 EMPTY DUSTBINS!

HONK AWK AWK BAM CLANK BAM

WOW! THAT'S A NOISE!

YOU BET! NO ENEMY IS GOING TO SURPRISE US WITH OUR WARNING SYSTEM

IT'S FOOL-PROOF

Z

DIK BROWNE   © King Features Syndicate, Inc.   World rights reserved

AS YOU KNOW, MY NAME IS HELGA

AND I AM YOUR SUBSTITUTE TODAY

I WILL NOT ALLOW BAD MANNERS!

I WILL NOT ALLOW FOUL LANGUAGE!

I WILL NOT ALLOW DRINKING ON THE JOB!

AND BEFORE WE GET THERE I WANT EVERYONE TO WASH HIS FACE AND COMB HIS HAIR!

I KNEW WE SHOULDN'T HAVE AGREED TO INVADE ENGLAND WHILE HÄGAR HAD THE FLU

DIK BROWNE

A selection of HÄGAR books published by Ravette

COLOUR THEME BOOKS
No 1 THE GREAT GOURMET	£2.95
No 2 TROUBLE AND STRIFE	£2.95
No 3 TAKES A JOURNEY	£2.95
No 4 CHILD'S PLAY	£3.50

POCKET BOOKS
TRIES AGAIN	£1.95
HAS A GO	£1.95
IN A FIX	£1.95
ON THE RAMPAGE	£1.95
TAKES AIM	£1.95
IN A STEW	£1.95
LEADS THE WAY	£1.95
TAKES A BREAK	£1.95
ALL AT SEA	£2.25
ON HOLIDAY	£2.25
GETS IT ALL	£2.25
IN THE ROUGH	£2.25
MEASURE FOR MEASURE	£2.25
SAYS IT WITH FLOWERS	£2.25

ALBUMS
THE HERO	£2.50
LETS HIMSELF GO	£2.50

BLACK AND WHITE LANDSCAPES
MEETS HIS MATCH	£2.50
IN A HURRY	£2.50

COLOUR LANDSCAPES
TELLS IT LIKE IT IS	£2.95
NEVER SAY DIE	£2.95
MAKES AN ENTRANCE	£2.95
WELCOME HOME	£2.95
VIKING HANDBOOK	£3.95

All these books are available at your local bookshop or newsagent, or can be ordered direct from the publisher. Just tick the titles you require and fill in the form below. Prices and availability subject to change without notice.

Ravette Books Limited, 3 Glenside Estate, Star Road, Partridge Green, Horsham, West Sussex RH13 8RA

Please send a cheque or postal order and allow the following for postage and packing. UK: Pocket books – 45p for one book plus 20p for the second book and 15p for each additional book. Landscape series – 50p for one book plus 30p for each additional book. Other titles – 85p for one book plus 60p for each additional book.

Name ....

Address ....

....